"A mother's worst nightmare on the page. For those who dare."
—*Kirkus Reviews*

"*The Best of Friends* gripped me from the stunning opening to the emotional, explosive ending. In this moving novel, Berry creates a beautifully crafted study of secrets and grief among a tight-knit group of friends and of how far a mother will go to discover the truth and protect her children."
—Heather Gudenkauf, *New York Times* bestselling author of *The Weight of Silence* and *This Is How I Lied*

"In *The Best of Friends*, Berry starts with a heart-stopping bang—the dreaded middle-of-the-night phone call—and then delivers a dark and gritty tale that unfolds twist by devastating twist. Intense, terrifying, and at times utterly heartbreaking. Absolutely unputdownable."
—Kimberly Belle, international bestselling author of *Dear Wife* and *Stranger in the Lake*

THE PERFECT CHILD

"I am a compulsive reader of literary novels—but this has been a terrible year for fiction that is actually readable and not experimental. I have been so disappointed when well-known writers came out with books that, to me, were just duds. But there was one book that kept me reading, the sort of novel I can't put down . . . *The Perfect Child*, by Lucinda Berry. It speaks to the fear of every parent: What if your child is a psychopath? This novel takes it a step further. A couple, desperate for a child, has the chance to adopt a beautiful little girl who, they are told, has been abused. They're told it might take a while for her to learn to behave and trust people. She can be sweet and loving, and in public she is adorable. But in private—well, I won't give away what happens. But needless to say, it's chilling."

—Gina Kolata, *New York Times*

"A mesmerizing, unbearably tense thriller that will have you looking over your shoulder and sleeping with one eye open. This creepy, serpentine tale explores the darkest corners of parenthood and the profoundly unsettling lengths one will go to to keep a family together—no matter the consequences. Electrifying and atmospheric, this dark gem of a novel is one I couldn't put down."

—Heather Gudenkauf, *New York Times* bestselling author

"A deep, dark, and dangerously addictive read. All absorbing to the very end!"

—Minka Kent, *Washington Post* bestselling author

THE
SECRETS
OF US

OTHER TITLES BY LUCINDA BERRY

THE
SECRETS
OF US

LUCINDA BERRY

THOMAS & MERCER

Published by Thomas & Mercer, Seattle

www.apub.com

Amazon, the Amazon logo, and Thomas & Mercer are trademarks of Amazon.com, Inc., or its affiliates.

ISBN-13: 9781542027960
ISBN-10: 1542027969

Cover design by Rex Bonomelli

Printed in the United States of America

To my COVID-19 writing crew, Natasha, Cris, and Lisa, with thanks and appreciation for all the writing sessions during quarantine. Love you, ladies.

ONE

KRYSTAL

I shut the bathroom door behind me and whisper-hiss into my phone, "This better be important." My phone's been vibrating with Theresa's calls for the last ten minutes. Judge Kern gave me the most annoyed look when I asked for a short recess, and she won't be pleased if I'm not back soon. I crouch down and quickly scan underneath the stalls for any signs of feet. There's none. Good. I'm alone.

"I'm so sorry to interrupt you," Theresa gushes before I can get another word out. "You know I wouldn't pull you out of trial if it wasn't important."

It's at that moment that I register the urgency in her voice. I assumed her call had something to do with the Wilkins estate. We've been waiting on the settlement terms for months. My annoyance instantly vanishes and is replaced with worry. "What's going on?"

"It's Nichole."

My chest tightens at the mention of my sister's name. "Nichole? What's wrong with Nichole?" Panic shoots through me.

She's the first person on my must-get-caught-up-with list once this trial ends. It has consumed the last month of my life. I've barely talked to her or anyone else, but domestic violence divorce cases are like that. There's a mountain of paperwork waiting for me after the long, grueling hours spent in the courtroom. I pass out from exhaustion the minute my head hits the pillow each night.

"I'm sorry, Krystal." Theresa's voice carries the weight of her news.

"Just tell me what's going on," I demand, coming off snappier than I intended.

"She's at Wright Memorial Hospital—"

I jump in before she has a chance to finish. "The hospital? What's she doing at the hospital?"

"There was a fire at their house last night and—"

"Oh my God." I bring my hand up to my mouth. "Is she okay?" I whip around and exit through the door I just came through seconds ago. My heels click on the tiled floor as I hurry down the long corridor. Thick courtroom doors line each side of the hallway. Judge Kern is going to be furious that I disappeared in the middle of closing testimony, but I don't care. I hold back the urge to sprint as Theresa talks because running will create a disturbance that will only draw attention to me and slow me down.

"She's not hurt. Well, at least not physically. She got out of the house in time. Aiden wasn't so lucky. He was trapped inside their bedroom and suffered severe smoke inhalation. He's at Wright, too, but he's in intensive care hooked up to a ventilator." Her throat catches with emotion. She's been my assistant for almost ten years, so Nichole and her husband, Aiden, are like family to her. She probably knows more about their personal life than she does mine since I spill more of their secrets than I do my own.

"What happened to Nichole?" I love my brother-in-law but only because he's married to my favorite person on the planet. I wave my way past the security officers at the parking garage entrance and push through the aluminum doors into the ramp, pressing the button on my fob and listening for the sound of my car. I never remember where I parked, and today isn't any different.

"This is where it gets weird." She lowers her voice like she might be somewhere close to people and doesn't want anyone to overhear what she's about to tell me. "She's not at the main hospital like Aiden. She's at Riverside East."

I stop in my tracks like I've slammed into a brick wall, the search for my car quickly forgotten at her shocking news. Riverside East is the psychiatric hospital on Wright Memorial's east campus. What could have possibly landed her there?

"Dr. McGowan is the one who's been calling because he's been assigned to her case," Theresa explains. "All he kept saying was that she was in a compromised mental state."

A groan escapes my lips.

Dr. McGowan is the last person I want working with my sister. He's the least approachable psychiatrist on the floor. He has no real interest in people and doesn't seem to understand them at all, so I have no clue why someone like him chose psychiatry. I'm familiar with most of the psychiatrists and nursing staff at Riverside East since I specialize in family law and represent mostly women. Divorce is one of the top three most traumatic life experiences, and sometimes women crack under the emotional pressure. I've met plenty of my clients in Riverside East hospital rooms for the first time after they swallowed a bottle of pills or walked into the emergency department and asked to be admitted because they didn't know what else to do with themselves.

"I know," Teresa agrees. She's the type of person who easily slips into other people's shoes, so she shares my disdain for Dr. McGowan since he rarely shows empathy. "He needs you to get down there and meet with him and someone from the hospital's legal team. Aiden's unable to make medical decisions for Nichole, and they need someone to speak on her behalf, given her current state."

"But I thought you said she wasn't hurt?" None of this makes sense. My head swirls with possible scenarios. None of them good. I spot my car in the next lane over and hurry toward it.

"It's because of the charges they might file against her."

"Charges?" I unlock the door and leap inside, quickly putting the car in reverse and pulling out.

Theresa clears her throat. "Arson and attempted murder. And I . . . I mean, I guess murder if Aiden doesn't make it . . ."

"What?" I almost hit a red truck coming out of its parking spot and force myself to focus on driving as I make my way out of the garage. "That's the most ridiculous thing I've ever heard."

"Dr. McGowan wouldn't give me any of the details. I barely got that out of him. He kept saying his 'scope of information' was limited. Who even says that? Anyway, the police are claiming she started the fire because apparently she admitted it to the first responders as soon as they arrived on the scene."

I shake my head, unwilling to let her words hold any truth. "That's impossible. Nichole would never do anything like that. Never."

Not only is she one of the most law-abiding citizens I know, but she's also madly in love with Aiden. They've been together over a decade, and she's as into him now as she was when they met. She can't stand being apart from him and stays with me if he's away on business for more than a night or makes me camp out over there with her until he gets back because she hates sleeping alone in the bed without him.

"I know," Theresa says, still on the verge of tears. "He wants you to come down to the hospital as soon as possible and suggested you bring a lawyer with you."

I flip on my hazard lights as the stoplight in front of me turns green and press my foot down on the gas pedal. "I am a lawyer." I pull onto the freeway, quickly moving into the fast lane. "And I've got her covered."

———

"I want to see her," I demand with my arms crossed against my chest, refusing to sit in the chair that Dr. McGowan keeps pointing at. He's on the other side of the table next to one of the hospital's attorneys, Robert

Barnes. I want to talk to Nichole before having a conversation with anyone else. How am I supposed to make any decisions for her before doing that?

"She's on a seventy-two-hour hold in isolation and unable to see anyone." Dr. McGowan repeats himself for the third time as if I don't understand what that means and he's irritated with my lack of understanding. His dark hair is combed straight back with a few thin strands stretched flat over a bald spot. He's wearing a crisp white shirt buttoned to the top with a dark tie and matching jacket. I've never seen him look so formal, and the gravity of the situation hits me in waves.

I nod, doing my best to keep the frustration from showing on my face because I don't want to appear combative. These men control Nichole's fate right now. "I understand the legalities of a seventy-two-hour hold. However, I don't want to visit her from the perspective of a friend or family member. I want to speak with her as her attorney."

Mr. Barnes shakes his head from his position at the head of the table. He's a big guy with a large pockmarked nose and small green eyes who didn't stand to greet me when I walked in the room. "That's not going to happen for a myriad of reasons. One, she's in no position to retain you as her attorney, and two—"

I can't help myself. I have to interrupt. "You keep saying that she isn't in any position to provide consent or make any kind of decisions, like she's an incompetent toddler. I understand she's gotten herself into something serious, but she still gets to have a say in what happens to her, no matter what kind of a state she's in."

"Perhaps we haven't been clear enough about Nichole's condition." Mr. Barnes's jaw is set. His eyes narrow even farther as he speaks. "Nichole is currently in one of our seclusion rooms for her own safety and the safety of those around her. She's in six-point restraints to keep her from harming herself."

"You have her tied up? I understand the formalities of trying to keep her safe, but come on." Fury lines my words. They can't treat her like she's some kind of animal. "None of this is necessary. You're completely overreacting." I mentally flip through my former cases for any kind of precedent but come up empty handed. I've dealt with some pretty awful divorces but never anything like this.

"Ms. Benson, with all due respect, we don't put our patients in the seclusion rooms or in restraints unless it is absolutely necessary. It's always a last resort to keep them from hurting themselves or someone else. We couldn't keep her safe," Mr. Barnes says and folds his hands on the table like the matter's settled.

"I find that hard to believe." All of this is impossible to wrap my brain around. None of what they're describing fits with anything Nichole would say or do, and I know her better than anyone else. We're practically twins, since our birthdays are only two weeks apart.

"It's true." Dr. McGowan nods, making sure Mr. Barnes notices his support. He sits at his right, still waiting for me to take a seat on the other side of them. "Nichole bit one of our nurses on the forearm while she was taking her vital signs. Not only did she bite her—she did it hard enough to break the skin. In another incident, we released her to use the restroom, and she clawed at her own face deep enough to draw blood. That's when she was put in restraints." He looks at me pointedly like he's daring me to disagree with him again.

I pull the chair out from underneath the table and slowly sink into it, conceding defeat for the moment, because there's no way they're letting me see her today. I'll work on that tomorrow once everyone's had a chance to calm down.

"Take me through everything that happened," I say, shifting into investigative mode. I pull a pen and notebook out of my Maestro bag, grateful I grabbed it and took it with me when I left the courtroom earlier.

All of us turn our attention to Dean Sparks, the detective assigned to the case. He introduced himself when I first arrived but has been quiet from his position in the corner ever since, and I almost forgot he was there. He steps forward and clasps his hands in front of him. His brown hair is closely cropped, and he looks more like a soldier than a detective.

"A fire in the bedroom triggered the Fischers' security alarm, and first responders were immediately dispatched to their home. When they arrived on the scene, they found Mrs. Fischer dancing on the front lawn, fully clothed, and singing songs. She became agitated when they questioned her about the situation and tried to attack the firefighters when they moved past her to rescue Aiden from the house. She jumped on one of their backs and had to be restrained by his partner until the police arrived. Her interference might have cost valuable minutes to Aiden's life." Each word is measured, careful, and deliberate, like his statement is being recorded as he rattles off the details.

"Upon entering the house, firefighters made their way to the bedroom where the fire was centralized. A desk had been placed in front of the Fischers' bedroom door that they had to push past in order to gain entry. Aiden was unconscious in front of the door. It appears he'd been trying to break through. Officers were still questioning Nichole and trying to calm her down when they brought Aiden out of the house. Paramedics immediately began working on him. At that point, she pulled away from the police and flung herself at the paramedics trying to save Aiden. According to their statements, she began attacking them and screaming for them to get off Aiden, that he was supposed to die. She ordered the firefighters to take him back inside."

"None of this makes sense." I haven't stopped shaking my head since he started talking. "Nichole would never hurt Aiden. He's the love of her life." Their story is a real-life fairy tale, and unlike most people's, it looks even better from the inside. It's more beautiful than their Instagram pictures. "I have no idea what's going on, but there's got to be an explanation. Did she say anything else?"

Dr. McGowan and Mr. Barnes exchange a knowing look.

"What?"

Detective Sparks takes another step forward and looks me directly in the eyes. "She said Aiden deserved to die because he was a murderer."

TWO

KRYSTAL

I've been in the hospital many times but never on the intensive care ward, and the anxiety of the place assaults me as soon as the elevator doors open. There's nothing still. Everyone is in motion—nurses sprint across the floor; assistants in brightly colored scrubs scurry around after them. Doctors stand at every corner, chatting animatedly with each other in their white lab coats. Patients in wheelchairs, some on gurneys, are rushed past. There's a buzz of static electricity humming underneath all the frantic activity. The elevator lets out an annoying ding, signaling that the doors are going to close on me, and I jump out before they do, even though I want to stay inside.

I stand motionless as the doors shut behind me. The receptionist area and U-shaped desk loom in front of me. *ICU* is spelled out in huge intimidating letters above it. I'm rooted to my spot, unable to move, because every step I take in the direction of Aiden's room is another step toward making this nightmare a reality. Detective Sparks's words haunt every thought. Why would Nichole call Aiden a murderer? That doesn't make sense. None of this does. It's like I got the wind knocked out of me and I still can't get it back. I force myself to move, and the situation becomes more real with each hesitant step to the reception station.

"Excuse me," I say to the nurse typing into one of the many computers on the desk.

"Yes?" she greets me half-heartedly without raising her eyes from her screen. Her fingers never stop moving on the keyboard. They glide with lightning speed.

"I'm looking for my brother-in-law, Aiden Fischer. He was brought in this morning," I say quickly, wanting to get the irritating formality out of the way as much as she does.

"I'm sorry," she says even though she doesn't look sorry, only annoyed as she flips her long black hair over her shoulders. She grabs the coffee next to her and takes a quick drink. "Only immediate family members are allowed on the unit with the patient, and even then, it's a one-person limit." She points to the hallway on the right of the intersecting corridor. "There's a series of waiting rooms provided for family and friends down that way. Aiden's are in room 211b."

"Thank you," I say, but she doesn't notice or respond since she's already returned her focus to the computer in front of her.

211b is easy to find. I knock lightly on the door before going inside. The room is filled to standing room only. Aiden's younger sister, Janice, takes up an entire wall with her brood. Her four kids are bookended between her and her husband, Gary. The kids each have a backpack splayed open in front of them with the contents spilling everywhere, and the youngest jumps up and down on her padded chair. She waves a Barbie doll in the air while her sister tries to grab it. More of Aiden's relatives fill the chairs on the other side of the room, and the rest stand in small clusters. The room smells like old french fries and dirty feet. A TV is mounted on the back wall, and an oval coffee table covered with Starbucks cups sits in the center of the room.

Everyone stills at the sight of me. All conversation stops.

"Hi," I say slowly as I stand in the doorway with all eyes on me. I didn't give any thought to my reception, but maybe I should've. There're lots of people in the room I don't recognize, so I focus my attention on Janice since she's the one I know best. "I just finished talking to Nichole's doctor and wanted to make sure that I came and checked on Aiden before I left." It seemed like a good idea at the time. Now, I'm not so sure. "How's he doing?"

Janice gives me a clipped nod. "Mom and Dad are in a meeting with his doctors right now to get the latest update. But from what we know so far, his lungs are filled with fluid, and he's started running a low-grade fever. The next twenty-four hours are critical." Her eyes fill with tears, and she shakes her head. "He barely made it out of there alive. We can't lose him. Not after he fought so hard."

"I'm so sorry." My words feel empty and flat—completely inadequate. I eye the room for any space, but almost every inch is taken, and nobody's moving to create a spot for me. Nichole always says Aiden has a close family, and most of them are here, watching me with hostility. His aunt is clutching her purse like I might steal it at any given moment. "This all just seems so unreal," I say after the silence stretches out and things grow even more uncomfortable. "I can't believe it's happening. They won't even let me see Nichole."

"At least she'll have something to say when you do. Aiden's got a tube jabbed down his throat. That makes talking pretty difficult," Gary mutters underneath his breath, but it's still loud enough for me to hear, even though I pretend I didn't.

"I'm sorry this is happening," I say again, because I don't know what else to say.

"Excuse me," Aiden's mom, Marlene, interrupts from behind me, and I cram myself against the doorframe to allow her into the waiting room. Shock distorts her face when she notices me, and she doesn't go any farther. "What are you doing here?" Her eyes are red and bloodshot from crying. Her husband, Saul, hovers behind her.

"I, uh . . . I was meeting with Nichole's doctors and just, um, wanted to make sure Aiden was okay." I stumble over my words, caught off guard by her response to my presence. She's always been so nice to me. All of them have. They invite me to all their events, even though I never go, and send me Christmas cards each year like I'm part of the family too.

"Well, he's not," she snaps. "Haven't you figured that out yet? You have a lot of nerve coming here!" She waves her arms wildly, pointing around the room. "You see all these people here? You see them?" I nod, unable to look away or stop her tirade. "You want to know why they're here? Do you?" She takes a step closer to me. Her chest almost touches mine. Her small frame shakes with emotion. "They've come to say their goodbyes because Aiden's doctors don't think he'll make it through the night. Did you know that? They think my son is going to die. And why is that?"

Janice jumps up and rushes to throw her arms around Marlene. "Mom, just settle down. It's not good for you to get this worked up."

"Get this worked up?" Marlene pushes Janice off her. "My son might die, and her sister killed him!" She shoves her finger into my chest. "Your sister. She did this."

"We don't know what happened last night," I say quietly because I don't want to upset her further, but I'm not allowing them to pin the blame on Nichole unless we have more information. I know it looks bad for her, but how can they possibly think she tried to kill him?

"Maybe *you* don't know what happened last night, but we do." Marlene's lips curl with anger, and her eyes fill with disgust as Janice tries to pull her away from me. "I always told Aiden he shouldn't marry her. Not with where you girls came from," she spits out. "Nothing but poor white trash. Both of you."

I raise my hand to my face like she's slapped me, searching for an invisible mark. She laughs at my shocked expression. "Oh, you didn't think I knew about that, did you? I know exactly where the two of you come from and the things you did—no-good, white-trash-looking girls. I always knew she'd find a way to bring my Aiden down." Her words hit me like bullets. Janice's mouth drops open in horror, but she makes no move to stop Marlene. "People like you?" She turns to scan the room and makes sure everyone is paying attention before shifting her eyes back to me. "It doesn't matter how cleaned up you get on the outside; your insides will always be dirty. You—"

"Marlene!" a man standing underneath the TV cuts in. "Stop. Just stop."

My lower lip trembles, but I won't cry in front of her. I'm not going to give her the satisfaction. I hold my bag against my chest like it's a shield against her.

"What?" Marlene asks in mock surprise. "I just—"

This time I'm the one to cut her off, saying the only thing I came into the room to say, the only thing I keep saying, even though nobody is listening. "I'm sorry."

"Just get out." Marlene shrinks before me as if the venom fueling her rage is slowly draining from her body. Saul wraps his arms around his wife to steady her, and Janice grips her waist to help him.

I drop my gaze to the floor and gingerly move around them, then step outside the room and into the hallway. My head spins from the assault of Marlene's words. Nichole can't ever find out about this. Her worst fear has always been Aiden's family discovering the way we grew up and what happened there. It's mine too. There's never been a way to hide that we were in foster care, since we're both without families except for each other and look nothing alike. Not to mention that we used it on every college application, hoping to win approval points in the "overcomer" category. Nichole told Aiden the same story we tell everyone else—Nichole's biological mother was a teenager who put her in foster care to give her a better life. I have an equally heartwarming story, and together we painted a beautiful rags-to-riches picture.

We tell everyone our foster parents died in a tragic car accident during our freshman year in college. It garners pity rather than shame and packs our childhood in a nice box that everyone tends to leave alone afterward. We never worried about getting found out, and the story was so much nicer than the reality that eventually the made-up stories about our childhood easily rolled off our tongues while the real ones faded into the background.

Until Aiden.

Aiden's family is old-money rich. His family owns one of the largest oil fields in West Texas and has over three hundred acres of land stretching across the state and into Louisiana. They'd been fine with her while they were dating, but marriage moved things to an entirely different level. They expected him to choose a certain caliber wife, and one who was raised by a drug addict mother, then spent the rest of her childhood on a foster farm filled with other messed-up kids, certainly didn't qualify. Nichole freaked out about getting discovered as soon as she and Aiden started talking marriage. I've always assured her that we'd be fine; as long as we kept our story straight, nobody ever had to find out.

But what if Marlene did?

Anxiety seizes my gut, and I tap the down button again, trying to hurry the elevator. I have to get out of here. The familiar surge of panic moves through me, and I press my toes against the bottoms of my shoes to center myself.

Breathe. Everything is fine. Nobody knows anything.

Usually that works. But not today. My heart only races faster until the elevator arrives, and I practically leap inside. The doors close before anyone has a chance to get in with me, and I breathe a sigh of relief to be sealed inside.

What exactly does Marlene think she knows about us? And what about Aiden? Did she tell him? What if that has something to do with what happened last night? I don't have any answers to the questions circling on top of each other. There's only one thing I know for sure—Aiden's family can't be trusted. We're not in this tragedy together.

THREE

KRYSTAL

I didn't sleep at all last night, and the pot of coffee I drank this morning twists my stomach in knots as I hurry down the hospital hallway searching for Mr. Barnes's office. Thankfully he agreed to meet with me first thing this morning, because I'm not going another day without seeing Nichole. They might've been able to talk me out of it yesterday, but not today. I'm finding a way to see her, no matter what he or anyone else says.

Yesterday shook me to my core. I've never been so grateful for the distraction of work as I was when I got home from the hospital. I put on my favorite sweats and reheated leftover pasta from lunch before setting up camp on the dining room table. I've been in my condo for almost three years and only used the table to eat dinner on twice. The entire room functions like my office, even though the loft is supposed to be my office.

I threw myself headlong into making phone calls. My first call was to the best criminal defense attorney in the county, William Jenkins. I didn't expect him to answer, so I left a lengthy message asking him to call me back as soon as possible. I emailed him and his legal team with the same information. I'm not taking any chances with Nichole's life.

Brenda Wilkins came next. She was as angry as Judge Kern that I'd walked out of the trial yesterday at such a critical point. Brenda retained me three years ago after her cousin recommended me. Dysfunctional relationships tend to run in families, so most of my business comes from word-of-mouth advertising, but Brenda's case was much worse than her cousin's, and she had even less support. Mr. Wilkins drained every one of their financial accounts as soon as he found out she was leaving him. She hadn't even filed for divorce yet, and he cleaned them out—completely destroyed her financially. He refused to leave their house, so she'd left with nothing, and he was determined to make sure that was all she ever got.

"What do you mean you have a family emergency?" she asked after I told her I was going to have to pass her case on to my colleague Mark for the time being and foreseeable future.

I could hear the betrayal in her question, and none of my reassurances that she was in good hands did anything to comfort her. It was a devastating blow to her, and I can't blame her for being upset, but what choice do I have? Nichole needs me, and I can't be tied up in court for eight hours every day. I have a sinking suspicion I won't get any more referrals from the Wilkins family.

I spent the next three hours talking Mark through the logistics of her case. We both have solo practices, so we're each other's backup. I've filled in for him a few times, but this is the first time I've had to use him since I rarely take vacations and almost never get sick. It was after one o'clock by the time we finished, and I was completely spent from the day. I'd been up for almost twenty hours and was hoping to fall asleep immediately, but my brain wouldn't let me. I couldn't get Marlene's words out of my head.

I still can't. They've burrowed their way into my consciousness and won't let go. I'm still trying to shake them loose as I scan for Mr. Barnes's name on one of the placards lining the identical doors in the hallway. I finally spot his name and tap on the aluminum.

"Come in," he calls.

He stands to greet me from behind his cluttered desk. Stacks of paperwork overflow in boxes scattered around the office floor. File folders lie on top of each other on the wooden desk. His computer is covered in yellow Post-it Notes. One side of the room is lined with bookshelves holding law journals and thick textbooks. His Stanford degree hangs proudly on the wall behind him. He motions to the wooden chairs in front of the desk. I slide into the one on the right, crossing my legs and folding my hands on my lap, sitting up straight like I'm in court—ready, prepared.

"I'd like to speak with my client today, and if that's not possible, I insist on seeing her even if we're unable to speak." I skip all small talk and pretense of a social visit. There's no time for those things when Nichole's in trouble.

"Well, Ms. Benson, it's like I explained to you yesterday—your sister is not in any position to speak with anyone. She's incapacitated." His skin hangs on his face like he's recently lost a lot of weight. He must've been really big before.

"Exactly." I nod my head in agreement. "That's all the more reason that I need to see her." He knows I'm right.

"I'm retaining counsel on Nichole's behalf in case criminal charges are filed against her." I lock eyes with his. "William Jenkins? You know him?"

Mr. Barnes stiffens in his chair and straightens his tie. "Yes, I'm familiar with him."

Of course he's heard of William. Everyone has. His face adorns all the billboards from Jackson Street to Oakland Avenue. I didn't come to play games.

"I expect to have formal documents to you by tomorrow, hopefully by the end of the day. Until then, I'm going to act on her behalf." He's no match for my years in the courtroom when he spends most of his time behind an office desk.

"Shift change finished on the unit right before you got here, and the head nurse informed me that Nichole had a very difficult night without any sleep. She became agitated numerous times and had to be sedated twice. Even under sedation, she still remained worked up. I'm not sure you understand the severity of your sister's condition or the seriousness of her situation." He rests his arms on top of the table. His sport coat sags on his shoulders like the skin on his face. A quick glance at his left hand reveals no ring. Probably recently divorced. That explains the weight loss. He hasn't even had time to buy new clothes, or maybe without a woman in his life telling him how to dress, he doesn't know that he needs to. Either way, he's in desperate need of skinny clothes to match his new frame.

"I'm fully aware of her situation and what needs to be done," I say with more confidence than I possess, but there's no way I'm letting him see that. Family law skirts criminal law, but the actual practice of them is like the differences between playing basketball and football. I lean forward in my chair. "Look, Mr. Barnes, we both know I can get permission from a judge to see my sister in any capacity I choose. It's only a matter of filing the paperwork, and I'm more than willing to do that if I need to. In fact, I'm fully prepared to walk out of here and down to the courthouse." I give him my most serious face—the one that says I mean business—and hold up a folder filled with blank paper, but he doesn't know that. They could be signed affidavits. "But that's not what I want to do because it wastes my and my sister's time. Not to mention how much it will hold up the investigation if I have to go that route."

Last night I considered appealing to his compassionate side and building a case about how inhumane it was to keep Nichole locked up like an animal, but ultimately I chose to play toward his lawyer self. His eyes bore into me as he considers what I said, and I jump at the opportunity when I sense the slight crack in his opposition. "There's nobody who knows her better than me, and I'm sure I can get her to calm down. All anyone wants is for her to give a statement, and I'm the person who's most likely going to be able to get her to do that." It's true and he knows it.

"She's still in the seclusion room and in restraints," he says, beginning to waver. I can see it in his posture, the way he's tilted his head to the side. "And I'm warning you—she's not pretty."

She's been in restraints for almost twenty-four hours. How can they keep her locked up for so long? Anger rises in my throat, but I swallow it back down because I'm getting somewhere with him and need to push forward. "I'm not worried about her condition. The doctors can treat whatever condition she's dealing with. I'm worried about protecting her and her rights."

That's what we do for each other. We've been doing it since my social worker brought me to Mrs. Wheeler's foster home in the middle of the night. I was seven and terrified. They'd taken me from my mom and put me in other foster homes before, but never in the middle of the night and never to a place so far from home. It was full of bad smells that made me want to gag. My mom had done something really bad this time, and somewhere within my seven-year-old mind, there was an awareness that I was never going back home. I'd never felt more alone.

Nichole had been there for a few weeks before me, and our connection was instant as she peeked out from around the corner in the hallway. She gave me a wink and put her finger up to her lips. I latched on to her big green eyes and didn't waver, drowning out the horrible things Mrs. Wheeler and my social worker said about my mom and what she did to me.

Normally, I was embarrassed when people talked about my mom because she couldn't help the way she was, and things weren't as bad as they made them out to be. It wasn't her fault she was allergic to the poison in the bottles she drank from or that she got those terrible headaches she needed to take sleepy pills for. She loved me no matter what they said about her. Whenever we went to court, my cheeks burned with embarrassment while the judge spoke about her, and I'd wish for the floor to open up and swallow me whole, but it wasn't like that with Nichole. I could see it in her eyes—she was like me.

"Come on, child, let me show you to your room," Mrs. Wheeler had said as she led me down a long hallway. She was a tall giant with linebacker shoulders and wore a nightgown down to her ankles like they did in the Christmas storybooks. My legs were no match for her long strides, and I hurried to keep up with her. She stopped at a door on the right side of the hallway and peered down at me. Weird patches of skin dotted her face. "This is your room. You'll be sharing it with another foster child. Her name is Nichole, and she's asleep in one of the beds, so don't wake her up. You'll have a dresser for all your things, but don't worry about putting anything in it until tomorrow." I nodded, but I didn't need a dresser because I didn't have any things. My mom didn't believe in me having things. She said they were only one more thing to grow attached to and lose. "So be quiet and hurry on to bed. You girls get up at six for chores."

I nodded again, trying to show her with my eyes that I understood as she opened the door and motioned for me to go into the room. She put her finger to her lips and gave me a stern look as an extra reminder to keep quiet. She didn't know how good I was at being quiet. I could move like a mouse. I showed her as I slid my way through the crack and stepped onto the wooden floor without making a sound. She quickly shut the door behind me.

A night-light plugged into the wall cast eerie shadows all over the room. The funny smell was trapped in here too. There was a twin bed against the wall on one side of the room, and a small lump lay curled underneath the covers. I tiptoed to the other side of the room and took a seat on the bed. It was hard. Not like my big comfy bed at home. My mom had gotten it from the neighbors after they moved and left it out on the street for somebody to pick up. She'd said we were lucky we came across it when we did, before someone else stumbled on it. I'd helped her drag it up to our apartment.

I wished I would've brought my sleeping shirt, but my mom had screamed at the people who came to take me away that everything had to stay in the house.

"You can't have my things!" she'd screamed out the door as they drove away with me tucked into the back seat. I was one of her favorite things. She'd told me that once, so she must've been really mad that they took me.

I peeled back the quilted bedspread and crawled underneath, fully clothed. I lay flat as a pancake and stiff as a board, just like I did when my mom had a friend sleeping over and she told me not to move a muscle or she'd make me sleep in the closet again. The quilt stank and scratched my cheek. I strained my eyes to see the ceiling, missing my glow-in-the-dark stars on the ceiling at home. My mom had said they gave them away for free from Kay-Bee Toys, but she might've done that thing where she put it in her pocket without giving money to the cashier.

Twenty-six stickers. Twelve planets. Eleven stars. Three moons. That's what I counted every night before falling asleep. Every night.

There was nothing on this ceiling. My heartbeat exploded in my ears. Short spasming breaths from my chest. Oh no, it was coming. Not again.

I flipped around, facing the wall, and brought my knees up to my chest, squeezing them against me before it got too bad. My body shook no matter how hard I tried to keep it still. The funny smell made it worse. Tears burned my cheeks. I squeezed my eyes shut so tightly that bright spots danced in front of the lids, and I whispered the prayer from children's church about little sheep over and over again.

A body slid into bed next to me. It was the little girl from across the room. She was warm. "It's okay, you're okay," she whispered quietly into the back of my head as she curled up next to me.

We slept that way for the first week until Mrs. Wheeler caught us and threw a fit about it. She forbade us to sleep together, but that didn't stop us from finding our way to each other on our hardest nights and sneaking back to our own beds by morning. We were like that all the way through college and even into our adult lives if something really bad came up.

That's why I can't stop wondering how Nichole got through last night alone. She must've been terrified.

I push Mr. Barnes's files to the side and lean across his desk. "You have to let me see my sister."

He lets out a deep breath, finally conceding. He flips his computer around and types for a few seconds. "I let the nurses on the unit know that you are on Nichole's list of approved visitors and can visit outside of visiting hours. We can head up there now."

FOUR

KRYSTAL

Dr. McGowan meets us at the nurses' station on the locked psychiatric unit at Riverside East. None of the nurses on the unit wear scrubs. They dress in regular clothes in an attempt to normalize themselves and help patients feel more comfortable, but it has the opposite effect on me. It just gives the place a surreal quality, and it's never been more pronounced than today as Dr. McGowan grabs a file folder from behind the desk. He's nicely dressed again in a well-cut suit. He shakes hands with Mr. Barnes first and then me before dropping his arms to his side. His arms dangle past his waist like he still hasn't grown into them yet, even though he's got to be over forty.

"I appreciate you taking the time to bring Krystal to meet with Nichole," Mr. Barnes says, but there's no one more appreciative than me.

Dr. McGowan gives him an eager nod. "Of course. Anything I can do to help. Are you coming with us?"

Mr. Barnes shakes his head. "I've got meetings all morning. I'll speak with you later this afternoon." He sticks his hand out to me. "And I'm sure I'll be speaking with you as well."

I take his hand in mine, squeezing it firmly. "Yes, we'll be in touch." Probably after this meeting, depending on how it goes.

I walk next to Dr. McGowan as we head toward the community room. They call it the community room because it's the space where the patients gather when they're not in their rooms or other scheduled activities. It's supposed to function as a living room, but it couldn't be less homey or inviting. Mismatched furniture donated to the hospital fills the space and is arranged around the room in no particular order. The games lining the shelves are missing important parts, and none of the puzzles have all the pieces. The TV screen is still a big and bulky box standing on a table that sags from the pressure of it. I'm surprised when Dr. McGowan walks right past the room and keeps going down the long hallway.

"Are we going to her room?" Hope stirs in my chest. Maybe they let her out during my meeting with Mr. Barnes.

Dr. McGowan shakes his head. "She's still in the seclusion room."

"How long can you keep her in there?" There's got to be a limitation on the number of hours they can be locked up like that. When does it start being inhumane?

"For as long as necessary."

I follow him to the end of the hallway, past bare walls and window-less rooms. The place is designed to be as unstimulating as possible, and anything with the potential to be a weapon has been removed. All the patient rooms are open, and I try not to look in case any of them are occupied. It feels like a huge invasion of their privacy.

We make a left followed by another right and come to a much smaller nurses' station than the main one out front. Unlike that one, which bustles with activity and multiple nurses, this one is quiet, and there's only one nurse. He's tilted back in his chair and scrolling through his phone like he doesn't have a care in the world. He quickly uprights himself at the sight of Dr. McGowan.

"This is Ms. Benson. She's the sister and attorney of Nichole Fischer." Dr. McGowan places the file he brought from the nurses' station on the desk.

The nurse scans me up and down, and I instantly feel exposed, even though I have nothing to hide. His inspection is unnerving in the same way that everything is unnerving about this place. A large whiteboard hangs on the wall beside him. I quickly spot *Fischer* with the notations *1x1* and *SI* next to it. What do the characters mean? I can't decipher the code.

"Betty just finished cleaning her up," the nurse informs Dr. McGowan as he hands him a different folder.

How did she get dirty? I don't know what that means, but Dr. McGowan nods like it's completely normal. He takes the chart from him, and we walk around the desk to a tiny hallway with three metal doors flanking the right wall, each with a small window. Nichole is behind one of those doors, and the impulse to rush forward and fling open each one until I find her surges through me, but I keep myself in line next to Dr. McGowan. He stops in front of the last door.

"This is her room." He moves aside so that I can look into the window slit.

Nobody's warnings could have prepared me for what meets my eyes. The room is a dirty white box with thick padded walls that remind me of an upholstered headboard. Even the ceiling is covered, as if someone could jump high enough to hit their head. There's nothing in the room except Nichole. She huddles in the corner in the fetal position, rocking in rapid, repetitive motions, back and forth, and back and forth. Her long red hair falls forward in ratty strings, obscuring her face.

She slowly lifts her head like she senses our presence. The air leaves my lungs. Angry red welts mangle both sides of her pale face, making her appear ghoulish. She bends her hands to her cheeks like she might be about to dig into herself again. Dr. McGowan instinctively moves past me to open the door and restrain her, but she suddenly stops like she remembered what happened last time and drops her hands to her lap in slow motion.

"Are you prepared to go inside?" He turns his attention to me.

"Yes," I answer, but I've never felt more unprepared for something.

Dr. McGowan slides one of the key cards in front of the scanner, and the metal door swings open. He motions for me to go inside while he waits behind me. I take a cautious step forward. My movement startles her, and there's a weird sheen to her emerald-green eyes as she stares at me without seeing me. The air is stuffy and smells like urine. I take another step forward and crouch to the ground so I'm not towering above her.

"Nikki?" I say softly, using her childhood name—the one we used until our junior year in college, when she decided she'd outgrown it.

My voice immediately registers, and she jerks like there's been an electric shock to her system. Life moves into her eyes as her soul slips back into her body.

"Krystal?" She lets out a small cry like she isn't sure I'm real and begins inching her way toward me, crawling on all fours in jerky movements.

"It's me, honey. I'm here now." I reach for her.

Within seconds, she's in my arms and buries her face in my shirt, clawing at me like she can't get close enough. I put my arms around her and hold tight; her frail body violently shakes against mine like she's freezing cold. I can feel the bones in her back. She's lost a lot of weight since the last time I saw her two weeks ago.

"It's okay. You're going to be okay. We'll figure this out together," I whisper into the top of her head.

She crumples in my arms and whimpers like a wounded puppy, too weak to even cry. I've never heard sounds like that before, and thick emotions strangle my throat, making it hard to breathe. Tears prick my eyes. The camera mounted above Nichole's head with its blinking red light tells me it's recording everything we do. I can't turn into an emotional wreck for everyone to see, or it will damage my credibility, so I force my feelings down and focus on her.

"Don't worry, sweetie. I'm here now, and I'm going to take care of you," I say as I rub circles on her back. "I'm going to help you. I'm going to get you through this." Another whimper that breaks my heart, but

I keep it together. "The first thing we need to do is get you out of this room, okay?" I wait for a response, but she keeps her head pressed into my chest and doesn't say anything. I can feel Dr. McGowan's presence behind us, reminding me that we're not alone. I choose my words carefully. "They're going to keep you here until they believe you're safe, so you've got to show them that, okay?"

She pulls back. "I'm not safe," she says in a pressured whisper as her eyes dart around the room without landing on anything. "I'm not safe. You're not safe. Nobody's safe." Her voice grows louder with each word. "They're still out there. They took Aiden." Her voice wavers with hysteria. I've never seen her look so terrified.

I lean in closer. "Who is still out there?"

She gives a quick nod and mouths, *"Help Aiden."*

"What happened to Aiden, Nichole?"

Her eyes widen. She rubs her hands up and down her arms like she's trying to keep warm even though she's sweating. Her face grimaces, and her tongue jerks out like a lizard's. For a second, I wonder if she's choking, but just as I'm about to react, she snaps it back inside, then puts her wrist up to her mouth like she's going to bite it. I instinctively bat her hand away and cry, "Stop that! What are you doing?"

"We have to get out of here. They're coming. He told them. I know he did," she hisses, fixing her eyes on Dr. McGowan blocking the doorway behind us.

"We can't do that right now," I say in an even tone, trying to keep her calm. "I'm going to get you out of here as quickly as I can, but I'm going to need your cooperation to do that. I want you to—"

She shakes her head, interrupting me. "Nonononononono . . ." She leaps to her feet and flattens herself against the wall. Her eyes dance wildly around the room. "Why are you looking at me like that? I like your tie. I want it for my collection. A pretty bow with a present for the top. You're still staring at me. Stop! You see?" She turns her head to the side like she's in a two-way conversation with someone, but there's nobody there. "The yellow rainbow's on his head. Just please. Go away. He can't play that song."

"Nichole, I'm going to ask you to settle down," Dr. McGowan breaks in, speaking for the first time since he unlocked the door and let me inside.

His voice makes something within her snap, and she lets out a piercing scream. She brings both her hands up to protect her face against an invisible threat. I step forward and reach for her. She whirls around and slaps me so hard that it hurls me backward. A male attendant appears from out of nowhere and is upon us instantly, stepping around me. He yanks Nichole to her feet in one swoop and pins both her arms behind her back. She arches against him and lets out a bloodcurdling scream, neck muscles strained, spit flying from her mouth. I slide back against the wall, stunned, as I watch her writhe and scream against him until I can't stand it anymore.

"Let go of her!" I shriek wildly. "She didn't mean to hurt me. Let go of her, please!" I can't keep the desperation out of my voice.

Another attendant appears in the doorway next to Dr. McGowan. He stands next to him, and they both watch Nichole as she kicks at the other attendant's shins. He lifts her up like she weighs nothing. She howls.

"Please, she's just scared. Let her go," I beg, unable to keep the tears from streaming down my face.

Dr. McGowan places his hand on my shoulder and pulls me toward the door. "This isn't helping. It's time for us to go."

———

I pace the hospital parking lot, waiting for Dr. McGowan's text. He promised to text as soon as Nichole's tests are finished and she's on the unit again. Everyone that gets admitted receives a full medical exam, a psychological evaluation, and an MRI and a series of blood draws to evaluate potential culprits for their symptoms, so it'll be a while before she's done. He had to practically pull me away from her room as she wrestled with the attendants. I thought those padded rooms were supposed to be soundproof, but her screams followed us all the way down the hallway and into Dr. McGowan's office. I couldn't stop crying, and there wasn't anywhere to hide, which only made me cry harder. Dr. McGowan kept handing me Kleenex and patting me awkwardly on the back until I finally pulled myself together.

He explained that Nichole's facial grimacing is because of the Haldol they're giving her. I googled it as soon as I got out here and found out it's a heavy-duty medication for psychosis. Calling her psychotic feels wrong, but it's the only description that fits what I saw today. I don't know how it's possible to go from the person she was to someone who's unrecognizable in a matter of weeks, and I keep replaying the scene from that horrible room over and over again. I wish there was something to do to distract me.

When there's a crisis, I hate sitting around doing nothing. There has to be something I can do. Maybe I can sneak onto the ICU without anyone in Aiden's family seeing me and check on how he's doing, since I'm dying to know. It's been radio silence from his family, and I'm too scared to text any of them, but the nurses might give me an update if I explain the situation, especially after I inform them that I'm Nichole's lawyer. At least it'll give me something to do while I wait. I turn around and head back inside just as Detective Sparks is leaving the building. I look down and move toward the other glass door, hoping he won't recognize me, but it's too late.

"Hello, Krystal," he says, stepping in front of me so there's no way around him and nowhere to hide. His button-down shirt is perfectly tucked into his wrinkle-free pants and doesn't match his unshaven face.

"Oh, hey—hi," I respond with enthusiasm like I wasn't doing my best to avoid him.

"This is my lucky day. You're one of the people on my list to call, so I'm really glad I ran into you," he says with a smile, revealing slightly crooked teeth in the front. "Maybe I should buy a lottery ticket."

I'm not amused. He's the last person I want to see or talk to. I don't want anything to do with anyone who's legally investigating Nichole until I speak with an attorney. I give him a polite smile, so I don't appear rude.

"Are you going up to see Nichole?" he asks.

I shake my head. "I saw her this morning."

He slides his hands into his front pockets and waits for me to say more, but I keep quiet, fully aware of his tricks. He's like a psychologist. Most people are uncomfortable when presented with silence and automatically start talking just to fill up the space, but not me. I can sit in silence for days if I need to.

"And how was she?" he asks after I don't provide any more information, and the silence grows longer than even he's comfortable with. His stare pierces me with so much concern that I almost start talking, but I force myself to count to ten before I do. It's an old trick I learned in graduate school.

"She's definitely had better days."

"Any luck getting her to talk about what happened?"

Does he really expect me to answer that question?

"How's Aiden?" I ask.

"He's definitely had better days," he says, lobbing my vague response back to me as if we're engaged in a tennis match. His lips twitch with a slight smile before returning to their straight line to match his stoic face.

"Do they think he's going to make it?" That's all that really matters. Everything else can be dealt with.

"The doctors are far more optimistic about his recovery this morning than they were yesterday."

Relief floods my body.

"Thank you," I say, acknowledging that he did a nice thing by giving me information he could've easily kept to himself. Should I tell Nichole? Will it help her to hear that he's getting better or make things worse? She hasn't said anything sensible about him, so there's no way to know what the information will do.

"It doesn't change the fact that somebody tried to kill him, though," he says, squaring his shoulders.

"Maybe . . ." I shrug noncommittally. "Something happened in that house for sure, but the two people that were there can't tell us what happened, and until that changes, I'm not willing to jump to any conclusions."

He raises his hands in a peaceful gesture. "Hey, I'm not either. Believe me, all I'm trying to do is read the evidence, and the evidence shows pretty strongly that it was an intentional fire set by your sister."

Every one of my muscles tenses. Dread fills my gut. Hearing a detective announce it is jarring. He doesn't give me a chance to recover before dropping the next bomb.

"The clothes she wore that night are covered in gasoline, which is the same accelerant used to start the fire. Her fingerprints are all over the lighter." He holds a finger up for each piece of evidence he recounts. "Not to mention that the lighter was found in her possession. They—"

"Where'd they find the lighter?" I interrupt, fixated on that detail as if it matters or means anything significant.

"In the pocket of her jeans." He gives his words a chance to sink in before continuing. "The fact that she made it out of the house before he did means that she was most likely the one who put the desk in front of the door. And . . ." His voice slows as he drops the final damning fact. "She admitted to doing it."

"Well, no offense, but you can't really trust anything that's coming out of her mouth right now." I raise my eyebrows at him and cock my head to the side. He knows I've got a point. "Besides, all of that may be true, and it still doesn't mean that someone else wasn't there and made her do it."

FIVE

KRYSTAL

Dr. McGowan stands by my side as I peer through the slit in the thick metal door of the seclusion room. Nichole looks peaceful. She's curled into the same corner as before, hugging her legs against her chest in a tight ball. Her morning tests stretched into the afternoon. It's almost three, and all I've done is twist myself in knots running through a hundred different scenarios of what might've happened, especially after running into Detective Sparks. William hasn't returned my call or replied to my email. I pulled Theresa off everything else to focus on finding other top criminal attorneys, because we need a plan B in case he doesn't work out or is too swamped to take on Nichole's case.

I stayed in the parking lot and didn't go back inside the hospital after my confrontation with Detective Sparks. My condo is only a few miles from the hospital, and I could've gone home, but I wanted to be near her. I want her to sense my presence even if I can't be with her physically, and three miles is too far for her to feel me. There're plenty of places to sit and wait comfortably in the hospital, but I don't like hospitals. I don't care how nice Dr. McGowan says the cafeteria is. I found a comfortable spot on the grass underneath a tree with plenty of shade where I could wait things out.

I spent most of my time scrolling through social media and trying to get a read on what people are saying about Nichole and Aiden, since their story is officially out. It was only a matter of time. Always is. In a town the size of Belmont, news travels fast, and it travels at lightning speed when it includes a woman burning her house down with her husband in it. There aren't any reporters or media at the hospital yet, but it's only a matter of time before the news vans start showing up. Theresa told me they're already lining the sides of Nichole's street and blocking the intersection before their house. This is the type of news the media loves to feast on. They'll sink their teeth into Nichole's story like it's an expensive steak and won't let go until they've devoured every bite. I've had lots of experience with the press. High-profile divorces get lots of publicity in small towns, so I spend hours coaching my clients on how to deal with the media. Thankfully, the hospital security will keep them from stepping foot inside here.

I turn to look at Dr. McGowan. "Will you tell her when she wakes up that I was here?" I hate not being able to talk to her or give her a hug, but she needs sleep more than anything else right now. He gives me a clipped nod, then goes back to his phone. His fingers fly on the screen as we leave the seclusion-room hallway and head toward the psychiatrists' offices. The walls on this side of the unit are painted an institutional blue because someone once said that blue was a calming color. It only makes everything more distorted. Psychiatric wards were originally called asylums, but there's nothing soothing or safe about this place.

Dr. McGowan's office is immaculate—clean, pristine, and orderly. There are no papers floating around or stacked in haphazard piles like there are in Mr. Barnes's office downstairs. There's not even a pencil or pen lying out. Two prints hang on each side of the window behind his desk. He takes a seat in the black leather chair behind the desk while I take one of the upholstered office chairs in front of it. He lays his hands out in front of him.

"What's wrong with Nichole?" I blurt out, eager for answers since I've been waiting all day for them.

"She's clearly in the throes of a psychotic episode. Her symptoms match the classic signs of what we see in someone who is experiencing psychosis—hallucinations, paranoia, delusions, tangential thinking, and difficulty distinguishing what's real from what's not. Her distorted cognitions are coupled with periods of mania and heightened anxiety, which makes her even harder to evaluate and assess. Her primary delusions center around Aiden. It appears she's convinced that he's not her real husband." He wears a neutral expression as he speaks.

"But I don't understand. How does that happen? She was fine when I saw her two weeks ago."

"We're not sure yet. Figuring out the cause of a patient's psychosis is difficult and complex, especially since there usually isn't a singular cause," he explains as he pulls a file out from one of the desk drawers and places it on top of his clean desk. "Sometimes individuals experience psychosis following seizure activity or because of an infection in their blood that's traveled to their brain, but her EEG and blood work came back completely normal. The only thing flagged on her blood work was mild dehydration, and that's an easy fix. We also look for any lesions on the brain as an explanation, but there weren't any abnormalities on her MRI. However, we've scheduled a follow-up CAT scan for her tomorrow because sometimes CAT scans pick up on things that the MRI missed. Her psychological treatment and evaluation will be ongoing while we work on finding the right diagnosis to explain her symptoms. That can take time, and things might be up and down with her until we do." He pauses, giving me a chance to catch up and making sure I'm digesting all the information. I nod for him to continue. "She did, however, fail both her neurological exam and her mental status exam." He pulls out a piece of paper from the file and slides it across the desk to me.

I pick it up and examine what looks like a preschooler's drawing of a clock. The circle is lopsided and misshapen like a kidney bean. The hands are on one side of the clock, and all the digits that would normally circle the clock are bunched up together in the upper corner. I've never seen anything like it. I hand it back to him, confused.

He sets it on his desk and points to it as he speaks. "This is just one of the many tests the neurologist gave Nichole this afternoon. It's called the clock-drawing test, and most people think of it as a screening tool for dementia, but we use it to look for other impairments in cognitive ability too."

I don't need to be a psychiatrist to see that she failed the test.

"We gave her other tests that clearly demonstrated similar cognitive impairments. She also isn't oriented to time and space."

I cock my head to the side and eye him quizzically, since his language has suddenly shifted into what sounds like science fiction talk.

He lets out a small smile before quickly returning to his stoic expression. "My apologies. Sometimes I can get carried away in my explanations, and I forget that not everyone understands what I'm talking about." Any other day his statement might've insulted my intelligence, but stopping him because I was offended and wanted to prove how smart I was would only slow him down, so I allow him to continue uninterrupted. "What that means is that Nichole doesn't know where she's at and she's unable to identify the correct day or date. She's unable to answer basic questions about herself or current events."

"So, where does all that leave us?" I ask.

"There're other differential diagnoses we haven't explored yet that may explain her psychosis."

"Like?"

"It's possible her symptoms could be due to something more organic. So, for instance, she might've had a stroke or a blood clot— some kind of injury to her brain. Perhaps she has a viral infection. Viral encephalitis is a definite rule-out. Mononucleosis is another option." He speaks in a clinical tone that I always mistook as uncaring and lacking compassion, but I appreciate his candidness now as he rattles off the facts without emotion. At least we haven't run out of options.

"What do we do next?"

"Our main priority is to stabilize her. Medication is tricky, and without a formal diagnosis it can be hard to find the right combination to treat her symptoms, but we'll get there. In the meantime, we'll engage in follow-up testing. I'll be sending her blood work out for a full autoimmune panel workup, and we've already sent samples off to Infectious Diseases. Those results should be back within the next forty-eight hours." He consults his notes before continuing, double-checking his facts. "We'll have to wait and see what the CAT scans show tomorrow. Hopefully, they will point to something helpful in aiding our diagnosis."

I let out a deep breath. "Is there anything I can do?" I just feel so powerless, and there's nothing I hate more than feeling powerless, especially when it comes to Nichole.

"Can you think of any time in Nichole's history that she might've demonstrated difficulty maintaining her grip on reality?"

The room shrinks, then spins, leaving me dizzy. I will my face blank. She had a tough time when we were seventeen, but it was nothing like this. And besides, our lives depend on us keeping that summer a secret. I hate lying, but sometimes there's no other choice.

I raise my eyes to meet his and shake my head. "No, she's never had any kind of mental illness."

SIX

NICHOLE

(THEN)

Mrs. Wheeler's daughter, Veronica, storms ahead of me and Krystal on our way home from school. She's stomping and kicking up dust behind her on the gravel road. She's been on a mission since we passed the Pattersons' house. That's when we're officially out of town and closer to home than we are school. Her arms swing like machetes in quick jerky motions, like pumping them harder will make her short legs go faster.

"How bad was it?" I whisper to Krystal out of the corner of my mouth when Veronica's far enough ahead so she can't hear me. She hates when we talk about how they bully her. How many times have we been through this crap since school started? Five? Six? I've lost count, but I've had enough. Our junior year in high school is supposed to be fun.

I was late for PE and missed all the drama because I was meeting with Mr. Peltier about doing extra credit in math. I got a B on our last test, and I've been doing whatever I can to bring my grade up. Most people would be happy with Bs, but this year's transcripts are the ones colleges look at the most, so I need to make sure I get straight As if I want any chance at an academic scholarship. I should've just skipped

PE and gone straight to English, but I didn't, and I knew something was going on as soon as I swung open the locker room door. Nobody was around. Just laughter coming from the back. I followed the sounds like an idiot, even though I knew what I'd find, and I did. There they were—Whitney and the HIT girls forming a circle around someone on the floor. People swarmed in like vultures to watch, like they always do. Sometimes they clap. It makes me sick. I hate people getting picked on.

Whitney and the HIT girls rule our school. They named themselves and won't tell anyone outside of their circle what the acronym stands for. The teachers either play along with them or look the other way. Krystal and I avoid them at all cost, and for the most part, they leave us alone. But Veronica's not so lucky. She's their favorite target, and the locker room is one of their prime spots to torture her. I knew it was her on the floor, and I got out of there as fast as I could before anyone saw me.

"It was awful," Krystal says, keeping her eyes straight ahead and barely moving her lips while she speaks. We perfected the art of pretending we aren't talking to each other years ago. "They were plastered everywhere on her locker. So disgusting."

"They were already up when you got there?" Word about what happened spread like wildfire, and it wasn't long before everyone knew that "someone" had squirted maxi pads with ketchup and taped them all over Veronica's locker.

She nods, tucking her long hair behind her ears. Her eyes are glued on Veronica like she might turn around and attack us at any time, but we're safe until we get home. "I was one of the first ones in there, and trust me, I wanted to take them down before anyone saw them so we could avoid this entire deal, but there was no way. If it had just been the pads, I could've easily grabbed them and thrown them into the trash, but I couldn't because of the ketchup everywhere. I tugged at a corner of one of the pads, and a huge glob fell on the ground. I just stood there."

She couldn't go anywhere since her locker is right next to Veronica's. Ever since we started high school, Coach has assigned us three lockers next to each other like all the other siblings, even though our last names don't match. It's probably also why they always put us in the back because we don't fit in the alphabet. It's so stupid and only makes Veronica an even easier target. We'll be getting punished for this one big-time because she hates when there's a crowd, and this one was more than just one grade. Seniors were there too. She probably spent all last period plotting the terrible things she'll do to us. We're going to have to be extra careful tonight. Full-alert mode.

"This is going to screw up my plans with Travis," I whine, trying to sound pathetic enough so that she'll feel sorry for me. Travis and I were supposed to hang out after we finished our homework, but that's definitely not happening. Veronica will have talked Mrs. Wheeler into punishing us by the time we're through the front door, and the first rule of punishment is always being banished to your room immediately following dinner with lights out at eight. Of course, we're the only ones who ever get the punishment since Veronica's never been punished a day in her life.

Krystal rolls her eyes dramatically at the mention of Travis. I punch her in the arm. "I don't care—he's cute."

"He's dumb," she says like she does every time we talk about him. "He doesn't even read books."

"So, not everybody has to like reading as much as I do." I roll my eyes right back at her.

I'm a freakishly obsessive reader. I can easily plow through two books a day if I have the time. All summer long I wait for people's garage sales to finish so I can swoop in on all the unsold boxes of books they give away at the end.

"Yes, but someone that dates you probably should." She gives me a knowing look.

"You act like I have so many options. Like boys are just lining up at my door to meet me."

This shuts her up. She knows I have a point. I'm boy crazy. I'll be the first to admit it. It started in second grade when I spent every recess chasing Joey Matzdorf around the playground, trying to kiss him. But just because I like boys doesn't mean they like me. I'm not the type of girl boys go for around here, and I definitely don't have the look. Small-town Iowa boys like girls with blonde hair and blue eyes. My orangish-red hair sticks out even more than my Goodwill clothes. There's only one other redhead in our entire school, but it's not the same. Her hair's a pretty red, and I wish I could dye mine to match hers, but dyeing hair is against Mrs. Wheeler's rules, even though I have no idea why. She could definitely use some brown color on all those gray roots. Some of her rules make sense, like no one is allowed to leave their boots in the entryway during the winter, or all the trash bins have to be taken out every Monday morning. There's no way to do it behind her back without getting caught. Showing up at dinner with pretty red hair would be obvious, and I'm too afraid she'd make me shave my head for breaking the rules. So, I'm stuck with my ugly brassy hair until I'm eighteen.

Just like I'm stuck with Veronica until then.

"It's not like I'm going to marry Travis or anything. He's only my starter boyfriend, and I think he's totally fine for a starter boyfriend, even if he's kind of dumb. I actually don't mind it all that much because it makes it easier to practice things with him. I look at it like he's preparing me for when my first real boyfriend comes along."

Krystal bursts out laughing at my explanation, but I'm being serious. Someday my Prince Charming is going to come along, and when he does, I want to be ready for him. Sometimes you only get one shot at true love, so I'm practicing just like we do before our track meets. I'll make all my big mistakes with the ones I don't really care about so I don't screw things up with the right one. But I don't expect Krystal to understand that. She doesn't care anything about boys. All she's focused on is getting us out of here and making sure we don't end up like our birth moms.

The farm comes into view as we pass the Stevenses' horses. Inky and Schlotzky are out in their pens. Those aren't their real names. Just the ones Krystal and I gave them when we were eight and used to sneak down to play with them every day during the summer. We thought their names were hilarious, and it doesn't seem right to give them better ones now. They love being petted, and since we have every other possible animal on the farm but horses, we stop to love on them most days. But not today. Obviously, not stopping today.

Krystal quits laughing about me calling Travis my starter boyfriend and turns serious again. "What do you think she'll do?"

That's the burning question of our childhood.

What will Veronica do?

It's an impossible question to answer because you never know what she'll do or when she'll strike. Everything they do to her at school she takes out on us at home like it's somehow our fault she doesn't fit in. Her system for righting the wrongs doesn't make any sense, either, but it hurts my brain trying to figure her out. We used to be naive and worked so hard at getting her to like us. I mean, it could literally be the three of us if she wanted it that way since she's barely a year younger than us. We didn't have to be sister twins. We could've been triplets. It's not like we ever excluded her. We were always trying to include her with things and used to apologize for what the kids did to her, going on and on about how amazing she was or how great she was. Lots of the stuff we said wasn't exactly true because she's not an easy person to like, but it didn't matter anyway. Saying nice things and being kind only made her more pissed off.

So, we stopped. Just like we stopped trying to make them leave her alone at school, because believe me, we tried.

Kids have bullied her since I came to live with the Wheelers in second grade and Veronica was in first. She's always been an easy target because she's so weird and socially awkward. She never says the right thing, and she makes these weird grunting noises underneath her breath that I don't even think she knows she's doing. It doesn't help that she doesn't dress right and smells like the farm. Not that me and Krystal don't smell like the same farm, but we're good in sports and we spend hours combing through the clothes at Goodwill for cool outfits so we don't stand out. People want us on their teams, so that saves us from most of the bullying by Whitney and her crew. Always has.

Their teasing used to be just kid stuff. They'd try to trip her, call her "Stinky pig!" and snort when she went by, but it wasn't anything that other kids didn't get too. They spread their meanness like an equal opportunity plague. That's just how they were. But things took a bad turn in sixth grade.

Ben's the male version of Whitney—entitled and privileged—except he's over six feet tall and punches way harder than she does. Whitney's petite and blonde; he's bulky and brown. Nobody's safe from his radar. He calls me and Krystal Stick 1 and Stick 2, and that's just fine with us. Usually people get labeled way worse, and once you've been labeled by Ben, it's almost impossible to get rid of. His labels stick.

Ben and Whitney teamed up to basically rule the school, and things haven't been the same since. Veronica is mean and vindictive, and she can be just as cruel as Whitney, but at least she has her reasons, even if her reasons are totally screwed up. Whitney likes to hurt people on purpose and for no reason. She gets a sick thrill out of it, and her sicko meter was triggered during the second week of school, when she decided to throw a spaghetti noodle at Veronica during lunch. It hit her face and stuck. Everyone laughed like it was the funniest thing they'd ever seen, just like they always do, because no matter how bad you feel for the person getting picked on, you're glad it's not you, and you'll do anything to keep it that way.

Veronica was embarrassed, but it seemed harmless. Until Ben threw something at her the next day, and then it was game on. Every day kids took turns throwing food at her. They developed a system for awarding points based on the degree of difficulty with the shot and the type of food used. Nobody from other tables threw food, but we all clapped and cheered while they did. Veronica started faking sick so she could miss school, and I felt so bad for her, but I didn't know what to do or how to help her, even though I wanted to. I started thinking it was never going to end, but then everything came to a head after one of the school cafeteria workers alerted the principal about what was going on. They had enough after one of Whitney's gang ran up behind Veronica and dumped the insides of an entire trash can on her head. The principal called Mrs. Wheeler and told her about the incident.

Mrs. Wheeler was furious, and Veronica was mortified. What happens to her at school is her biggest secret with her mom. She has to maintain her image as the golden child—the miracle girl who can do no wrong—and I totally get why. Mrs. Wheeler tells anyone who will listen, which means I've heard the story like ten thousand times, about how she and Mr. Wheeler started trying to get pregnant when they were twenty and had nothing but problems. All their failed pregnancies are buried in small graves behind our house, which I avoid whenever I'm on that side of the yard. Eventually, they gave up on having kids. Mrs. Wheeler thought she was in menopause when she found out she was pregnant at forty-two.

That's why Mrs. Wheeler doesn't see Veronica the way everyone else does. In her eyes, she's the blonde-haired and blue-eyed little darling who she waited over twenty years for. In reality, her hair isn't anywhere near blonde. Some people call it dirty blonde, but I'd call it mousy brown. And her eyes aren't blue. They're a boring murky brown.

But who cares about her looks? There're plenty of ugly people, and others like them just fine. It's her personality that's the worst part of her, and I'm pretty sure you can't change that. She's never happy. Like never. I've only seen her smile a handful of times, and it's always because someone's making her do it. Most of the time her lips are set in a thin line. I mean, she's scowling in her baby pictures; what does that tell you?

I've never seen Mrs. Wheeler get so mad as she was the day she found out about the cafeteria, not even when the butcher ripped her off over the beef order. I could see her pulse throbbing in her temple, and Krystal thought she was going to have a heart attack because of the way she paced around the living room that night with her eyes bulging out. We were all shocked when she showed up at lunch the next day and sat next to Veronica. She did it for the entire week, no matter how much Veronica begged her not to. And Veronica begged. I heard her crying about it to Mrs. Wheeler in her bedroom. That's where they go for all their private talks, and it's the only time Veronica ever cries. It's totally fake because I'm not sure she knows how to cry for real, but Mrs. Wheeler was determined to go, and when her mind is made up about something, there's no changing it. She was making a statement—if the school couldn't protect her daughter, she would. They stopped throwing food at her in the cafeteria, but their bullying got way worse instead of better, and it hasn't stopped.

We reach the end of the driveway and watch as Veronica runs up the porch and into the house. I grab Krystal's hand and turn to look at her. I know every inch of her face. From the scar on her forehead that she got from flipping over her bike's handlebars in the drainage ditch to the small mole on her upper lip that she tries to freeze off with ice cubes. I can't imagine living here without her. She's the best friend you could ever have. I give her hand a squeeze. "You ready for this?"

———

Dust from the cow feed fills the tiny room and steals the air from my lungs. My pulse races as my eyes search the darkness for any sign of light. There's none. How could I have been so stupid? Panic thrums my chest. My hands grope underneath me for solid ground, but fistfuls of ground corn slide through my fingers like sinking sand.

Breathe. This isn't the first time.

I'm not being buried alive. It just feels like it.

I was being so cautious tonight. Krystal and I hurried through our chores in stealth mode, always looking over our shoulder for Veronica. She creeps around like one of the other barn cats even though she's not supposed to be in the barn because of her allergies. She has terrible hay fever that acts up anytime she gets near it, but that doesn't stop her. Chore time is one of the best times to get us because we split up to get things done.

Never turn your back to the door.

How many times have we told each other that?

All I was thinking about was Krystal. I wanted to fill my wheelbarrow with the feed and get back out there as fast as I could to check in with her before I fed the cows. She always comes through the barn on her way to put the pigs down for the night, and I know exactly how much time it takes between barns.

Nine seconds.

That's all I was thinking as I darted in.

Click.

Instant darkness surrounded me. I held back the urge to scream. I used to scream. I don't scream anymore.

Old barns weren't built with windows, so when you snuff out the light, there's nothing but black space. Tight, compressed air fills my lungs. You could die in here if you were allergic to seed. Or never found.

I tell myself the same things I tell Krystal to tell herself whenever Veronica locks her up. It's been her favorite thing to do to us since the early days—our foolish little-girl days. It was halfway into our first summer on the farm, and she asked if we wanted to play hide-and-seek. We jumped at the chance, thinking she finally liked us after months of pretending we didn't exist. Krystal and I hid together in the linen closet. We tried to be quiet and not giggle as we waited for her to find us. Seconds drew into minutes. Then the minutes stretched even longer until we started wondering if she was ever going to find us. Both of us were shocked when we tried the door and discovered it was locked. Krystal freaked out first. We all have our phobias. Fear of enclosed spaces is definitely hers.

It wasn't mine before. It is now.

I inch on all fours, doing my best to steel myself against the terror surging through me. All my self-talk does nothing to calm the fear that she might've killed Krystal. Or have her tied up somewhere. Given her something to knock her unconscious. Anything to keep her from getting to me. And if she can't get to me, then there's nobody to come looking for me. Eventually I'll run out of air in this feed room before anyone finds me.

Something brushes up against my leg as my fingers touch the spikes from the pitchfork—the one we stack against the door for a marker like we have in all the rooms and just for this reason. I work my way to the handle, then follow it up to the top as I stand. I feel my way along the wall a few inches to the door. I reach down with my other hand and tug the handle.

Nothing.

She's done it again, but I always hope that this time the door will open when I twist the knob. I move to the side of the door and slide down the wall to the seed underneath me. I pull my legs up to my chest and hug them against me, reminding myself to breathe.

Krystal will find me. She always does. I just have to wait.

SEVEN

KRYSTAL

My cat, Hobbes, paws my chest, waking me to sheets drenched in cold sweat from my disjointed nightmares, but at least I slept. I took two melatonin before I went to bed because I wasn't taking any chances with a repeat performance from the night before. All I did was lie there with my head spinning, and I wasn't going through that again. Normally, I'd spend a few minutes cuddling with him, but I don't have any time this morning. There's only a short window of free access to information before everything gets tied up with the lawyers, and I don't want to waste a single minute until then.

"Sorry, buddy," I say, pushing Hobbes aside and throwing the covers off me. He lets out a loud meowing protest, but his upset will be gone as soon as we get downstairs and he sees me heading to the pantry for his food. I grab my bathrobe from the gray armchair and tuck it around me to keep warm before plodding down the hallway. The smell of coffee greets me on the stairs as I make my way down and into the kitchen.

I grab my phone from the charger plugged in next to the coffee maker on the counter. Years ago, I stopped keeping my phone in the bedroom with me after a *New York Times* article described how the alpha waves disrupted your sleep and that your brain still listened for the sounds of your phone even while you slept. I quickly tap out a text to Mark, asking how things are going with the Wilkins case, before opening my unread emails.

The first one is from Dr. McGowan, informing me that Nichole was taken out of the seclusion room last night around midnight and transferred to a patient room.

"She's out, Hobbes!" I squeal, jumping up and down in the kitchen. Dr. McGowan doesn't give any more details, and I email him back, letting him know I'm on my way up to the hospital. I don't care if it isn't visiting hours. Somebody's working there, and they're going to let me see Nichole.

I answer client emails in between showering and getting myself ready for the day, draining another two cups of coffee in the process. Theresa's doing an amazing job keeping everything together, and gratitude for her washes over me. I'm so fortunate to have her as my assistant. There's nothing I can do that she can't, and she knows more about law than most lawyers I meet.

The sun is starting to rise as I leave home and rush to my car. I'll probably get there so early the nurses won't have changed shift yet. Maybe they'll let me eat breakfast with her since all their meals are in the community room. I hurry through town, making the green at the only two lights in Belmont, and arrive in the empty parking lot of Riverside East before seven. I grab another coffee from the lobby and take it with me to the fourth floor.

"Excuse me," I say to the receptionist behind the desk with a tone of authority like I'm supposed to be here at this hour.

She's young, somewhere in her early twenties, and looks like she's been up all night. Her ponytail, which was probably tightly pulled back at the beginning of her shift, is haphazardly piled on top of her head, and loose strands fall around her round face. She holds back a yawn as she greets me with a hello.

"I'm Nichole Fischer's lawyer, and I'm here to see her." She narrows her eyes. I don't give her a chance to interrupt. "I spoke with Dr. McGowan this morning, and he should be up to join me shortly."

Not entirely a lie. Nowadays, emailing qualifies as speaking, and even though he never said he was on his way up, I'm certain he's not going to be able to stay away either.

The nurse quickly looks me up and down. "Nichole is in room 41; however, patients aren't allowed to meet with anyone in their rooms while they're on one-to-one supervision, and she is currently on one-to-one. I will notify one of our staff members to wake her and bring her into the community room. I—"

"No, no, no," I jump in. "Don't wake her up. I mean, get her if she's awake, but if she's sleeping, just let her sleep until Dr. McGowan gets here."

She gives me a confused look like she might be reconsidering giving me permission to see Nichole, but her lack of energy works in my favor. She points to the hallway leading to the community room. "You can have a seat in the first room on your left. I'll have one of the staff check in on her and get back to you."

"Thank you," I say, giving her a grateful smile.

The place is eerily still as I walk down the hallway. My footsteps on the linoleum echo behind me. Everything in the community room is violence- and suicide-proof. The windows are unbreakable Plexiglas sealed at the edges and locked to keep the patients safe. The walls are bare except for a clock that mercilessly clicks away each minute. The patients eat all their meals here, so the smell of hospital food has seeped into the walls. It mingles with the smell of body odor.

There's only one other person in the room with me—a man who nervously paces in front of the row of windows, smacking his cheeks every few seconds and muttering to himself. I find a table on the other side of the room, as far away from him as possible. His agitation is infectious, and I turn the other direction so I can't see him. The minutes stretch out endlessly until I finally hear motion outside.

Nichole shuffles into the community room like an elderly person. Her head hangs so low her chin is almost touching her chest. A paper-thin white gown droops on her small frame. Her legs jut out stiffly like she's forgotten how to walk overnight, and the staff member next to her puts his arm around her and guides her over to me. He's got at least forty years on her and could easily be her grandfather, but she's the one struggling to make it across the room.

He places her delicately into the chair, and her body slumps so far to the right side that he has to quickly grab her and pull her back up before she slides off the seat. He tries to press her down on the chair upright, but it's obvious she'll tip over again if he lets her go. He eyes the room, but there's nobody here except me and the other patient, who's clearly no help, so he decides to keep his hands on her shoulders and stand behind her chair.

"I'm sorry," he says. "I never know what to do when this happens, and I hate that it happens as often as it does." His voice is thick, and he draws out his *a*'s like he might be from the Deep South. He leans forward conspiratorially. "I can't stand when they get them so doped up that they act like this." He has kind eyes and a soft voice. The smell of stale coffee is on his breath.

I move over to their side and kneel down beside Nichole, holding her forearm so she's steady in the chair and can't fall if he lets go. "I've got her. We're good," I say, but he doesn't release his grip or step away from the table.

"That's okay," he says as his face breaks into a gentle smile. His bright eyes are framed by thick white eyebrows, and he looks like the kind of man who sits on his porch watching out for his neighbors. "I don't mind helping you girls, and she's my one-to-one, so I can't be further than two feet from her at any given time."

"Really?"

He nods. "That's how it'll be until she's off restriction. I'm Earl, by the way."

"Hi, Earl," I say, forcing a smile for his benefit because nothing about Nichole's present state makes me happy. She sits unflinching in her chair with no recognition that I'm crouched next to her. "I'm Nichole's sister, Krystal."

"Poor thing. I just hate seeing them this way."

Tears mist my eyes. "Nichole?" I say tentatively and as softly as I can, hoping the sound of my voice calling her name will bring her back from wherever she's disappeared to, but she still says nothing, doesn't move. Her hands are bent at her wrists in forty-five-degree angles on her lap. Red chapped rings circle her mouth from continually licking her lips. She lets out a weird smacking sound every few seconds when she does it.

"Nichole?" I try again. She stares straight ahead, rarely blinking, face flat. "Sweetie?" My voice warbles with emotion.

"My daughter used to get like this whenever she was first brought to the hospital." Earl's voice breaks in instead of Nichole's. "She'd go through real bad spells. Real bad ones. Her brain would start telling her all these things that weren't true, so she didn't always act right, and she ended up in places like this many times. This is a good place, though. Some of the best doctors work at this hospital. Betcha didn't know they bring people from up north and all over the country to get treated here, did ya?" He gives me a wide grin, and I can't help but smile back. Some of the tension in my back releases. "Sometimes we even get people from New York." He says it as if New York is an exotic place. "Your sister's gonna get good care here. Real good care. You just watch. Trust me. They'll figure out what's wrong with her in no time."

I'm afraid I'll start crying if I speak, so I nod my gratitude and allow myself to feed off his hope and encouragement. He smiles back as though he senses my appreciation. I tuck Nichole's red hair behind her ears with my free hand, then softly rub the back of her head like I do Hobbes's. I take deep breaths in and out, trying to gather myself and think clearly. I'm no good to Nichole if I turn into a puddle of tears on the floor.

I'm not quite centered when the sound of footsteps approaches from behind. I turn around. Monk-strap dress shoes lead up to Dr. McGowan's face, and I've never been so relieved to see him. He takes one look at

Nichole and shifts into a doctor mode I've never witnessed. Earl gladly steps back as Dr. McGowan swoops in. He crouches beside her and turns her chair so they're facing each other.

"Nichole, you've met me before, but in case you don't remember, I'm Dr. McGowan. I'm a doctor at Riverside East, and I'm here to help you," he speaks slowly, enunciating his words. He pulls a pencil light out of his shirt pocket and shines it in each of her eyes. He does it two more times, like he's not satisfied with the response he's getting from her pupils. He tucks the implement back into his shirt and lifts up his pointer finger in front of her face. "I want you to keep your eye on my finger, okay? Don't look away while I move it; just follow it as best you can." He moves his finger from one side to the next. Nichole remains faced forward, oblivious to the movement in front of her. I watch as a droplet of drool forms at the corner of her mouth, horrified that she seems unaware of it. I pull my sleeve down and use the back of my hand to wipe it off.

"Can you tell me what year it is?" he asks.

A long, drawn-out pause follows.

"How about the month? Are you able to tell me the month?"

I fight the urge to grab her shoulders and shake her—wake her up from this drug-induced stupor. I can't stand looking at her this way. I want to shove her into the bathtub and spray her down with the shower like she used to do to me in college when I stumbled in late and needed to sober up by 8:00 a.m. for my biochemistry class. This isn't right.

The breakfast cart arrives after his next question, which she meets with silence. We might as well not be in the same room. Other patients begin trickling in. Our conversations are no longer private.

"I think we should get right to it this morning," Dr. McGowan says, finishing his exam and rising to his feet. There's no change in Nichole's expression. He picks up his iPad and types for a few beats. "She's the first person on the list for CT this morning, so the technicians should be here immediately following breakfast to bring her down. She'll meet with Dr. Bernstein afterward. She's the neurologist Nichole met with yesterday and should be the one officially assigned to her case after our team meeting at eleven."

"Okay," I say as I stand to meet him, keeping one of my hands on Nichole's shoulder in case she topples over. I point to her with my other hand. "But first and foremost, even before breakfast, what are you going to do about this?"

"I can understand why her condition might be upsetting."

"Upsetting?" My voice shakes. "She's on so many drugs right now she's probably peeing on herself. She can barely walk." This time I point to Earl, who stood as still as a statue two feet away from us throughout the entire conversation. "He had to help her in here. This isn't right. You can't keep her—"

Dr. McGowan interrupts. "Can we step outside? I don't want to have this conversation around the other patients."

I glance down at Nichole. I don't want to leave her even if she has no idea I'm here. I bend down and whisper in her ear, "I'm going to go talk with Dr. McGowan outside in the hallway, but I'm not leaving. I'm coming back. Promise."

There's no change in her expression.

I can't kiss her on her mangled cheeks, so I press my lips to the top of her head instead. "I love you," I whisper, before standing back up and following Dr. McGowan out of the community room.

He walks a few paces down the hallway and stops in front of the patients' phones. They aren't allowed to have their own phones on the unit, and there're two old-fashioned rotary phones provided for them. The young people who get institutionalized probably have to be taught how to use them.

"You have to do something about that," I say bluntly now that I don't have to hold back. "That's ridiculous. I've never seen someone so high in my life. If that's what it takes to get her out of the seclusion room, then put her back in there."

He nods his head in quick succession. "I understand your concern. I'm going to decrease her Haldol and see how she does if we replace her clozapine with an SSRI instead to treat the anxiety."

"Okay, good, because I don't ever want to see her like that again. It was awful." Thinking about it makes me feel sick to my stomach.

"Yes, I'm sure it was." He pauses the conversation while a nurse walks by carrying a cart loaded up with vials of blood. "There's something I left out of my email because I wanted to tell you in person." He clears his throat as I stretch forward, hanging on his every word. "Aiden took a turn for the worse last night, and his condition still hasn't stabilized."

"Seriously? What happened?" I checked on how he was doing before I went to bed last night, and all the reports were positive. There were plenty of local news and social media reports since Aiden's family is so well known in the community. They aren't a family anyone outside of Texas would recognize, but they are big fish in our sea.

"He's developed an infection in his lungs due to the fluid buildup. It's causing all kinds of problems with his blood pressure, and his other major organ systems are beginning to shut down," he announces in the same monotone.

"That's awful."

"You know what's going to happen then, right?" he asks.

"I mean, I'm assuming it's going to get really bad?" I have no idea what happens to people when their organs shut down. Obviously, they die eventually, but Aiden can't die. He just can't.

"They're going to charge Nichole."

"No way. How could anyone think of charging her with anything, given the condition she's in? Nobody's charging her with anything."

He cocks his head to the side. "That's not why they haven't charged her yet." He gives me a strange look like I'm dumb. "They're waiting to see if Aiden lives so they know whether to charge her with murder or attempted murder."

EIGHT

KRYSTAL

"Coming!" I yell to the sound of the phone ringing on the other side of my office door as I struggle to turn the key in the lock, silently cursing myself for not getting it fixed. Normally, I wouldn't care so much about missing a phone call or letting it go straight to voice mail, but there're too many important people trying to get ahold of me. I drop my bag on the chair, and grab the phone on the reception desk before it cuts off.

"Hello?" I answer breathlessly.

"May I speak with Krystal Benson?"

"This is she," I say, hoping it's William Jenkins. If what Dr. McGowan said is true, then I need his help more than ever.

"Oh, hi. Good morning, Krystal. This is Detective Sparks."

I curse silently under my breath, regretting that I picked it up and wishing I'd let it go to voice mail. I quickly step through the reception area and into my office. "What can I do for you this morning, Detective?" I ask, shutting the door behind me. My office sits untouched from how I left it two days ago. It's only been a short time, but it feels like an entire lifetime has passed.

"I'd like to follow up on our conversation from yesterday, if we might," he says, as if I have a say in the matter.

I wait for him to continue, but he doesn't. His silence won't be nearly as effective on the phone. I turn on my computer and wait for all my files to load on the desktop.

"How's Nichole?" he asks.

"She's progressing," I say, knowing a medical status update isn't his motivation for calling.

"That's great. Glad to hear she's getting better. I plan on stopping by the hospital later on today myself." His answer isn't any more about her health than mine.

My breath catches in my chest. Can he do that? Is he allowed to talk to Nichole without a lawyer present if she's not even capable of asking for a lawyer? If I don't get in touch with a good attorney soon, I'm going to get stuck with a slimy used-car-salesman lawyer because I need one now. I can't manage these issues on my own.

"I should be there most of the afternoon," I say so he knows she won't be up there alone. Maybe knowing that I'm going to be around will keep him away. "Looks like we'll probably get to see each other in person today too."

"How nice. Two days in a row," he says with a hint of amusement in his voice, and I can't tell if he's flirting with me or just being sarcastic. He doesn't wait for a response from me before continuing. "I spent some time yesterday out at Crestview interviewing her colleagues and students. Your sister was very well loved by both."

Outside of Aiden, Nichole's life centers around her students at Crestview High School. She loves teaching her history classes, but she's the most passionate about coaching track. She says it's about running, but it's because she gets them for four years—ninth grade to graduation. Nichole suffers from primary ovarian insufficiency so she can't have any children of her own. She's always loved her students, but after the life-changing diagnosis, they became her babies, and she channeled all her mothering instincts into them. She nurtures her team members all the way through high school and goes through empty-nest syndrome every summer.

"How are her kids holding up?" I ask. She talks about them like they're her own, and I grow attached to them over the years, too, because most of her stories revolve around what's happening in their lives.

"They organized a GoFundMe campaign for her and created a Facebook page that's filled with supportive messages." I can hear the smile in his voice, and I can't help but smile too. They love her as much as she loves them. "But everyone I've talked to says you're the one who knows her best. Sounds like you're not just her sister, but the closest person to her too. Would you agree?"

"We're pretty close." I don't tell him we're close enough for me to read her thoughts sometimes and know what she's going to do before she does it. I've never understood people who aren't friends with their siblings as adults. How do you survive childhood together and not grow an intimacy unlike any other? But then I remember. Not everyone's like us. Lots of siblings hate each other for the same reasons we love each other.

"Most of them haven't seen her since school ended for the summer, so they couldn't say much about what the past month has been like for her. They said it was usual for them to maintain their distance over summer. Have you noticed a similar pattern?"

"Nichole spends her summers hanging out with Aiden as much as she can. They take all of their vacation time during the summer because they're both so busy during the year. Aiden travels a lot for business, and Nichole takes on her students' problems like they're her own, so when Aiden and her are together, it's intense and all-consuming. I guess that's what happens when you give yourself a chance to miss your partner," I say like I have experience knowing what's good or bad in a relationship. Hobbes is my longest relationship besides Nichole.

"Do you see her during the summer?"

"Absolutely. Sometimes I even travel with them on weekend trips." We were supposed to go to Galveston next week after my trial ended. Aiden's family has always thought it's weird that I travel with them and that we spend so much time together as a threesome, but I've never felt like a third wheel. Aiden's the one always complaining about being left out and how we easily slip into our own private song and dance without making room for anyone else at the party.

"Did you notice anything off with her behavior?"

"No."

"Any problems in their relationship?"

"They were happily married." His disbelief comes through the phone without him saying a word. "Believe me—nobody happily married sets their house on fire with their spouse inside. I get that. I'm aware of how bad this looks for her."

He lets out a compassionate sigh. "Sometimes it's the people closest to us that have the hardest time accepting that someone we love could do something so terrible. I see it happen all the time, especially with parents, but those two things can coexist. We can still love someone even if they've been bad." His voice is syrupy thick with pity.

That's fine with me. He can pity my perceived denial all he wants. While he's busy examining Nichole's life under a microscope, I'm going to find out what really happened that night.

NINE

NICHOLE

(THEN)

Krystal's hair falls out in clumps in my hand as I work my way through it. "It's not that bad. Really, it isn't." I'm trying to sound convincing, but she can't stop crying.

Stupid Veronica.

Her appetite for revenge wasn't satisfied by punishing me. Oh no, that wasn't enough. She had to make Krystal suffer too. She gets like that sometimes.

It had taken Krystal almost an hour before she got to the feed room and let me out. She apologized over and over again for how long it took her to get to me, like it's her fault Veronica is such a crazy psycho. I hate when she does that.

"I'm so sorry," she said for like the thousandth time. "One of the cows got stuck in an old barbed wire fence down by the creek. His left hind leg was all tangled, and Mrs. Wheeler asked me to run the clippers to Judd. Worst timing ever."

I'd stumbled out of the room without saying a word, gasping for air and racing to the bathroom. Once I peed my pants when Veronica locked me in an antique chest for three hours. She kept me in there for so long that I didn't have any other choice. There was no way to do it without peeing all over myself. Definitely one of her top three most humiliating ones. Now every time my brain goes into terror mode about being locked up, it also goes into have-to-pee-so-bad-I'm-about-ready-to-die mode too.

Veronica had won the lottery with the cow getting tangled, and she'd leapt at the opportunity to corner me alone. At least that's what we'd thought. But apparently she wasn't smirking with pride and satisfaction outside the heavy door while I tried not to have a heart attack in the darkness. She went into the house and filled our shampoo bottle with Nair or some other kind of formula that makes your hair fall out on the spot.

Krystal jumped in the shower after we got back inside. Her screams sent me flying from our bedroom and racing to the bathroom door.

I pounded on the door. "What's going on? Are you okay?"

"My hair's falling out! My hair's falling out!" she shrieked from inside.

"Open up so I can help you." I glanced over my shoulder to see if Veronica was standing at the end of the hallway watching us from the family-member side of the house. Mrs. Wheeler's home is a ranch-style house. The kitchen and living spaces are in the center of the house with a wing off each side. Foster kids on the right. Family on the left.

Veronica stood at the intersection in the middle. Her lip was turned up slightly, the closest she gets to smiling. Of course she wouldn't miss this moment. I flashed her a dirty look while I banged on the door with my fist.

Krystal flung it open and held her towel out for me to see. Her chestnut-brown hair lay in clumps and swirls in the middle of it. "Look! I took my towel off, and half my hair fell out. See?" She shook the towel in front of me like I wasn't getting the depravity of the situation.

Krystal loves her hair as much as I hate mine. She's been growing it out since we were in seventh grade and takes meticulous care of it, brushing one hundred full strokes every morning and one hundred more before bed each night. Besides her running, it's the thing other people comment the most about since it's so shiny and goes halfway down her back. Everyone wants to know the secret to her great hair, but she refuses to tell anyone but me. She uses the same conditioner that we use on the cows when they get yeast infections. Mrs. Wheeler refuses to buy conditioner for us. She says it's a luxury we don't need, so Krystal is always trying to find ways to use products we have lying around the house. Once she tried regular hand lotion on her hair. I tried the cow conditioner, too, because it worked so well for her, but it made my hair frizzier.

I moved inside the small bathroom and quickly shut the door behind us. I slid the brick in front of it—another one of our tricks, since we're not allowed to have a lock on the door; at least it slows things down and gives us a warning.

So far, Veronica's left us alone.

I grab the towel from her and examine the piles of hair like I don't already know who did this. "It's okay. It's not half your hair. You probably won't even notice."

But it's pretty bad.

"How didn't we think of this?" Krystal cries.

We spend hours brainstorming all the possible ways Veronica might attack us and then figure out what we can do to protect ourselves from them. There's a small pink notebook stuffed underneath my mattress, because sometimes ideas come to me in the middle of the night and I'm too afraid to wait until morning to add them to our master list in case I forget. We keep the master list in the hayloft in the barn, the same place we keep everything that we want safe, because Veronica hates going up there. It was our favorite spot to play when we were kids. It was perfect because it was the one place that guaranteed we'd always be alone. We spent hours creating elaborate towns out of the hay bales. We built skyscrapers to the roof, pretending we lived in the cities we dreamed of visiting someday. A couple nights we even slept up there with the hatch open so we could see the stars. We trained ourselves to overcome the stifling heat in the summer without any ventilation and turned the mice into our friends during the long winter months because we were determined to have space that was ours.

"I don't know, but she's never going to get us with it again. Every time we get in the shower, we have to check the shampoo and the conditioner to see if she's put something in it," I say.

"How are we supposed to do that?" she asks, doing her best not to cry, in case Veronica has tiptoed down the hallway and is listening outside the door. We don't want to give her the satisfaction of knowing how badly she hurts us. Crying's the only thing we have control over.

"Easy. A sniff test. Whatever that stuff is, it has to smell super bad because it's got to be strong enough to make your hair fall out."

I remind myself to add this one to the master list as I work the comb through her hair as delicately as I can, doing my best not to pull out any new hairs. The stuff Veronica used was potent. A small bald patch is growing on the back of Krystal's head. I don't want to break the news to her, but I have to.

"So, there is a spot back here where it's just a teensy bit bald. Not bad at all, and you can barely see it. I wouldn't have even noticed it if I wasn't back here working on it so—"

"What?" She shoves me off her and grabs the handheld mirror on the counter next to the sink. She hops up on the counter with her back to the mirror on the wall, holding the smaller mirror in front of her face as she tries to angle it just right to see the spot. "I can't see it."

"It's because it's so small. See? I'm telling you, it's nothing." She's still moving the mirror around like she doesn't believe me. I grab her arms and pull her down. "Come on, sit. Let me finish going through your hair."

She puts the lid down on the toilet and takes a seat on it. She's got her sad-puppy face on. That one crushes me. "What are we going to do, Nichole?"

I run the comb softly through her hair. "We're going to keep going like we always do. One day at a time. We're almost there. Only a year left, and we're getting out of here."

———

Krystal pulls the baseball cap down to her ears and glares across the dinner table at Veronica. She stabs at the peas on her plate like she wishes she was squashing Veronica's head. It took me over an hour to calm her down this afternoon, and the sight of Veronica has sent her through the roof again. I don't blame her.

I mean, she has a bald spot on her head. Thankfully, Krystal's got a lot of hair, so she can brush over it and hide it pretty easily, but it's there. You can see it if you look closely, especially in a certain light, but I didn't tell Krystal that. At least it's on the back of her head where she doesn't have to see it every day and be reminded of it.

Veronica returns her glare with an equally hostile stare. Her brown beady eyes fixed on Krystal. She looks like a rat. Pointed nose. Squinty eyes too close together. Mousy hair. She takes measured and calculated bites back at Krystal.

"You girls are awfully quiet tonight," Mrs. Wheeler says from her spot at the head of the table. Mr. Wheeler used to sit there, but she took over his spot once he got sick. I never got to meet him. He was gone before I got here. Mrs. Wheeler and Veronica never speak about him, so sometimes I wonder if they made him up altogether. There's not even a picture of him in the house. Well, not in our part of the house, anyway. Maybe Mrs. Wheeler's bedroom is filled with framed photos of his face.

It's hard to imagine Mrs. Wheeler being married. She doesn't wear any makeup, not even lip gloss, and I don't think she owns anything pretty. She wears blue jeans and a flannel shirt every day. It doesn't matter if it's ninety degrees in August; she's still out there in the fields with her sleeves rolled up. Besides her jeans-and-flannel uniform, she only ever wears long nightgowns like they did in the Little House on the Prairie days. I don't get to see her in them very often. Only those rare times when I'm sick or a kid gets brought to the farm in the middle of the night, since waking Mrs. Wheeler is reserved for emergency situations. I did it once when Krystal's ear was hurting so bad she said it felt like knives were stabbing inside her head. We've never been in Mrs. Wheeler's bedroom, though. She keeps it locked no matter what and only opens it a crack to speak to you until she's ready to come out.

Krystal's convinced her bedroom is covered in pink and full of flowers. She swears that underneath her weather-beaten skin and dirt-crusted fingernails, she's secretly this girly girl who puts on dresses and dances around in front of a mirror. But that's just because Krystal is too much of a romantic at heart and automatically thinks the best of people. I couldn't disagree more about Mrs. Wheeler's room. She's probably got dead carcasses hanging on her walls just like the beheaded deer above the fireplace in the living room. It's my least favorite room in the house because these huge sad eyes stare down at me, and all I can wonder is, *What was he thinking in the moment before they shot him? Did he know he was going to die?* The head is so realistic. It looks like any minute he's going to find the other half of his body hidden somewhere, attach it to his head, and go walking around the living room. That's what I think her bedroom is full of. She spawned Veronica, so how could she not have an evil side?

We've thought about sneaking in there, but we're never alone at the house. Never once. It's strange to have never been alone in your own house, but then I guess this really isn't our own house. It's theirs.

"Sorry, Mama," Veronica pipes up in that syrupy thick voice that she only uses when she's talking to Mrs. Wheeler. "I've just been so preoccupied thinking about school today that I haven't been paying attention to dinner."

"Oh really? Did something fun happen?" Mrs. Wheeler comes alive in her chair.

She's fascinated with anything Veronica says or anytime she gives her attention. She always has been. She oozes with desperation for Veronica's love and approval. It's the strangest thing to watch, because Mrs. Wheeler is a stone wall of emotional expression unless it has something to do with Veronica. Then, it's like she got plugged into an outlet, and her whole body fills up with light.

Veronica doesn't return her feelings. Not in any real way. I'm not sure she can feel things. Mrs. Wheeler is desperate for her own kid to like her, but I'm not sure Veronica likes anyone.

Veronica nods, enjoying that Mrs. Wheeler is hanging on her every word. She loves her power. That's what feeds her. I see it in her eyes and the way she glances our way before continuing the escapade she's about to walk Mrs. Wheeler through. We've seen this scene before.

"Me and Morgan were up to give our presentation on Mount Vesuvius that we've been working on all semester. Remember I told you how Sarah and Jessica were dying to be my partners, but I could only choose one?"

Krystal kicks my shin underneath the table, like I need any reminder that our partners for our history projects were assigned by Mrs. Abbott and Morgan let out a groan when she found out she was being paired with Veronica. People stopped wanting to work with Veronica somewhere around fifth grade, when they started realizing it put a target on their backs.

Krystal's rage radiates from her body and across the table at Veronica as she weaves the details of her made-up story for her captive audience. I'm just mad that I'm not going to get to see Travis tonight. There's no way I'm going anywhere since Veronica made sure my other chores weren't done on time by locking me in the barn. That's an automatic loss of privileges.

Travis and I finally worked up to second base, and I'm dying to get him to third, but he's so shy. He still gets embarrassed that he gets hard whenever we kiss and apologizes like it's something to be sorry for. Not even. I love the power and thrill of exciting him. It means I've done something right. He's a terrible kisser. All gums and teeth, but I want to know how things work, so I don't mind.

I could sneak out, but Krystal would kill me if I did. She's going to want to have another emancipation talk tonight. We turn seventeen next month, and that's when kids can file the papers on their own. She's been talking about the Emancipation of Minors Act since she found it two years ago at the library. Mrs. Wheeler allows library visits during the summer as an approved activity, and she handed it out years ago, thinking it'd be a punishment, but it was our salvation. We learned things no one was ever going to teach us. While I buried myself in made-up stories, Krystal combed the nonfiction shelves and became obsessed with all the books in the legal section. She says it makes her feel like there's an order and structure to the universe, that there are rules to ground us.

That's how she stumbled on the act that would set us free, not just from Mrs. Wheeler but all county control. No more social workers. No more judges. No more staying in homes where we're not wanted.

Krystal is so smart, and she's done all the research. All it takes is filling out a bunch of paperwork that we get from the courthouse downtown. She has a list of everything we need already put together. All she's waiting on is the green light from me. At my go-ahead, she'd be down there on our birthdays and have the paperwork signed and submitted by the end of the week. But I'm just not so sure.

Don't get me wrong. Sometimes living here makes me feel like I'm going to split into a thousand pieces. I love the idea of being out on our own. Finally. Just me and her. No rules. Nobody else's regulations. And we get to live in a house where we get to go on both sides. But most importantly, no more Veronica or Mrs. Wheeler. They're out of our lives forever, and every evil thing they've put in it can go too.

Except, as bad as they are, we're almost through our junior year, and then we only have one more year left until we're free. If we get emancipated, we are totally on our own, which means we both would have to quit school and work full time to support ourselves. We'll get our GED while we work. Krystal's convinced we can earn our way up in the world, and I'm sure we can, but what about all the hard work we've already done? We've always gotten good grades. We work really hard, and we help each other with the difficult subjects. We've been on the honor roll since ninth grade. All we've ever done is build our high school transcripts in hopes of getting scholarship money for college. That started in eighth grade. What if we could go to college?

If we make it to state in track this year, there's a good chance we can both get athletic scholarships. Our 4x4 team has gone to state every year since Krystal and I joined the team in tenth grade. We were the only two tenth graders to make the varsity team. The scouts started looking at us last year. Do we really want to give up our chance at college? Because that's what we're doing if we get emancipated. We're starting all over and basically saying we're not going to college. I'm not sure I'm okay with that.

"What did you think, Nichole?" Mrs. Wheeler's voice interrupts my thoughts. I have no idea what they've been talking about, but she only ever wants to hear one thing—how amazing her daughter is.

"School was great," I say, plastering a fake smile on my face. It's the same one I practice in front of the mirror in the morning as I'm getting ready for my day. "Veronica is an amazing student. You should be really proud of her."

TEN

KRYSTAL

I creep around the side of Nichole and Aiden's house, doing my best to look normal and go unnoticed, but I still feel like a criminal even though I'm not doing anything wrong. I would've gone through the front door, but it's blocked with yellow crime scene tape, and I didn't want to disturb it. All the forensic evidence has been gathered, so it's not an active crime scene anymore, but the fire marshal still hasn't cleared it for occupancy. Technically, you're not supposed to be allowed inside without an escort, but I don't plan on taking anything or doing anything dangerous. I just want to go through their security camera footage and look around the house for myself. It's not like I don't trust the police to do their jobs, but they don't know Nichole and Aiden like I do.

I slip in through the sliding glass doors on the back patio and quickly tap the code into the wall unit to deactivate the alarms. The overpowering smell of smoke immediately assaults me and burns my nostrils. They're probably going to have to get all new furniture because I don't know how they'll ever get this smell out. Their house is an open concept with one room easily flowing into the next, so I can see almost everything on the main floor. My eyes quickly scan the rooms—kitchen to dining room to living room, then back to kitchen. Nichole is a meticulous housekeeper, so everything is neat, tidy, and in its place just like always, except there's a thick layer of black soot covering everything, making it look dirty.

I slowly make my way through the house. It's over three thousand square feet, but Nichole made it homely and inviting despite its size. The entire place is airy and bright with a mosaic of bold colors sprinkled throughout, but all of that has been dampened now like a cloud of darkness has taken over the place. The police and detectives left footprints on the hardwood floors, and I follow them throughout the house as they weave in and out of the rooms. I do my best to keep in step with them so nobody knows I was here. I don't even know what I'm searching for, but there has to be something, some kind of clue.

The majority of the activity leads in and out of the office, which is where I find myself after my search of the kitchen and living room turns up nothing. The office is large with bay windows overlooking the garden. Their home library is encased in built-in bookshelves on each wall. Most of the books are Nichole's since Aiden doesn't like to read, and I can't help but smile when I spot her Ramona Quimby books that she's had since we were ten. She discovered the entire collection at a garage sale, and you would've thought she'd found a winning lottery ticket.

I haven't seen their laptops anywhere. The police might have taken them, or they could be upstairs, but I still haven't decided if I'm going up there. I'm not sure if I trust the stairs to hold me since they get more and more charred as you move up. The last thing I want to do is fall through and draw attention to my snooping around. Aiden and Nichole share a PC, and thankfully, the police left it sitting on the huge mahogany desk in the center of the room. I was hoping they wouldn't take the computer, and I cross my fingers that they've kept the password the same as I jiggle the mouse to bring it to life.

I type in Nichole's birthday and watch as the home screen lights up. I'm always on her to change her passwords to something more difficult, but I'm so glad that she didn't listen to my advice. I go straight to the home security system. I'm not tech savvy. Neither is Nichole, so Aiden made accessing the security cameras easy. I click on the folder and open them up. Thankfully, I've been in the system more than once. A few years ago, I stayed with her for a week while Aiden was away working on business, and raccoons kept getting into their trash at night, scaring us half to death. We thought someone was in the backyard because they were so loud, and I learned my way around the system then.

I immediately go to video of the day of the fire. My eyes are glued to the screen as I watch it unfold in front of me like I'm watching a horror movie. I move the time back to the morning. Aiden leaves out the front door at seven. There are six cameras mounted around the house, and I rotate perspectives throughout the day. Nichole doesn't leave, and there's no other activity. There's nothing until Aiden comes home again at six. Even though I'm expecting it, the smoke that starts billowing in thick clouds from the upstairs windows at eleven still floods my body with fear. It isn't long before Nichole opens the front door and steps out.

She walks into the yard and turns around. It's not lost on me, as I'm sure it wasn't lost on the investigators who watched the same clips, that she's not running or moving fast. There's nothing about her that's panicked. You can't see her face, but you don't need to in order to see that she's enjoying watching her house burn. She dances lightly on the balls of her feet, moving side to side like she's listening to music. It isn't long before she actually starts dancing around the yard—leaping, running, and twirling.

I watch the entire scene play out in blurry images as the police arrive. It's just like they explained. She attacks them when they come near her and goes after the gurney carrying Aiden when they bring him out.

"What the hell were you doing?" I ask out loud to her image on the screen as though she can hear me and answer.

I'm more confused than ever. I don't bother watching the firefighters put out the fire. Instead, I rewind to the day before, hoping there's something in the days leading up to it that will give me a clue. But Nichole doesn't leave the house that day either. Or the day before that. My heart starts racing as I go as far back as the system allows. The cache stops at ten days. Nichole doesn't go in or out of the house for an entire week leading up to the night of the fire. The last image of her going into the house shows her walking up to the front door with a bag of groceries in her hand. She furtively looks over her shoulder before heading inside. Then, she never takes another step outside for seven days. Seven whole days. She doesn't even go in the backyard, and that's her favorite spot because she spends hours reading books by the pool.

How is that possible? Nichole has walked three miles every morning for the last ten years. She even does it on vacation and when she's sick, and her backyard is her personal sanctuary. And then it hits me like a sucker punch to the gut. What if Aiden or someone else was keeping her trapped inside? What if the fire was the only way for her to get out?

———

The sound of footsteps coming down the hospital corridor behind me pulls my attention to the doorway. Nichole's being led in by a petite Latina woman. I can barely contain my excitement. I've been waiting for her for over an hour, trying to still my racing heart. I came directly to the hospital after I left her house. My clothes smell like smoke, but I don't care. I have to find a way to get through to her.

I watched the footage three more times to be sure I didn't miss anything, but it was the same every time. Aiden was the only person who moved freely in and out of the house in the week leading up to the accident, and all I can think about is how she told the police that Aiden deserved to die because he was a murderer. Was he keeping her a prisoner?

Nichole's eyes dart around the room until they land on mine. The recognition is immediate, and tears flood her cheeks as she tries to hurry toward me. She's still unsteady on her feet, and my knee-jerk response is to rush to her with a huge hug, but that would cause too big of a commotion and break the rules. All visitors are given a list of unit rules after signing the liability waiver, and the first one is to do your best to stay in your seat and not incite extreme emotions. I wait to stand until she's closer.

"Krystal!" she cries and throws herself into my arms.

I hold her carefully because she feels even frailer than she looks, and I'm afraid to hug her too hard in case I hurt her.

Her attendant sticks out her hand and gives me a huge smile that takes up most of her face. "I'm Mia." Her attire is even more casual than the nurses'. She has dark wavy hair tucked into a baseball cap and jeans slung low on her hips.

I give her hand a quick shake. "Krystal."

I pull two chairs together so that the edges touch and our seats are almost one. I slide in on the left one and motion for Nichole to sit next to me. She plops onto the chair and sits so close to me that she's almost on my lap. She strokes my arms and rubs my thighs like she's not quite sure I'm real. I keep trying to grasp her hands and hold on to them, but she can't keep them still long enough to hold hands.

She motions for me to get closer, and I lean in. "He's turning into different people to play tricks on me," she whispers into my ear.

"Who is?" I ask, doing a quick scan of the room to see if there's anything going on around us. It's usually frenzied around this hour because it's right before medication time, and everyone gets anxious when it comes to their drugs. The weird thing about madness is that it follows a schedule too. But besides the increased pacing and meaningless chatter in the room, nothing out of the ordinary is happening.

"Shhh." She brings her finger up to her lips. "He's sitting right there. He'll hear you."

I moved a table to the far side of the room before she got here so we'd have as much privacy as possible. The nearest person is a morbidly obese woman sitting three tables over. Her swollen belly is pushed up against the table, and she wears a huge necklace on her chest that's strung with pictures of babies cut out from magazines. I want to get through this experience without ever knowing her story.

"He's changing. He's changing people again. You see that? Huh?" Nichole nudges me harder and harder with each question. Her eyes have a weird sheen to them, and her pupils are huge. "Do you?"

"Who? You mean Aiden? Is he here?"

She grabs my forearm. Her fingers dig into my skin. She whispers through gritted teeth, "Aiden's gone. That's what I'm trying to tell you. He's gone. They took him."

Does she mean the Aiden upstairs breathing on a ventilator and fighting for his life or the Aiden she sees in the room with us that nobody else does?

"Where did he go?" The thought leapt in my brain, and I spit it out, wondering if I should be wandering this trail of madness with her, but the truth about what happened is somewhere inside her.

"I don't know." Tears swell in her eyes. Her love for Aiden is carved deeply into her beat-up face. "What if we can't find him again? What if he's lost forever?"

"It's okay, honey. We'll figure this out," I promise. I caress her back, trying my best to calm her.

"I think a demon got him. He jumped inside his body." She looks as terrified as she did when we watched *Nightmare on Elm Street* for the first time and Freddy killed Tina. "Isn't it so creepy how he does that?" Her legs jitter underneath the table. She twists her hands on her lap like it's painful to sit still.

"It is. Really is." I try to keep my expression normal, but I can't believe she's the same person from this morning. How can she have bounced to this extreme in such a short period of time? Is this the mania Dr. McGowan was talking about?

Mia stretches across the table, not even pretending that she isn't listening to every word we say and watching the scene play out in front of her. Can she be asked to give a statement about things she overhears between us? What if she can? Nothing between Nichole and me is privileged. That's not good.

"How did things go today?" I ask, trying to steer the conversation to more neutral ground and abandoning the idea of getting through to her today. She's in no condition for sensible conversation.

"Remember today in *Batman Returns*?" Nichole asks. She's frighteningly pale with huge black circles underneath her eyes, and her red hair only makes the effect more dramatic and pronounced. I nod slowly, unsure where she's going with this. "Just like it, or maybe I could say that about the red rain too. Don't you think?"

I nod even though she's talking nonsense. Agitation surges through her body. Every muscle is tight. I can feel her bones through her gown.

"Did you eat today?" I ask, hoping it's a safe topic. She furrows her brow. "Did you eat?" I ask again to help her stay focused.

"Food today . . . I did . . ."

I latch on to the connection grounded in the present moment. "What'd you have?" I bite my tongue and hold back the urge to rapid-fire questions at her. There are so many things I want to ask, but the questions will have to wait.

She furrows her eyebrows even farther together, concentrating on pulling a memory from her bank. Frustration lines wrinkle her forehead as she struggles to come up with anything.

"Who cares what it was," I say. Hold on to her. Don't lose her. "Did you like the food?"

A small smile peeks out of the corner of her mouth. "I did."

I don't hide my smile. She's always loved to eat. She taught herself how to cook the summer before our freshman year in college. She refused to live off dorm food after we'd survived on nothing but sandwiches and split pea soup most of our childhood. I suffered through so many bad meals that summer—overcooked chicken, tasteless vegetables, and countless failed desserts—but by the end of the summer, she'd grown into an amazing cook and hasn't stopped since. Nothing makes her happier than preparing a good meal. She cooked every night for herself and

Aiden whether they ate together or not. No matter what time he came home, there was always a plate saved for him in the refrigerator.

"I heard you get dessert for dinner," I joke.

She lets out a giggle, and I squeeze her against me, forgetting for just a second that we have an audience. "You're going to get through this. You will. I promise."

A male attendant arrives to take her downstairs for her blood draw. They've sent out so much of her blood that they ran out and need more samples. The timing is perfect since it gives me a chance to sneak away and get more details from Dr. McGowan about how things went today.

I squeeze both her hands in mine. "You run off and let them take your blood. I'm going to chat with Dr. McGowan while you're gone."

She freezes. Her eyes skirt the room. "He's playing tricks on me. I told you."

"Dr. McGowan?" Her pupils have shrunk. Terror has returned to her eyes. She wildly shakes her head, bringing her fingers up to her mouth to shush me.

Mia shifts her attention back and forth between us as we talk. Can she record any of this? What if she's got her phone in her pocket? The paranoia of this place is contagious. I shove the thoughts down. I bring Nichole against me and speak to her softly, even though there's no way to keep Mia from overhearing. "This man is safe. I promise. I would never let you go with anyone who is unsafe. Do you understand me?"

She nods. Her lower lip quivers, and her eyes fill with tears. Little Nichole appears in front of me, and it's everything I can do not to break down in front of her, but I pull myself together. I have to stay strong for us.

I place my hands on her cheeks and stare into her eyes. "You're safe. I'll be here when you get back. I promise."

She looks over her shoulder multiple times as she leaves, clearly not wanting to go, but she does because she trusts me. The weight of responsibility and the magnitude of the task in front of me weigh heavily on my chest, but I give her a smile and mouth, *"You got this."*

I wait a few minutes, giving her plenty of time to get on the elevator, before heading to Dr. McGowan's office. His door is shut, and Detective Sparks opens it right as I'm about to knock. We both jump back, then laugh nervously at our responses. He's not as clean cut today. A thin layer of scruffy facial hair covers his chin.

"Excuse me," he says, recovering quickly.

His presence fills the doorway, and unlike him, I can't recover. I don't know what to say. There are no books for situations like these. I open and close my mouth twice.

"Coming to see Dr. McGowan?" he asks.

I nod. "Yes, I just came from seeing Nichole." I want to slap myself for disclosing any more than he asked for. What a rookie mistake.

"How's she doing?" Kindness coats his question.

"Better." Much smarter response from me this time. He doesn't need to know that I mean better than the comatose patient she was this morning.

"That's good. I'm glad to hear that." His blue eyes are warm and compassionate, but I don't doubt for one second that they aren't continually scanning and watching me for any sign that I'm lying or know more than I'm letting on—an eye twitch, the tensing of a jaw, any involuntary movement.

We stand facing each other and decide at the same moment to step around each other. We bump our chests as we move aside in the same direction, making the moment incredibly more awkward than it already is. I'm close enough to smell his aftershave. Can he smell the smoke on me? What will he think if he finds out I went to Aiden and Nichole's house? We manage to move around each other in a way that lands me in Dr. McGowan's office this time and him in the hallway.

"How are you holding up in all of this?" Detective Sparks asks.

"It hasn't been easy." No wonder he's a detective. His kind eyes and calming voice make me want to spill all my secrets immediately—that I ate a package of Oreo cookies for dinner three nights last week or that I stuff my recycling in my neighbor's bins whenever I run out of space in mine. Not talking takes conscious effort.

"Dr. McGowan just filled me in on everything that's happened. All her tests came back negative again today." He tilts his head and places his hands casually in his back pockets like he's in no hurry to go anywhere.

Normally, negative test results are an opportunity to celebrate, but my heart sinks. How do we fix her if we don't know what's wrong with her? And she's got to be fixed. I can't help her when she's like this. Nobody can.

"That's unfortunate. It's been a roller coaster of emotional states today, and that's not who she is. Nothing about her behavior right now is remotely close to anything I've ever seen her demonstrate." Even though I told him she was better, I don't want him to think she's not sick.

"Is there any history of mental illness in her family?"

I freeze for a second. What's he found out about her family? Has he talked to Marlene? I haven't forgotten about her threatening words. "There's nothing in her family besides lots of drinking."

"Hmm . . . that's interesting. Usually these types of illnesses run in families." He rubs his chin like he's deep in thought. "She's way out of the normal age range of when you would see a person have their first psychotic break, so something else must be going on," he says with the authority of someone who's studied psychology for years, and I can't help but wonder if he has. That makes him more dangerous.

"There's got to be an answer for it somewhere. Sometimes these things are complicated." I try to mirror his confidence, as if I have any experience in diagnosing psychiatric disorders.

"Any chance she's faking it?" Detective Sparks asks.

His question throws me off, and I stumble to rearrange my face. "Why would she do that?" I ask like I don't already know.

"She's faking crazy to get away with murder. It's the oldest trick in the book."

"No way. Not a chance." I shake my head in obstinate denial. I'm vehemently opposed to the idea. Except there is one thing—I know how well Nichole lies.

ELEVEN

NICHOLE

(THEN)

My pulse thrums in my temples as my heartbeat explodes in my ears. Krystal rounds the corner of the blacktopped track on her way to finishing the last one hundred meters of the relay race. Rebekah Swan from Bradbury High is inches in front of her, barely holding on to her lead. Everything is muted like the sound's been turned off on a film as I watch Krystal's muscles strain to catch her.

"Go!" My scream rips through my throat.

The air is warped and wobbly around me beneath the bright afternoon sky. Krystal's arms pump; her feet blur underneath her. Every muscle strains forward. I take a quick glance at the stands. The three college scouts—Baylor, Iowa State, and Westchester emblems blazing on their chests—stand with their timers clutched in their hands as close to the finish line as you can get. This is it. The moment we've spent months training for.

"GO KRYSTAL!"

Just like that, she gives the kick she's famous for—the one everyone came to see. It got us all the attention in the first place. I'm just here as her teammate and moral support. Second leg in the 4x4 is nothing. She's the real deal. She's the one who packs the stands every Friday afternoon. This is why they put her picture in the local newspaper and plaster her face on the evening news, even though we never get to watch because TV is only allowed on the weekends.

Perspiration lines her forehead. Sheer determination marks every step as she shifts into high gear like only she can. Instantly, the crowd is on its feet, lit. Screaming, yelling, chanting her name. I jump up and down as Krystal flies past Rebekah and races over the finish line. Screams erupt from everywhere. The rest of the 4x4 team and I rush to her, throwing our arms around her and smacking her back in congratulations. She doubles over with her hands on her knees, trying to catch her breath. Everyone talks on top of each other. The excitement bubbles over as Coach joins in the celebration, lifting Krystal up and twirling her around. The rest of the team and all the fans from the bleachers storm the field.

"You did it!" our team captain, Meghan, shrieks. "We're going to state my senior year!"

Our 4x4 race gave us the win we needed to qualify the entire team for state. Bradbury High was the school to beat out, and we did it. This was the tie-breaking win. I've never been prouder of Krystal.

Meghan gives Krystal another hug after Coach sets her down, and Krystal catches my eye as she does. She gives me a huge smile, and I give her an even bigger one back. Meghan might be thrilled about going to state because it's her senior year and she's never been, but nobody's more excited than us. Krystal's win assures us a scholarship to at least one of the colleges that's vying for us. Not that anyone really wants me, but Krystal's made it clear she won't go alone. We're a package deal.

I breathe a sigh of relief as the adrenaline subsides. Everything is falling into place. I retook my SATs last weekend and got a 1512 combined. Even if the athletic scouts don't include me in their scholarship offer to Krystal, my grades put me in the running for an academic scholarship at whatever school she picks, so it'll give them an incentive to take me. She's going to have multiple options even though she thinks she'll have to grab at whatever offer is thrown her way. She's so hard on herself. I wish she could see herself the way everyone else does.

The hair on the back of my neck tickles. Electricity shoots through me. I turn my head in the direction of the feeling. Veronica stands off to the side of the bleachers, holding the team's water bottles. Mrs. Wheeler insisted she join the team last year because it'd be a good social activity for her and we could help her make friends with the other team members. Mrs. Wheeler constantly forces Veronica into situations where she doesn't fit, which only makes sure she sticks out more.

Her lips are pursed in a straight line as she watches the scene unfolding in front of her, and I search her face for clues to what's going on in her head. Is she planning on spiking our water to get us disqualified? I never have any idea what she's thinking. Her eyes catch mine. She raises her thin upper lip in a smirk—her version of a smile. The closest she ever comes to the real thing. But there's nothing friendly about it. There never is. She's plotting something. She hates anything good that happens to us almost as much as she hates Whitney and the HIT girls.

There's been a bit of a lull in their attacks against her. The spring formal is coming up, and Whitney and her crew have been so obsessed with it that they haven't had any time to torture Veronica. It's been a nice reprieve. I just wish it would last, but the look on her face tells me it's about to begin all over again. I quickly turn away, refusing to allow her to ruin this day, and put my attention back on Krystal. I'm so happy for her. She deserves every ounce of success that she gets.

I stand on the small disc platform and hold on to the metal rail of the flatbed trailer, staring at the rows of freshly tilled dirt behind the old John Deere tractor. Krystal's up front in the driver's seat with the radio blasting and singing along at the top of her lungs to every song that plays. AM radio is the only kind that comes in out in these fields, so it's nothing but oldies. Doesn't bother her, though. She belts them out without a care in the world, even though she's tone deaf and can't carry a tune to save her life. Her happiness radiates from the cab. She's still high from yesterday's win.

Today is a perfect day to follow her success since rock picking is her favorite chore. Every spring we till the soil, bringing all the rocks to the surface. The rocks can't stay in the fields because they damage all the other equipment and screw up the crops, so somebody's got to get them out. We've always been the somebodies. She loves the days spent in the black, hot dirt underneath a blue sky in the sweltering heat. I'm not a fan of the black soil that sticks to every part of you including your eyes, ears, and nose.

She can barely wait for spring now that she gets to drive the tractor while we make our way through the acres of rolling hills surrounding the farm. We waited for years to be able to drive it. One of the hired hands used to drive, and we got a new driver every year—sometimes two—because no one was ever to Mrs. Wheeler's liking. Her standards are nearly impossible. We've had two Joes and three Bills. Then, we turned thirteen, and we haven't had anyone since. We're the only hired hands she needs now.

She never minds that we're girls driving the tractor, even though people in town look down their noses at her for it. Around here, heavy farm labor is reserved for the boys, but that doesn't bother Mrs. Wheeler. How could it, considering she's been running the farm by herself since Mr. Wheeler died? Tongue wagging never bothers her, though. Lots of people say they don't care what other people think about them, but she really doesn't.

I spot a rock and jump off my stand to grab it. This one takes both hands, and I have to do a full squat to come up with it. Krystal catches my movement in the rearview mirror and shifts down to first gear. I lug it back to the trailer and toss it on the bed along with the others I've gathered. I give her the thumbs-up sign, and the tractor lurches forward into motion. I can't see her face, but I'm sure there's a huge smile on it because she hasn't stopped grinning since we left school yesterday.

All three scouts circled around her when she came out of the locker room after the win. I stood off to the side, beaming with pride and reciting the answers to their questions in my mind while she reported them out loud. "What's your fastest 400? Interval sprints? How are your grades? Ever lived out of state?" Her face flushed red through all of it because she hates being the center of attention, but we prepared in advance, so she wasn't as nervous. She did great. Nobody but me could even tell she was nervous.

Maybe after today she'll ease up on her crusade for emancipation. She's been relentless since the hair incident, and yesterday she gave me the papers to go over since my seventeenth birthday is only days away. She assumed I'd sign them and get them back to her, but I'm still not sure it's the best choice. I didn't mention it on our walk home. She deserved to have the moment she worked so hard for, even though she kept trying to lob it back to me, as if I had any credit for it. All I do is scream at the top of my lungs for her to run faster.

"I never could've done this without you, Nichole," she gushed as we logged the miles back to the farm just as the sun was beginning to set. Staying in shape during track season is easy since we basically have two practices every day. Mrs. Wheeler said we could run track, but she wouldn't pick us up after practices or games, and that we would still be responsible for chores at night. We've had to walk home in the dark plenty of times, but we don't mind. It just means longer time away from the farm, even if we have to hurry through our chores on the nights we have meets and don't get to sleep until after midnight. All of it is worth it.

"You totally destroyed Natalie today, by the way," she told me. "Your exchange with Polly was flawless too." Her hair was pulled into a messy bun on top of her head; loose strands twirled around her rosy cheeks still flushed from all the excitement.

I smiled at her. I didn't do anything special. Not like she did. But she always refuses to see how amazing she is. She chattered on about all the things she wanted to do differently at our next race, but this was the one that mattered. It was the one Coach recorded for her reel that would go to all the college scouts who weren't there. Coach was as nervous as Krystal.

Her win feels like the universe giving us an answer about emancipation. I want out as bad as she does, and it's so tempting to go now that we have a real opportunity to get out, but I want to go to college. Like really want to go to college. And she does too. It's all we've talked about since second grade. It's just hard for her to switch her brain into a different gear when she's got it set on something, and the last incident with Veronica pushed her over the edge. Her hair still hasn't fully grown back. But sometimes she can only see what's in front of her and doesn't look at the bigger picture. I don't want to make the wrong move. Not after we've worked so hard.

The tractor stutters and sputters as we round the corner and head down the next row. The rocks jostle in the trailer. She sticks her hand out the window and waves. The sun shines directly in my eyes in this direction, and I squint as I wave back. The horizon is nothing but blue skies divided by earth. Tomorrow, I'll tell her we should stick with our original plan.

Tonight, we'll enjoy this.

TWELVE

KRYSTAL

"How is she?" Aiden asks as soon as I walk into his hospital room. He made a dramatic turnaround six hours into his intravenous antibiotic treatment, and they moved him out of ICU and onto the burn unit last night.

It's no surprise he doesn't know how Nichole's doing because not a single one of his family members has come to see her. I check her visiting log every time I'm there, and I'm the only one who's visited since she got admitted three days ago. That's why I was so shocked to get Janice's text when I turned my phone on this morning:

Aiden's out of ICU. Wants to see you.

I don't know how many different responses I typed out and erased before finally settling on a simple thank-you coupled with the praying hands emoji. I skipped my shower and headed straight to the hospital. While I drove, my thoughts danced in a hundred different directions like they'd been doing ever since I saw the security camera footage. I forced myself to calm down. If I couldn't talk to Nichole, he was the next best thing, but I had to act normal. By the time I reached the parking lot, I'd managed to slow my heart rate and breathe regularly again, but all that left the minute I stepped into his room and saw him.

His face is covered in thick white bandages with two small holes for his eyes and a larger one for his mouth. He looks like he's wearing a padded white ski mask. His left hand lies limp next to him, and it's covered in thick bandages similar to those on his face, but the right hand is the most disturbing. The fingernails are cracked and look painful, the fingers themselves ripped open in angry sores. They testify to how desperately he worked to get out of that burning room.

"We'll talk about her in a second. How are you?" I ask, doing my best to keep my voice steady and even. He's attached to a monitor recording his vitals, oxygen, and heart rhythm. An IV stand drips a steady stream of fluid into his veins. There is an upholstered chair on either side of his bed. No windows in the room.

"Being in a coma and having a tube down your throat is a nightmare." His raspy voice bears the scar. "But I guess burning to death is probably worse, so . . ." He shrugs his shoulders playfully and tries to smile, but it looks like it hurts. He points to the chair on the right side of his bed. "Sit down. You look so tense."

I barely slept at all last night. Melatonin had no effect. All I did was lie there staring at the ceiling and trying to wrap my brain around the possibility that Aiden was hurting Nichole. I need real legal guidance, but I'm not any closer to getting it. William's assistant sent me a formal email a few minutes ago saying that their law firm found a conflict of interest between one of the firm's lawyers and the Fischer team, so they can't represent Nichole. I immediately texted Theresa and told her to move on to our plan B—Eric Parker—and we should hear back today after they run a similar check.

I take a seat in the chair that Aiden indicated and angle it slightly so I have a better view of his door and anyone coming in. Always have to see the door.

"Tell me how she is." His eyes look weird peering out from the two holes in his face covering, and it takes me a second to notice it's because he doesn't have any eyelashes. Another half second to realize why. How much did he suffer before passing out?

I take a deep breath and try to maintain eye contact. He has to think I'm on his side. It's hard not to flinch at his appearance. "It's been such a crazy three days. It feels like an entire lifetime has passed, and I don't even know where to start."

"Just start at the beginning," he prompts.

Another deep breath. This one centers me more. "Okay, well, she was totally freaking out when they first brought you guys to the hospital, so they put her in the seclusion room on the psychiatric unit. Apparently, she attacked the paramedics and the emergency personnel who tried to treat her in the emergency room. I didn't get to see her until after twenty-four hours had passed, and she was still messed up. Super agitated. Angry. Very confused, saying all kinds of crazy things. She'd put huge scratches on her face and was doing the same thing to her arms, but luckily they caught her in enough time before she got too carried away like she did with her face." The image of her mangled face scars my brain and is constantly intruding into my thoughts without my permission. No doubt Aiden's face will take a turn in the rotation of invading images. "They're still trying to figure out the right medication combination for her, so it's pretty much like she's suddenly bipolar on top of whatever else is going on with her mental state. But I'm not complaining. I'd rather have her this way than whatever they had her on in the beginning. That stuff made her drool." His eyes widen in horror. "It's true, and we can't ever tell her because she'll be mortified." He nods in eager agreement. "Hopefully, they'll get it right soon. I mean, if you try enough combinations, eventually you have to, right?"

"What has she been saying about things?" I can't tell how he feels or what he's getting at. It's impossible to read someone's facial expressions when you can't see their eyebrows.

"Most of what she says still doesn't make any sense. Half the time she doesn't know where she is or what's going on around her." I purposefully leave out the parts about him.

He grimaces and grinds his jaw while he talks. "As soon as I'm cleared by my team, I'm going to see her." He cringes again and reaches for the black control lying on his chest and presses it. The air stills as we wait for the morphine to kick in. His arms tense. He starts coughing and works himself into a fit. He raises his unbandaged arm to his mouth and coughs into his elbow. A pitcher of water with plastic cups is on a tray beside the bed. I rush over and fill him a cup. His cough has worked its way into a wheeze.

"Should I call the nurse?" I ask as I hand it to him.

He shakes his head, taking a quick sip, followed by another. He holds his breath, trying to stave off the cough like it's the hiccups. Gradually, he settles down. Why does talking about Nichole work him up? Is it concern? Guilt?

"Sorry." He wipes his mouth with the back of his unbandaged hand.

"Don't apologize." I twist my hands on my lap, nervous all over again because I don't have any idea how to do this and one of his family members could show up at any time. "What happened, Aiden?"

"It's like I told the police. I don't remember much of it. I was really tired that night, so I went to bed early. I knocked out right away, and the next thing I know, I was waking up coughing and there was smoke everywhere." The mention of coughing sends him into another brief fit that has to calm before he's able to continue talking. "I went to grab Nichole and wake her up, but she was gone. I jumped up and ran to the bathroom to see if she was in there, but she wasn't there either. That's when I ran for the door and discovered it was locked. I was trapped inside and couldn't get out. That's when I panicked. I beat the hell out of that door until I passed out." His shoulders sag with defeat.

"There was a desk in front of the door. That's why you couldn't get out."

"I know. The police told me that."

"Any idea how the desk got there?" I try to ask the question in the least lawyerlike way, but it's impossible.

"I'm assuming Nichole." He breaks eye contact.

"Is that what you told the police?"

"Of course it's what I told the police," he says. My inability to read his expressions is infuriating. It's like talking to a still life painting. "I've got nothing to hide."

Implying he doesn't but that Nichole does? Or what? I search his bandaged face for clues to what's going on inside him, but come up with none.

"Look, Krystal, I know in any kind of domestic situation everyone always looks at the husband. I know everyone's already thinking she tried to kill me to protect herself from me. I—"

"Nobody's thinking that," I lie.

He motions for me to shut up. "Please. We both know that's what the investigators are trying to figure out. My parents and immediate family are the only ones who see me as the victim here and aren't secretly wondering if I did something to get myself into such trouble with my wife, but I didn't do anything. I swear I didn't. She's sick, Krystal."

"Okay. Well, then tell me what's going on, because the last time I saw her, she was perfectly fine, and now she's someone unrecognizable." There's no hiding my accusatory tone.

"It all happened so quickly and spun out of control before I even had a chance to wrap my brain around it." He drains what's left in his Styrofoam cup. "I was just stumbling around in shock when she first started acting weird and didn't know what to do. Still don't. I was hoping she would come out of it, Krystal. I really was. At first, I thought it was a drug reaction. Or something she ate. I even googled it." He lets out a dry laugh that brings another flinch of pain. This one makes him clutch his side. "I know it sounds ridiculous, but we ate chicken at a new restaurant the night before her first episode, and I had an upset stomach afterward. So, I started thinking that maybe the salmonella traveled up to her brain and infected it. There're people that believe that theory, you know"—he cracks a smile—"just not any credible ones."

"Yeah, I'm pretty sure this isn't bad chicken." I wish he'd stop making jokes, but I'm not surprised. He laughed at a funeral once. "But what was she doing when everything started? What made you think something was wrong with her?"

"There might have been things going on that I didn't notice before, but the first time I noticed anything strange was a little over two weeks ago. I came up behind her in the bathroom while she was getting ready in the morning and scared her. I put my arms around her waist like I always do, and she literally jumped back like I'd burned her. That's how scared she got. It was way more scared than a normal jump-scare, but it made sense given . . . well, you know . . . all her issues." He shifts his attention away from my eyes and to an imaginary spot on the bed.

He doesn't like talking about Nichole's childhood. He's not an emotional guy, and anything intense is too much for him, so he avoids going there or spends all his time making stupid jokes to ease the tension. It was one of the traits Nichole loved so much when they were dating and things started getting serious. He didn't drill her with questions about what she'd been through like she was a circus freak. That's why he was so safe for Nichole. She knew he'd never press her. She told me that once.

"So, you really scared her, and then what?" Nichole getting jump-scared doesn't seem all that unusual to me. We both have a half-second startle response. How could we not with everything we've been through?

"She looked at me like she had no idea who I was. It was the oddest thing, but I was in a hurry and knew I'd scared her, so I couldn't stay to see if anything else was going on. I gave her a quick peck on the cheek and took off. I thought about it on my drive to work, but I forgot about it as soon as I got there. Besides, it wasn't anything that was too dramatic or over the top. You know what I mean?" He searches my eyes like he's looking for approval. "It was like that for a couple days. She was weird and distant. I'd catch her muttering underneath her breath like she was talking to someone. And she was always on edge. Like really on edge. I noticed that it was strange, but things were so busy at work that I let it go. I noticed it, but I let it go . . ." He trails off as he disappears into whatever memories are playing in his mind. "I keep kicking myself about it. Like maybe if I did something about it in those first few days, I could've stopped it. All I've done since I started getting better is research psychotic breaks. And you know what everything I've read says?"

It's a rhetorical question. He doesn't wait for me to answer. "Early intervention is the key to successful treatment whenever you're dealing with psychosis. The key. Do you know how many times the experts said that? And I did nothing. What if I could've stopped this? What if this is all my fault?"

"You can't do that to yourself. It's not your fault." I will a straight face as my insides scream, *How could you?* If what he's saying is true, why didn't he do something about it the minute he noticed something was off with her? He might've been able to stop it. He *should* be kicking himself. He should be punching himself in the face right now.

"Things kept getting weirder and weirder. She wasn't herself. She was paranoid. Wouldn't let me near her. She'd say things like, 'Get away from me,' and I never knew if she was talking to me or somebody else. Every noise made her jump. I kept asking her what was wrong, begging her to tell me, but she'd scream at me to get away from her, not to touch her." His voice thickens with embarrassment that takes over the room. "Then, about a week ago, I came home from work, and she'd locked herself in our bedroom. She taped a note on the door telling me to stay in the guest room and leave her alone. She'd moved all my clothes and things into the closet while I was at work. I hadn't seen her for an entire week up until the night of the fire."

"Are you serious?" He nods, refusing to make eye contact. "Why didn't you call me? I could've helped. I could've gotten her out of her bedroom. Even if we couldn't figure out what was going on with her, at least I could've taken her to my house to stay. What were you thinking?"

"I was embarrassed. I know it sounds stupid, but I was embarrassed and so overwhelmed with all of it. You know how I get. I kept hoping she'd snap out of it. That it wasn't real. That I was making a bigger deal out of things than it was. I told myself a million different things while it was going on." There's no hiding his shame. "Even as scared as I got when she was locking herself up, I never imagined anything like this happening."

"You didn't see her at all for an entire week?" How was that possible? There'd been many times when they'd gone without seeing each other for a week when he traveled, but never when they were in the same house.

"Nope, but she came out of her room while I was at work, so that made me feel a little better. She was always back upstairs when I got home, but I could tell she'd been in the house because she'd leave the coffee maker on, or one day she left her favorite throw crumpled up on the sofa where she'd been. Little things like that. It was the one thing that gave me hope that maybe she'd pull through whatever it was she was going through."

What was she doing in her room all that time? We texted a bunch of times that week, and she never once hinted she was in trouble. Not once. Why didn't she tell me she was in trouble? That's the part that doesn't add up.

"What about the night the fire started? Take me through it."

"It was pretty much a regular night for what was becoming the new normal. I came home to an empty house, made dinner, and ate it in front of the TV in the living room while I watched golf. She came downstairs halfway through the highlight reel and said she was having trouble falling asleep—"

"Did she look sleepy?" I interrupt.

"Not really. She still had that half-crazed look in her eyes, but I didn't care because I was so happy that she wanted me anywhere near her. I tried to get her to sit down next to me, but that's not what she wanted. She asked if I would go upstairs and lie with her until she fell asleep. I jumped at the opportunity. I was literally giddy on my way up the stairs, but I kept trying to play it off like I wasn't." His expression falls. "I should've known something was up when she asked me to come upstairs with her. That should've been my first clue."

Yes, it should have, dummy. He probably thought he was going to get laid, and that pull drowned out everything else. How can men be so stupid?

I try not to show my disgust when I ask, "What was she like when you got up there?"

"She didn't want to talk or do anything else. She turned off the lights and got straight into bed. It felt nice to tumble into bed with her because I was so exhausted. I wanted to touch her, but I was scared. Not because I wanted to have sex." He pauses and makes a dramatic production to make sure I've gotten his point, since he knows how I get about men getting hyperfocused on sex. I give him a look that says I don't believe him. "All I wanted to do was hold her, and I was shocked when she let me put my arms around her. I remember thinking how good she smelled, how much I'd missed her . . . I miss her . . ." He gets choked up.

I put my hand on top of his bandaged hand since it seems less painful to touch than the other one. "I know you do," I say, patting it lightly. "I do too."

Questions chase each other and fight for space in my head. His story lines up perfectly with what I saw on the videos. Is it because it's the truth or because he knows that's what everyone will find so he has to create an explanation for it that fits?

THIRTEEN

NICHOLE

(THEN)

Krystal shakes with sobs and claws at my chest like she's trying to crawl inside my body and hide. I'm crying as hard as she is, and there's snot everywhere. We're a disgusting mess because we don't have any Kleenex, so we just keep rubbing our snot on our sleeves. The high from yesterday crashes to the ground and takes all the light with it at the sound of the pigs squealing. Mr. Johnson showed up with his truck today, and we both know what that means—but it wasn't always that way.

The pigs used to be our favorite animals. Krystal read in one of her library books that pigs are smarter than dogs. I don't know about all pigs, but our pigs are way smarter than the two collies running around the farm, and I've never seen any of the pigs chase their own tail. We have at least six sows on the farm at all times, so one of them is always pregnant and having babies. There's nothing cuter than a little pink piglet after birth.

They have huge litters, and the last one born usually dies, but sometimes it lives. Krystal and I used to rescue all the runts that survived so they wouldn't die. Pigs aren't like other animals that abandon their runts when they're too small, but their chances of survival are just as bad. They've got to be strong and quick enough to move out of the way when their six-hundred-pound mamas sit down, or they get crushed.

We bottle-fed the little ones to give them extra nutrients and fatten them up, making up for the milk they couldn't get from their mamas. We carried them around with us underneath our T-shirts, pressing their hot little bodies against our chests and falling asleep with them at night after we successfully snuck them into the house. And they survived. Every single one. We'd watch proudly when they rejoined their siblings after they were strong enough, and they almost always overtook them in weight. They started out smaller than the bunch, but our love made them bigger and stronger.

Until the day we had to stop loving them because it hurt too much.

We might've lived a few more years in blissful ignorance if Veronica hadn't taken it upon herself to tell us what happened to the pigs when they disappeared. See, every now and then, we'd get up in the morning and half our pigs were gone, like they'd vanished without a trace during the night. Mrs. Wheeler told us she raised pigs for money to be adopted by other families, so once they were a certain age, they were sent to other farms like ours to be raised by their forever families. It made sense to us since we figured maybe Mrs. Wheeler got paid per pig, so that's why she kept letting the mamas have more, and we couldn't have the pigs taking over the farm, so why not?

One of the sows had just delivered another litter of twelve piglets. She was a beast through labor, and Krystal and I were over the moon because we'd gotten to be there the moment it happened. We'd learned to recognize the signs that they were pregnant, and it definitely wasn't hard to recognize the signs at the end, since they looked even more ginormous and ready to burst. Catching a live birth was one of the best things to look forward to on the farm, and we bolted out of bed at five every morning to see if we'd missed it during the night.

This was the third birth we'd caught, and we'd watched as Mrs. Wheeler moved the sow into the farrowing crates for the mama to nurse now that it was over. Tears glistened in both our eyes. Veronica came around the corner and caught the moment.

"You know what they're doing with the pigs tonight, don't you?" she asked as she took in our bloodied clothes and turned up her nose in disgust. She didn't care about watching live births. She didn't care about any of the animals. Not like we did.

Krystal and I looked at each other, trying to communicate without speaking, but neither of us had any idea what she was talking about. Was it a trap? We turned our attention back to her.

"They are all going to die tonight," she announced with smug satisfaction, crossing her arms on her scrawny chest.

I recoiled in horror. "Don't say that! That's awful."

She let out a dry laugh. "That's what they do to all the pigs. You didn't know that?" She shifted her gaze to Krystal, who shared the same horrified expression as me. "And you didn't tell her?"

"Shut up, Veronica. There's nothing to tell," Krystal snaps. Veronica loved pitting us against each other.

Veronica shook her head and gave us her most pitying stare. "Poor sad souls. You really don't know, do you?"

My knees trembled. Insides shook. I wanted her to go away. Just go away. Stop talking with her ugly, skinny mouth in her stupid voice. Hate filled me.

"They kill every single one of those pigs that's born here. All your little babies?" She made a slicing motion across her neck.

Krystal jumped at her like she was going to punch her, and I pulled her back before she could. She strained against me, swinging wildly at her. I squeezed even tighter as she bucked, bracing my feet so she wouldn't make us fall.

"Don't believe me? Why don't you have a look in the barns tonight after you go to bed and my mom thinks you're sleeping?" She didn't wait for us to respond before walking away.

We did everything we could to get her words out of our heads and just go to bed that night. We really did. We tried pretending she was lying, that we didn't believe her. Krystal kept saying it was just another one of her dirty tricks. But we couldn't shake the seed she'd planted. We had to know if it was true.

We pretended to go to bed like we always did and held our breath after we'd turned out the lights, waiting for any sound of movement in the house, still holding on to the last shred of hope that Veronica was only trying to hurt us, that she'd made it all up. As time stretched on, it looked like we might get our wish. And then we heard it. The loud creak of the living room floor where you crossed the living room and moved into neutral living space.

Someone was up.

We strained our ears in silence as we heard the front door open and close. We didn't speak as we followed each other outside and crept along in the dark after Mrs. Wheeler's bulky frame. She was out of her nightgown. Dressed in her usual uniform of flannel and blue jeans. Krystal and I clung to each other, relying on memory and moonlight to get to the barn. We eased our way all the way to the back, where the water tanks hummed. It was the best odds for not getting caught. All the lights were on in the barn. We should've just stopped.

But we didn't.

Steam rose up from the huge tubs that we bathed the sows in before every county fair in the summer. The air was stuffy like a sauna. Why did they have it turned up so hot? They couldn't put them into tubs that hot. It'd burn their skin. The barn door slid open, and one of the hired hands pulled Bessie along into the barn. We had raised Bessie since she was a baby, and she'd grown into one of our most prized pigs. Mrs. Wheeler pulled out a Taser gun and shot her in the butt with it. Bessie let out a squeal that will be seared in my brain for eternity.

I turned on my heels and pushed out the door, running as fast as I could with Krystal right behind me. She was always faster, but she couldn't catch me that night. I flew through the forest behind the barn instead of heading to the house, stumbling and tripping over things in the darkness while I tried to outrun the screams of my beloved pig being led to slaughter. My lungs burned, chest heaved. My legs were on fire. But I couldn't stop. Didn't stop. Not until Krystal fly tackled me from behind, coming to land on top of me. She rolled off me quickly.

"Stop," she said in between gasping breaths.

How had we missed it? It'd been right under our noses all along, and we'd never seen it. Hadn't imagined. It was crueler than any prank Veronica had pulled on us.

We stopped eating all pork. The smell of it made me gag. Once Mrs. Wheeler made us eat hot dogs, even though I cried and begged her not to make me do it. I got it all down—the entire thing, but my body betrayed me, and within seconds, everything from my dinner was heaving onto the table and splattering all over the floor. I sprinted to the bathroom, spraying vomit along the way. Mrs. Wheeler never made us eat pork again. Our days of ham sandwiches were over. Peanut butter and jelly sandwiches became our staple lunch.

The memories replay themselves on repeat like they've done over all these years since making our first discovery. We thought it'd get easier if we stopped taking care of the pigs, if we tried to treat them like they were nothing and we didn't care anything about them or what happened to them. But it doesn't matter.

Two days of slaughter every three months still shake us to our core.

———

Krystal and I stare in silence at our bowls of cereal in front of us, still reeling from the night before. Neither of us will eat today even if we try. Mrs. Wheeler already left to go fishing. Her fishing days coincide with the quarterly slaughters. They take all night, and she heads to the river when it's finished like fishing is some kind of redemption for her sins. I don't know how sitting around killing fish while the sun rises makes up for killing pigs, but it doesn't do any good to ask questions. It's better to just accept things as they are and move on.

Veronica sits at the table, flipping through her history textbook and going over her notes for the test she has in third period. Last year we discovered that she sneaks out during these nights to watch. It hadn't taken us long to figure out the pig-farm process. The clues had been there all along. We'd just never imagined something so horrific could exist. As soon as the piglets are around six months old and fattened up, Mr. Johnson starts coming around. He used to pretend to take pennies out of our ears when we were little girls, and it was creepy even before we knew what his presence signaled on the farm. We had no idea he had anything to do with the "pig adoption." It wasn't until afterward that we put the two together. Mrs. Wheeler told us that the pigs were shipped off during the night while we were sleeping so we wouldn't have to see them get taken away.

Thoughts of Mrs. Wheeler summon her presence, and she walks through the mudroom at the back of the kitchen. I keep my eyes glued on my bowl. I'm not ready to look at her again yet. It's moments like these that she feels like a murderer and the hate that I usually keep buried surges to the surface.

"Good morning," she says as a formality to Krystal and me, before changing her focus and tone to Veronica. "Darling, I forgot to tell you that I ran into Alice Greer's mother yesterday at the supermarket. We got to talking about how the two of you are so in love with the new *Cowboy Bebop*, which made me think that we should get you girls together on Friday to watch the new episode. What do you think?"

Veronica glares up at her from her spot at the table. "No thanks," she says, but everyone at the table already knows where this is heading. Normally, Veronica is the boss and what she says goes, no matter what, except when it comes to this.

Mrs. Wheeler doesn't miss a beat. "I knew you'd be happy about it. I'm going to take a shower to wash the smell of fish off me, but as soon as you girls are at school, I'll give her mother a call. Hopefully, we can arrange it for Friday. Won't that be so much fun?" She skips off down the hallway before Veronica has time to answer.

I catch Krystal's eye and shake my head.

"Here we go again," I mouth.

Mrs. Wheeler will set up some awful playdate for Alice to come home with us after school, I'm sure, and it will only end disastrous. They always do.

FOURTEEN

KRYSTAL

Time is warped in the regular hospital, and five days of psychiatric visits are unlike anything I've experienced before. Life on the ward means you adjust to the weirdest stuff without even trying. Like Hilda. She's a middle-aged white woman who walks around the community room spitting on the floor. I barely notice her anymore, and even when I do, there's no reaction. I asked Dr. McGowan once, "Why spit?" and he told me she thinks it's poison, so she's trying to kill the nurses with it.

I'm alone in the community room and grateful for a chance to collect myself before they bring Nichole in. I've been sitting here for the last hour trying to figure out how to bring Aiden up in a way that doesn't set her off. It's my job to keep her safe, but I can't keep her safe if I don't know who I'm keeping her safe from, and I'm still on the fence about whether or not Aiden was telling the truth this morning.

Dread fills my gut when Nichole walks into the room with Mia. Staff providing direct observation have to be specially trained and certified, so there's only a few of them on the unit. I'm getting more familiar with them as they work their way through their rotations. I like Mia because she's so friendly, but she's also one of the nosiest. Most of them take a chair and slide it within the two-foot distance that's allowed between them and their assigned patient, but not Mia. She snuggles up close and gets right in on the conversation. I was hoping we'd get Earl or Derek. Sandra would've been best. She couldn't care less about your conversations and might be the only person I've met in real life who could sleep with their eyes open.

"Hi, Krystal," Mia says, lighting up when she sees me.

"Hi, Mia. Good to see you," I say, watching as Nichole shuffles into the room with her head hung low and her eyes glued to the dirty linoleum floor. Nichole pulls out the chair and sits next to me, eyes still downcast. She clutches her stomach like it hurts.

"Hey, hon, how are you?" I ask, giving her a side hug. She's stiff and rigid against me. Mia takes a seat across from her.

"Hi," she says in her new tiny voice—the only one she speaks in now when she's calm. She lays her head against my shoulder. Normally, I'd run my hands through her hair, but it's too matted with knots, so I stroke the side of her head like she's Hobbes.

"Rough morning?" I ask, even though they all seem rough to me.

She gives an almost imperceptible nod. Mia eyes the room before pulling her phone out of her pocket and holding it underneath the table. She busies herself trying to peek at something on her screen while still pretending to watch Nichole. Staff aren't allowed to use their phones during their shifts for obvious reasons, but they're always trying to grab a quick fix like a bunch of crackheads who've gone without a hit for too long. I can't believe my good luck. Nichole is much more likely to talk to me if no one else can hear.

I lean my head down near her face and whisper into her hair. "We need to talk, and it's really important." I rub my hand up and down her arm, hoping to ground her, get her present. Her lids are heavy. Her face slack. They must've given her something to calm her nerves for the test. "Did you hear me, honey?" I ask, keeping my eyes on Mia. She's still occupied.

No response.

"Nikki, if you're in there and you can hear me, can you just hold my pinky? That's all. Just take my pinky." I hold my breath for what seems like minutes until I feel the softness of her pinky hook itself with mine. I hold back the urge to squeal. "Okay, good, sweetie. That's good." I speak in a frenzied whisper. Now that I've got her, I have to keep her. "You don't even have to say anything. All you have to do is squeeze my pinky if the answer is yes." I take a deep breath. "Was Aiden hurting you? Did you set the fire so you could escape?"

She shoves me off her and jumps up, instantly springing to life. She towers over me. "Did he tell you to say that?" Her eyes dart around the room. Every muscle in her body is tense, ready to fight.

"No, no, no . . . he didn't. Nobody told me to do anything. I'm sorry." I grab for her hand, but she jerks it away and steps backward.

Her eyes bulge. "He did, didn't he? Where is he? How do you know? Why her? That one. Jesus."

Mia gets up from her chair and takes a slow step in Nichole's direction, motioning for me to stay in my seat. "Nichole, let's have you sit back down, okay?" She takes another cautious step toward her like she's an animal needing to be tamed. "I want you to focus on my voice and on what I'm saying to you. Can you listen to my voice and be here with me?"

She shakes her head wildly as Mia moves closer to her. Nichole leaps back just as she's within Mia's reach. Her pupils widen until her eyes look almost black, and then she's gone—crossing over some invisible line in her mind. The madness contorts the features on her face. She starts inhaling rapidly with no exhale. Her fists are clenched at her sides, arms shaking.

Mia reaches into her pocket and triggers the alarm fob that staff carry with them at all times. Within seconds, the security team—one white, one black, both huge—appears in the doorway. Nichole senses their presence and scuttles to the back of the room. She grabs one of the chairs and stands behind it, plastering herself against the wall. Her entire body tenses and moves in jerking motions like she's having some kind of spasm.

And, just like that, the security men attack.

Their muscled bodies envelop hers, and she lets out an ear-piercing scream. It takes two of them to restrain her, even though she's nothing but bones. Arms and legs flail everywhere. I don't want to watch, but I can't look away. The one with the crew cut grabs her arms tightly around her back and pins her to the floor.

My scream bubbles out of me. "Don't hurt her! Please, stop hurting her!"

As soon as she's down, his partner moves in with a needle that seems to appear from out of nowhere. In one swift movement, he pulls up her nightgown and stabs the syringe into her thigh.

In the movies when that happens, the person immediately gets knocked out. End of story. But that's not the case with Nichole. It does nothing to stop the fight coursing through her. The sounds coming out of her mouth aren't human. Crew Cut digs his knee into her back while his partner gives her another shot. Her face is smashed against the nasty floor, and spittle hangs from the corner of her mouth as she lets out muffled screams.

Mia puts her hand gently on my shoulder, and I appreciate the kind gesture. It's hard to watch Nichole struggle against the drugs making their way through her body. I instinctively move toward her to help, but Mia motions for me to sit down.

"I know this is hard to watch, but you either have to leave or stay in your seat," she says like she wishes she didn't have to.

Nichole lies on the ground. A knee in her back. Face smashed on the floor. Her body spasms and stills. Spasms and stills. Eyes unseeing.

"It's okay, Nichole," I cry just as her eyes roll back in her head and she disappears into a land where I can't follow.

FIFTEEN

KRYSTAL

I'm trying to appear calm and collected as I wait to meet Eric Parker, but the jiggling of my leg is a dead giveaway, and it's out of my control. I've met with high-powered attorneys when millions of dollars were at stake and wasn't this nervous. But this is Nichole's life, and she's circling the drain. Part of her may have already gone down.

The fit she threw in the community room was nothing in comparison to the one she threw as they dragged her down the hallway. The shots that knocked her out in the community room only got them halfway down the corridor before she sprang back to life like she'd been infused with electricity. I was at the nurses' station signing myself out when her bloodcurdling screams shook the unit and reverberated down the hallways. A patient in a room adjacent to hers let out a responsive scream that was equally chilling, followed by another one. Within seconds, staff were rushing to his room to contain him while the attendants battled through round two with Nichole.

Their large bodies were no match for hers, and she bit at them like a rabid dog when they came near her. It took all their combined strength to hold her hands behind her back and press her up against the wall. In one swift movement, Nichole bashed her head into the nose of one of them, sending blood squirting everywhere. She let out a squeal of glee. In that moment her eyes caught mine, and she suddenly popped into reality with a look of pure terror. They tore her off the wall and threw her into her room.

I couldn't get out of there fast enough. Theresa called just as I made it through the parking lot, and it took her over ten minutes to calm me down on the phone, another ten for me to figure out the reason for her call. We'd gotten the green light to proceed with retaining Eric Parker because he doesn't have any connections to the Fischer family.

I glance at my watch for the third time. It's only been two minutes since I checked, but it feels like so much more time has passed. I'm still reeling from Nichole's explosive episode. They get more disturbing every time I see them, and my words do nothing to soothe her or bring her back to reality. I'm supposed to be her anchor to the ground. What happens if that's gone? Before I have a chance to spiral further down the rabbit hole of what-ifs, the door opens and a tall, lean man struts confidently into the reception area.

"I'm Eric Parker," he greets me, sticking out his hand. He's got a firm grip, strong shake. That's what I like. "And you must be Krystal?"

"I am," I say, standing and smoothing down the front of my skirt. Thankfully, I had enough time after Theresa's phone call to go home, take a shower, and get myself together before this meeting, because I was a mess. I cried the entire way home from the hospital.

"You first," he says, making a sweeping gesture to the door and into his office. Muscular biceps peek out from underneath his shirt.

His office is smaller than the reception area. A boxy wooden desk takes up most of the space, and the bookshelves lining an entire wall give the place an even more claustrophobic feel. The blinds on the windows are closed, and if I knew him better, I'd ask him to open them, since I hate enclosed space and artificial light. Windowless rooms are the worst.

We easily slide into our designated spots. Me in front of the desk. Him behind. A standing fan in the corner blasts air throughout the room and creates a hum in the background. If I didn't trust Theresa's judgment so much, I'd be second-guessing her decision at calling him our best plan B. But she swears he has raving reviews, and she spoke personally with some of them.

His desk is meticulously uncluttered, and he pulls a yellow legal pad out of one of the drawers. "So, why don't you just take me back to the beginning and tell me what's going on," he says, grabbing a pen out of his shirt pocket and getting poised to write, like a therapist taking notes.

"My sister is Nichole Fischer, and her house started on fire last week, but I'm pretty sure you already covered that with Theresa." He nods. His red shirt complements his brown skin. "She got out, but her husband, Aiden, was trapped inside for a while before he was rescued. He was in pretty bad shape up until yesterday, but thankfully he's made a turn for the better, and doctors are hopeful for his recovery." Aiden texted me on the drive home from the hospital to let me know he had Janice's phone with him and to give him a call as soon as I could.

"My sister didn't get hurt, but she freaked out on the paramedics and first responders at the scene. They put her on a seventy-two-hour hold at Riverside East that has now come and gone, but the psychiatric hold is still in place because they consider her dangerous. And as much as I hate it, she needs it. She's bashed her head on things more than once since she's been admitted. She's even attacked me." My words come out so fast they trip over each other. I just want to bring him up to speed as quickly as possible so we can start figuring out how to help Nichole. "She's in really bad shape. She hears voices and sees things that aren't there. Her level of paranoia is off the charts, and she freaks out anytime you ask her about Aiden, going into these explosive rages. It took three grown men to restrain her this afternoon."

Eric's eyes haven't left mine. They're attentive and kind as they peer out from black-rimmed glasses, the opposite of William Jenkins's hard eyes leaping off the billboard screen. Shouldn't Eric have a little bit of an edge to him?

"She's a shell of a person when she isn't psychotic. She never smiles or frowns. Doesn't give any sign of wanting anything. It's like she disappears in and out of herself all day long." Talking about it brings all my emotions to the surface, and I fight back tears. Crying in front of him is the last thing I'm trying to do.

"I'm sorry you're having to go through all this," he says.

"Thank you," I respond, appreciating his kindness. "The detective assigned to her case is convinced she's the one that started the fire, and that she did it on purpose."

He raises his eyebrows. "Why is that? Because of her mental state?"

"No, it's because of the evidence they found at the scene. The fire was started with gasoline that had been dumped all over their master bedroom, and she was covered in gasoline when the paramedics arrived. She had a lighter in her pocket, and she admitted to doing it."

"What do you think?"

"Honestly, I'm pretty sure she was the one to set the fire." It's the first time I've said it out loud, and it strips away my last shred of denial about the seriousness of her situation. The world shifts underneath my feet. Nichole will never be the same, no matter how this ends. The life we knew is gone. This is a marker in the sand.

"Are you sure?"

"I mean, I'm not one hundred percent sure, but I've gone through all the security footage, and nobody comes in or out of their house on the night of the fire. In fact, no one goes into their house except Aiden the entire week leading up to it, so they were definitely the only two people in the house at the time. There's no way Aiden did it, because there was a desk in front of their door barricading him inside, so it'd be impossible. I just don't know why she did it."

He jots something down on his pad. "Any ideas? Was he hurting her? Drugs? Her mental break?" There're lots of other potential reasons, but he cuts his list short at the most probable.

"Definitely not drugs. She doesn't touch them. Never has. There's no question that she's in the throes of a psychosis, but here's the thing—she's genuinely terrified of Aiden. I've never seen her so scared. She loses it if you even mention his name. She's called him a murderer on more than one occasion. At first, I thought it was just part of her psychosis like everything else, but what if there's some truth to her terror? What if he was hurting her?"

"Self-defense?" He cocks his head to the side.

I nod and lean forward in my chair. "I don't know how much of the past footage the investigators looked at, but I went back as far as I could go, and Nichole doesn't leave the house for an entire week leading up to the fire. That's really unusual for her. No, not unusual—unheard of. She walks every day and spends most of her time during the day sitting outside in their backyard, but she doesn't do any of that. I can't help but wonder if Aiden was keeping her locked up inside so that she couldn't get out."

"So, she had to start the fire to get free?"

Relief passes through me that he doesn't think my idea is crazy. "It's definitely a possibility."

He takes a moment to think before speaking. "I checked the court docket this morning to see if any charges have been filed against Nichole because the first place they'll show up is on the register, and so far nothing's been filed. Have any police or detectives spoken with her?"

"Detective Sparks has tried, but I don't think anyone else has. As far as I know, anyway. But there's no way to tell whether what she's saying is based on fact or whatever delusional world she's living in at the moment. That's why I don't think anyone should be able to talk to her. Can we stop that from happening?"

"Not exactly, but we can prevent anyone talking to her without me present." He scribbles something down again. "Our first order of business is to file a notice of application with the court for mental incompetency. It's a lengthy process, just like any other motion, and sometimes a verdict can take a significant amount of time. Filing a notice puts her competency trial on the calendar for within thirty days of filing, and it alerts everyone involved in the case that we are approaching the case from a place of mental incompetency."

"What happens then?"

"Mental incompetency works in her favor. Anything she may or may not have said to incriminate herself while she's been in the hospital is going to be considered within that context and not considered valid testimony about what happened. It's going to make sure any interviews with investigators happen very differently than how they would normally occur, given the competency issues. Mainly, she'll never be alone, and a psychiatrist will always have to be present for any type of questioning or formal interviews. She'll be entitled to breaks and other things that other people in her similar position wouldn't because we've established her fragile mental state."

Nichole would be insulted about being referred to as anything remotely related to being fragile. People think of redheads as fragile and exotic. Maybe it's the pale skin that they associate with frailty, but Nichole is anything but fragile—she is fierce. Her personality matches her fiery red hair, exploding like lava when she gets upset.

"The most important part is that we've established from the very beginning that she's mentally incompetent and therefore didn't know the difference between right and wrong at the moment she was committing the crime. In addition, she didn't have the ability to recognize that her actions were happening in the real world with real-life consequences. Her incompetency will already be confirmed before any trial happens."

"How do you know they're even going to press attempted murder charges? I mean, Aiden looks like he's going to be fine. He's got some serious rehabilitation in front of him, but none of his injuries are permanent except the burns on his face."

"Charging Nichole can happen whether or not Aiden is better. Attempted murder is attempted murder regardless of Aiden's condition.

It's not based on the severity of his condition after the attempt, and they don't need his permission to charge her. He's not the one who gets to decide."

The information is coming so fast. "Then, who gets to decide all this?"

"Ultimately, it's up to the district attorney's office." He leans forward across the desk and speaks in a furtive tone. "And I'm going to be really honest with you, Krystal: The Fischers are one of the most prominent families in the community. It's highly unlikely that this case is not going to result in attempted murder charges against your sister."

My mouth goes dry. "Even if Aiden is fine and doesn't want her to be charged?"

"Even if Aiden is fine." He nods. "He doesn't get to decide what they do."

I let his words sink in. "And remind me what that carries?"

"First degree is life with the possibility of parole, so most first-degree-ers usually do around ten years. With second degree, she'd be looking at anywhere from five to seven years." He props his elbows up on his desk and folds his hands, resting his chin on top.

"Once she's declared incompetent, does that stay on her record forever? I mean, she's a schoolteacher. I'm not sure if you know that or not, but something like that on her record would ruin her career."

He reaches across the table and takes my hand in his in a commanding yet comforting way. "Krystal, her career is over. Forget the murder charges and mental incompetency—she's looking at felony arson no matter what if she started that fire."

I slowly exhale. "Sometimes I still can't believe this is happening."

He nods and gives me a moment of pause before continuing. "I hate to ask you this, but it's going to come up, especially if the Fischers are digging around." His eyes peer into mine. "Is this the first time she's done something like this, or does she have a history of violence and mental illness? Anything in her past that might hint at a pattern?"

I force myself to maintain eye contact. He doesn't have to tell me that it will be more difficult for her if there is. "I'm not saying she's a perfect person. She definitely has her flaws just like everyone else, and there're times when she's not the happiest person, but not anything that isn't within the realm of normal experience. She's never sought any kind of mental health treatment or been through anything like this."

"How about violence? Any aggression?" He's studying my face in the same way I sit across the table and study my clients when I want to know if they're telling the truth.

"She's got one of the biggest hearts on the planet, and she'd never hurt anyone." My deceit settles like a cold stone in the pit of my stomach, but I can't open that box. Not now. The last pieces of our life will come crumbling down. I've never been more grateful that our juvenile records are sealed.

SIXTEEN

NICHOLE

(THEN)

Alice's chubby legs hurry to keep up with Veronica as we leave school, but Veronica isn't making any effort to slow down. She hasn't said anything to her since we left the lockers. Even then she only mumbled hi and then said she liked her elbows, which is about the weirdest thing you could say to someone. Why can't she at least try to be normal?

Alice gives up trying to catch Veronica and starts walking next to Krystal and me instead. She's already breathing hard, and the farm is over two miles from school. Probably closer to three. She has no idea what she's gotten herself into, and I feel sorry for her. I feel sorry for all of them.

Freckles dot her pudgy cheeks. She has long dirty-blonde hair that swings past her shoulders as she struggles to keep up with us even at the slower pace.

"I saw you in the paper last week, Krystal. That was a great picture. I can't believe how fast you can run," she gushes. She's got the same starry-eyed look that all the nerdy younger kids get when they're around Krystal.

"Thanks," Krystal says. The tips of her ears are red. She gets so embarrassed when people compliment her. You'd think she'd be used to it by now, but nope. Not even close.

"I'm no good at running. Never have been. Do they make you run the mile in PE here?" Her questions are punctuated by her hurried breaths. "My old school made us run the mile twice every year. So awful. I hated it. I hope I don't have to do it here. You guys probably love doing it, though, huh? You're like, 'Yeah, please can we run?'" She giggles nervously and waits for one of us to say something, but we keep silent, smiling and nodding in unison.

We plod past Al's Diner on the corner of Ninth Avenue and make it halfway down the next block before Alice can't take the silence any longer. She cuts in at Saint John's Presbyterian Church and rattles on for the next two miles, barely stopping to take a breath. She goes on and on about all the characters in the anime she watches, assuming we're into it, too, since the playdate hinges on anime, but it's not my thing. Krystal can't stand it, either, because she hates anything with subtitles, but we nod and smile in the appropriate places like well-trained puppets.

She's one of those kids who has always lived in town and never been in the country. They act like Vernon is the size of New York City and coming out to the farm is a foreign trip. Once they get here, they want to run all over the farm because they *love* all the animals. So, we make the rounds with them through the barns so they can pet the cows and feed the sheep grazing in the back. The chickens are always a big hit until they step inside their pens and realize how much it stinks. The chickens aren't nearly so cute then.

All of them ask to do chores with us because they think it will be fun, which always makes Veronica mad because she hates doing chores. At least the outside ones. She tries to stop them, but they never listen to her. All they imagine is the cute little petting zoo at the county fair each summer where you pour seed in your hand like a cup and let goats and pigs nibble from it.

But we're the real deal.

Feeding the animals involves wheelbarrows and lots of shoveling. Most of them don't get any farther than the barn and all the manure squishing on their shoes before they start having second thoughts. Veronica trails along until they tire out, making loud and dramatic sighs the entire time. There's only been one who ever made it through all the chores. Once one of the playdate friends was in the barn when the vet came to inseminate our cows. Her eyes as she watched where he stuck his arm left me and Krystal squealing with laughter for the next three days. But that's not how I want tonight to go, especially since it's a sleepover.

Usually after chores, there's only about half an hour before they get picked up by their parents, but it's a totally different deal with the sleepovers. That's when things get really tough. What was Mrs. Wheeler thinking, making it a sleepover? Doesn't she remember how the last one ended?

Hopefully, once we get in the barn, Alice will be one of the kids who gets completely grossed out by all the smells and weird sounds. Those are the easy ones because all they want to do is play inside after that. Krystal and I get off the hook then because we make sure we don't step foot back in the house until they're gone.

I size her up as the farm comes in sight. Her pale skin is a dead giveaway that she doesn't get outside much, and the extra roll around her waist means she doesn't exercise much either. Still. You never know. I've been surprised before.

———

Alice wolfs down her dinner, shoveling the mashed potatoes into her mouth between bites of chicken. She's already on her second plate. The girl is impressive. She made it through chores and never complained, even though I know she had to be dying. She was covered in sweat while we emptied the feeding troughs, and it was like ninety degrees in the barn, but she just huffed and puffed right through it. That's why you can never underestimate people, and you definitely can't judge them by how they look. Veronica pretended not to be impressed by her, but I know she was. Poor thing has no idea what she's in for in the morning after she sleeps on that lumpy roll-out bed. She'll probably be so achy and stiff she'll be walking to the breakfast table like an old man.

I'm holding myself back from tearing into my food like her because I want to savor every bite. I hate playdates, but I love the dinners that go with them. We don't have guests over to the house like regular people. Supposedly, Mrs. Wheeler has parents, but I've never seen them, and they don't visit. She says they're living up north, but who knows. The only people who come to the house are social workers dropping off kids, but we haven't had a new kid in over a year.

Mrs. Wheeler outdid herself tonight, which is easy to do when there's nowhere for you to go but up. Most of our vegetables come out of cans, and she's a huge fan of Tuna Helper. I'm not sure if you can actually call what she does cooking if everything comes out of a can or box. But she goes all out for Veronica's friends, cooking to impress them in case their parents ask what they had for dinner. Tonight, she cooked an actual chicken, and she made gravy to go with the mashed potatoes. It's not homemade, but it's still delicious.

"I've set everything up in the living room for you girls to watch *Cowboy Bebop* after dinner," Mrs. Wheeler announces. "You can make some popcorn, and I even bought some diet soda pop that's getting cold in the fridge while we eat."

"Mom," Veronica groans from across the table.

I can't help but cringe with Veronica. Luckily, Alice is too buried in her food to notice how hard Mrs. Wheeler is trying or the needy desperation in her voice.

Mrs. Wheeler looks surprised at Veronica's response and ignores her embarrassment. "I was thinking you might want to watch a movie after your show ended. How does that sound? I can put the tapes out on the coffee table."

"Mom." Veronica groans even louder this time, but Mrs. Wheeler is unfazed by her embarrassment. She always is.

There's only going to be one movie on the coffee table since we only own two VHS movies—*Back to the Future* and *Dirty Dancing*. Mrs. Wheeler doesn't allow us to watch *Dirty Dancing*. That's reserved for her own guilty pleasure, although I've never seen Mrs. Wheeler in the living room alone, so I have no idea when she watches it.

"That sounds fun." Alice matches Mrs. Wheeler's enthusiasm. She's just as committed to making this playdate a success.

Krystal and I start clearing dishes as soon as we're finished. Krystal loses at rock paper scissors and gets stuck separating the leftover chicken from the bone. It's the grossest job, and we'd both rather haul manure than touch animal bones, but someone has to do it. I lost the last two times, so it's about time she had a turn. I fill the sink with soap and start soaking dishes while she separates the chicken from the bone, making sure she gets every piece and nothing goes to waste. There's nothing Mrs. Wheeler hates more than waste, especially when it comes to food. It's one of the reasons she keeps the cupboards locked. We keep our heads down while we work, hoping they'll forget about us if we're quiet and we can sneak off to our bedroom once we're finished.

Alice gets up from the table and brings her plate to the trash, scraping it off before carrying it over to the sink and placing it in the sudsy water. "Where's a towel?" she asks, scanning the kitchen. "I can help dry. You just have to show me where everything gets put away."

Mrs. Wheeler lets out a nervous laugh and stands behind her, placing her hand gently on her back. It's so weird to see her touch someone besides Veronica. "Oh, nonsense, sweetie. You don't have to help with dishes. Why don't you and Veronica go take a seat in the living room? Maybe there's a program on TV you can watch while we get the kitchen cleaned up."

She says *we* like it implies she'll be helping us, but I can't remember the last time she cleaned the kitchen. We're not just her hired hands on the farm; she relies on us as her housekeepers too. She'd have us cook meals if she trusted us with the food.

Alice shakes her head and gives her a smile. "It's okay. I love doing dishes."

She stands next to me at the sink and starts rinsing the plates, taking great care as she places them in the strainer. I catch Krystal's eye at the refrigerator, and she gives an almost imperceptible shrug. Mrs. Wheeler's eyes bore into me from behind as if I have something to do with Alice's wanting to help, but it's not my fault. Alice has fallen under the assumption that we're one of those regular happy families she sees on TV who does things together. She's an only child and spent half of chores complaining about how lonely she is in her house because her parents work all the time and how she wishes she had siblings. She's ready to join the fold. All she needs is an invitation.

"Drying is my favorite part, anyway. Sometimes my skin can get sensitive with certain kinds of soap, though. The doctors say I don't have eczema, but my mom wants to take me to a specialist anyway because she's convinced I do, but I don't really care. I just try not to let my hands get too dry. I use baby lotion on them, and that seems to help. You ever tried baby lotion on your skin? Everyone always thinks it's for babies, but it's great for our skin too. I mean, you have to think about it: babies are super sensitive and pure. Like super pure, so they can't have anything in their lotion, so why wouldn't it be a good thing to use? Have you ever tried it?"

"I haven't," I respond even though I'm not sure which one of us she's directing the question to. It's like all the words Alice has stored up over the weeks alone in her house have to come out tonight. Veronica sits at the table, waiting to be excused and looking to Mrs. Wheeler to tell her what she should do. None of the kids have ever offered to help with the dishes before, and it's thrown everything more off balance than it already is.

"Veronica, would you like to help?" Mrs. Wheeler asks with a slight hesitation in her voice that you wouldn't be able to detect unless you knew her.

I don't need to turn around to know Veronica is wearing a shocked expression. I can't remember a time when Mrs. Wheeler asked Veronica to help with anything.

Alice turns around. "Yeah, Veronica, come help me dry," she says eagerly.

Veronica walks slowly over to the row of drawers next to the sink. She pulls out two drying cloths like she's in a daze and gives one to Alice. Alice beams as the two of them start drying together. Mrs. Wheeler falls in line and starts putting dishes away in their designated spots once they've wiped them.

The giggles bubble inside me knowing how thrown off Mrs. Wheeler and Veronica are. I don't dare look at Krystal to see her reaction because I'll burst out laughing if I do. Veronica's annoyance is a palpable force, but Alice is oblivious to the weird tension around her. She's grinning like it's Christmas and she's having the family moment she's been asking Santa Claus for every year.

It's amazing how fast things get cleaned up when there're five of us doing it. Veronica and Alice move into the living room. Mrs. Wheeler looks almost as pleased as Alice at how well things appear to be going. Veronica wears her usual scowl.

"Well, good night," Krystal says to Mrs. Wheeler, even though we never tell her good night. Normally, after we've cleared and put away the dinner dishes, the two of us retreat to our room as fast as we can. I don't even know what the two of them do at night because we don't cross over to the other side once we're on our side of the house.

"Good night, Krystal." Mrs. Wheeler's reply is as awkward and out of place as Krystal's. "You too, Nichole," she adds as an afterthought.

"Wait—aren't you guys watching the movie?" Alice asks from her position on the couch, turning around to look at us.

Krystal and I freeze.

"I, uh . . . we just have a lot of homework to get done," Krystal says, thinking quick on her feet.

"But it's Friday," Alice counters with a puzzled expression on her face. "You have all weekend to do your homework."

"Yeah, but we really like to get ahead on Spanish," I say.

Alice wrinkles her forehead. "We didn't get any Spanish homework."

Veronica glares over her head at us. Joining them in the living room is the last thing she wants from us. But I forgot Alice is in our Spanish class, and she's right. Mrs. Aravello didn't give us any homework this weekend.

"Oh," I say, letting out a fake laugh and hoping it sounds convincing. "You're right. That was last week."

She pats the space on the couch between her and Veronica. "Come on, there's plenty of room, right, Veronica?"

"Sure, lots of room," Veronica responds without any emotion in her voice.

Krystal and I turn around, looking to Mrs. Wheeler for permission. She nods her consent, and we head back into the living room.

SEVENTEEN

NICHOLE

(THEN)

Krystal scored a bottle of gin from Scott at school today, and we waited until Veronica and Alice were settled in her bedroom before sneaking out our bedroom window. We spend most of our Friday nights in the hayloft. It's my favorite part of the week. Krystal's too.

I take Krystal's hand and help ease her out the window. We plop onto the grass and eye the house. No lights. I nod to her, and we don't speak as we tiptoe across the grass and head toward the barn. Just as we're nearing the driveway, Alice leaps out from behind the woodshed.

"Hi!"

Krystal and I jump back.

"What are you doing out here?" Krystal asks, keeping her voice low and eying the house to see if any lights turn on or there're any signs of movement.

"What are *you* doing out here?" Veronica echoes as she slides around the corner and stands next to Alice. She puts her hands on her hips. She's wearing her full smirk tonight.

I shove the bottle of gin down the back of my jeans and pull my shirt over it, making sure to stay out of their sight. Thankfully, the moon is only a sliver and there're tons of clouds, so it's almost pitch black, making it easy to hide.

"You were so right, Veronica. They totally snuck out. She said you guys were going to, but I was like 'No way.' The two of you seem like such Goody Two-shoes." She puts her hand over her mouth. "Oh my gosh, I hope I didn't make you mad. I didn't mean anything bad by it. I think it's super cool that you're sneaking out." She's so giddy she bounces as she talks, dancing on her tiptoes. "Can we come with you? Where are you going?"

"Shhh!" I whisper. "You're going to wake Mrs. Wheeler."

Veronica shakes her head. "No, she's not. We could yell right now, and she'd probably sleep right through it. Mom's a superhard sleeper." She reads our surprised expressions. "You didn't know that? You think you guys are really that quiet when you sneak out?"

"What are you talking about?" Krystal asks, feigning innocence, but even in the dark you can tell she's faking it.

"You don't think I know about all your little parties in the barn? Truth or dare?" She wags her head back and forth mockingly as she says the last part.

My stomach rolls in on itself. It doesn't matter what she's seen us do. What's she heard us say? Does she sneak out and spy on us in the same way she sneaks out to spy on the pigs?

Alice grabs my arms. "Oh my gosh, you guys play truth or dare? Is that what you're going to do tonight? Can we go with you?" She looks at Veronica for permission, not even trying to hide her eagerness. "Is that okay with you? You want to play, too, right?"

"It's kind of a dumb game. I mean, like you say you're telling the truth, but how does anyone really even know you're telling the truth?" Veronica says in her typical sourpuss fashion. "It's not like there's any way you can tell."

Alice frowns. "Don't you want to at least have a little fun tonight?"

Our fun is ruined. All I want to do is turn around and run back into the house, whip open the window, and crawl into bed. We never should've done this.

"Maybe we should just go back inside." Krystal speaks my thoughts.

"Yeah," I quickly agree. "It was one thing when it was just us, but we don't want to take the chance of getting caught and getting you guys in trouble."

"No, come on, guys, let's do it." Alice sounds like the football cheerleaders during the pep rallies. "We're already outside, so we might as well do something, and everyone knows that it's not a real sleepover unless you play truth or dare."

Nobody wants to be the first to move. The four of us stand in a circle as the moment stretches out among us. Finally, Veronica gives in.

"Okay, fine. We might as well," she says with a half-hearted shoulder shrug.

"Yes!" Alice squeals, throwing her arms around her. "This is going to be so much fun."

———

Travis Tritt plays in the background on the small portable radio that we keep tuned to the local country music station. It's tied with string to one of the rafters so we don't knock it down. It's been up there for so long cobwebs have grown around it. The sweet, musty odor of hay and cheap gin fills my nostrils. My thoughts are fuzzy and slip sideways.

"Nichole, truth or dare?" Alice giggles. Her cheeks are flushed from the booze and the heat up here. Beads of sweat glisten on her forehead. She shares a bale of hay with Krystal. The bottle of gin is wedged between them. Nearly empty. Krystal's just as sweaty, and they wear identical grins.

Krystal's met her match in Alice. Turns out Alice raids her parents' liquor cabinet on a regular basis when they're gone, and she was proud to show us how much she could drink. The two of them are giggling like they've been best friends forever and keep trying to get me pumped up, but I'm too tired. Drinking makes me sleepy, and I want to go to bed, but they don't show any signs of slowing down.

Veronica is hunched over next to them on a hay bale. Her hands cup her face as she rests her elbows on her knees. The moonlight streams through the cracks in the barn, casting strange shadows on her face. I sit across from them, and she shoots me dirty looks every few seconds, like I have any control over the two of them. They're in their own world. Drunk people get like that. You just have to wait it out. They'll come back to us eventually.

The Travis Tritt song ends, and the first few beats of Shania Twain's "Any Man of Mine" sends Alice flying to her feet. Krystal leaps up, too, since Shania Twain is one of her favorite country singers. Her hair is frizzy from the heat.

"I love this song!" Alice squeals, clapping and stamping her feet.

Krystal jumps around, focusing on her feet as she moves them out of sync with the music, trying to remember the steps to the dance I taught her. She's doing it all wrong, as usual. She can run, but she can't dance to save her life. She's as uncoordinated as she is tone deaf. So is Alice, but the two of them belt out the lyrics at the top of their lungs as they stumble awkwardly through the line dance.

I burst out laughing. "Oh my gosh, you're doing it all wrong. Let me help you." I get a burst of energy and stand to join them. They hoot and holler when I do, jumping up and down and reaching out to me. I arrange us all side by side. "You have to do it like this," I say, demonstrating each movement. "Put your left hand out like this, then jut your hip out, and one, two, three, tap."

They give it a try and do it all wrong again, tripping over each other and giggling.

"Come on, Veronica. Dance with us!" Krystal gestures for her to join us.

Veronica shakes her head. "I'm okay."

"Come on, you party pooper!" Alice runs over to Veronica. She grabs her hands and pulls her up, looping an arm around her shoulder. Alice sways to the song with her eyes closed like she's really feeling the lyrics. Veronica stands next to her with her arms at her sides, shifting from one leg to the next, doing the stiffest two-step I've ever seen.

I catch Krystal's eye at the same time, and we burst out laughing. Krystal's goofy grin is plastered on her face, and she can't stop giggling. I give her a sloppy kiss on the cheek.

"I love Drunk Krystal," I say, and she laughs like I'm kidding, but it's true. It's one of the rare times she lets the weight of the world off her shoulders. I love watching it happen as she eases into her body, and for just a few hours, her insides uncoil and she stops working so hard.

"And I love Drunk Nichole," she slurs.

"Except I'm not drunk." I laugh. This is as far as I get, and it's nothing.

"You don't know what you're missing, right, Alice?" Krystal calls to her.

Alice runs to the bale and grabs the bottle. She raises it in the air before taking another pull, wiping her mouth when she's finished. "Totally. Whose turn is it next?"

I point to Veronica and smile. "Guess it's your lucky night." I shouldn't tease, but I can't help myself. She'll punish us for it later, but I don't care. I just like feeling like I'm in control in my own house.

Veronica makes a face. "I'm not playing."

"Come on, Veronica, you have to play," Alice whines like a toddler. "You haven't done a single dare, and you—"

"That's not true," Veronica interrupts. "I made it all the way across that." She points to the rafters above the connecting ties, where she scooted across on her butt the entire way even though the dare was to walk.

"Come on, that doesn't count because you did it wrong. Right, guys?" Alice turns to us for confirmation.

"Yep, doesn't count," Krystal agrees. Any other time we wouldn't think of agreeing with Veronica's guest over her, but none of the rules apply tonight. We're in uncharted territory.

Veronica rolls her eyes as she agrees. "Fine. Whatever."

"Yeah!" Alice jumps up and down. "All right, then . . ." Alice's eyes roam the barn.

We've used up all the good dares already—do five cartwheels in a row over the furnace vent, take a sip of one of the goat's milk bottles, crawl along the rafters without falling, and of course all the other ones the others purposefully didn't do because drinking was the alternative if you lost, and they wanted to drink. Not me. I only had to drink twice, but that was enough. Alice finally lands on the hayloft door.

"Does this open?" she asks, her eyes lit with an idea.

Krystal doesn't bother answering. She unlocks the door, and the wind whips it open, smashing it against the side of the barn. I rush over to latch it on the side of the wall before it knocks into her. "Be careful," I say, pushing her back, sounding like a paranoid grown-up, but I don't care. It's almost two stories up, and there's nothing but concrete on the landing below. The grappling hook dangles from its pulley cord.

Alice stands on the edge and sticks her head out of the opening into the night sky. "I didn't realize how far up we are," she says, then quickly returns her attention to Veronica. "You have to stick your butt out here and moon the Big Dipper."

"Bare butt?" I ask.

Alice hoots. "Total bare butt."

"Oh my God, yes!" Krystal shrieks like a cheerleader. "That's such a good idea." She flips around to face Veronica. "Come on, you have to do it."

"I don't have to do anything," Veronica snaps, sounding even more like a grown-up than me, and the three of us squeal with laughter. Her face contorts with rage.

"Are you seriously not going to do it?" Alice asks.

"Yeah, Veronica, come on," I say, giving her a playful shove from behind. We have to do this with every single dare. It takes ten minutes just to talk her into doing it, and by the time we get her to agree, it's not even worth it.

Veronica glowers at me. "I want to go back inside."

"No." Alice's face falls. "We're just starting to have fun. Why are you trying to ruin it?"

"I'm not trying to ruin anything," Veronica shoots back.

"Seriously?" Alice raises her eyebrows. "That's all you've done since we left school."

"You're just drunk," Veronica says in a disgusted tone. "You don't even know what you're talking about."

"Really?" Alice's eyes flare with anger. "All we've been trying to do is have a good time. You're the one that's ruining it."

"You call this a good time?" Veronica points to Krystal, then me. "Hanging out with these losers? You must be desperate."

Krystal steps toward Veronica like she wants to smack her, and I pull her back.

"Let's get out of here," I say to Krystal. Things are spiraling, and I don't like it. Krystal tugs her arm away from me and goes to stand next to Alice to show her support.

"You're the one that's a loser, Veronica," Alice says. "Krystal is way more fun than you'll ever be. I only said yes to coming over so that I could hang out with her." She turns and high-fives Krystal.

Veronica's face is red. I don't know if it's from the heat or from rage. Maybe both. She takes a step toward Alice. My insides curl.

"Shut up," she spits out. "Just shut up!"

Alice throws her head back and laughs in her face. "You know what? Everyone at school said you were a freak, and they were right."

The air stills.

Suddenly, Veronica lunges at her and grips her throat in one fist, squeezing tightly. Alice's eyes bulge in shock and surprise. She lets out a strangled breath, frantically batting at Veronica's hands. In one swift movement, Veronica shoves her backward and flings her through the opening. One second Alice is in front of us, and in the next second she's gone, hurtling into the darkness. Alice lets out a bloodcurdling scream as she free-falls, disappearing over the edge.

"Alice!" I yell at the top of my lungs.

The moment stretches in slow motion.

A loud crack ricochets into the night.

"Alice!" I scream again, racing to the hayloft door.

The muscles in Krystal's neck fan in and out with each frantic breath. Her nostrils flare. She's rooted to her spot, gaping at the opening. Veronica is frozen next to her. Blind panic in her eyes.

And then I do it.

I look down.

Alice's body is splayed on the concrete below. Her arms spread wide out. Her left leg bent at a ninety-degree angle at the knee.

"Krystal, go get help!" I scream and grab her, pulling her away from the opening and snapping her out of her stupor.

She bolts through the hayloft with me right behind her. We're down the ladder in seconds. She races through the barn and toward the house to get help. I sprint to where Alice's broken body lies twisted on the cement ground. I kneel beside her, too scared to touch her in case I hurt her. A frozen shriek of terror contorts her face. Blood pools underneath her head. Her body gives a small twitch.

"It's okay, Alice. You're going to be okay," I say as the circle of red grows larger, working its way around my shoes. Her eyes match those of the deer hanging in our living room. The color has disappeared.

Pupils huge. "Krystal ran to get help. She's fast. I promise you she's fast. Remember all that stuff you were saying about her tonight?" I hear Veronica coming down the ladder from the hayloft. "Krystal's running as fast as she can now to get to the house. She'll get you help. I promise she will. Just hold on, okay?"

Veronica reaches us quickly and stands over us. She's out of breath, huffing and puffing from all the work it took getting down by herself. "Is she okay?" she asks between wheezes.

"No, of course she's not okay! You shoved her out of the hayloft!"

"I didn't mean to. It was an accident." She crouches beside me. "Is she okay? Alice, are you okay?"

She goes to touch her, and I smack her hand away before she can. "Don't! That's super bad to do when your head is messed up."

"Is she breathing?"

"Her chest is moving." I point to it. There's a slight rise and then fall. "See that?"

"Why are her eyes like that?" Her voice wavers like she might cry.

"I don't know, but it's not good. Eyes aren't supposed to look like that." I want to close the lids, but I can't do that. That's what you do to people who are dead, and she's not dead. She can't die.

"God, where's Krystal?" Veronica searches the area like she might be hiding somewhere. "What's taking her so long?"

I snap my head up and glare at her. "Don't you dare get mad at her. This is all your fault."

Her face is scrunched in a way I've never seen. Tears swell in her eyes. She chews on her lower lip.

Suddenly, Alice kicks me as her body stiffens.

"Alice? Are you okay?" I ask as her body stiffens again. She clenches her teeth and something white spurts from between them. "She's puking! We need to turn her over so she doesn't choke."

"No, she's having a seizure! Don't touch her!" Veronica shrieks before I can do anything.

"How do you know that?" I ask, but my question answers itself as Alice's body starts dancing in jerking motions on the concrete.

"We have to make sure she doesn't hurt herself. Get behind her and watch her head," Veronica orders.

I move behind Alice and sit cross-legged, carefully moving her head to my lap. Veronica sits at her side. Alice's body trembles like an earthquake is roaring through it. Gargling noises come from her throat while she spasms. Her body gives a final jerk and then stills. I wait for it to move again, but it doesn't.

"Alice?" I call to her like she's disappeared somewhere inside herself and I have to get her back.

Her pupils are dilated. No response.

"Alice?" Veronica tries this time. Fear lines every inch of her face. She reads the fear mirrored in mine as we stare at Alice's body.

"You're going to be okay. Krystal is going to be here soon." I take the hand closest to me and stroke it gingerly. The skin is soft, relaxed. Something about her body isn't right. Her chest isn't moving. The gasps are gone. There's no rise or fall.

"Oh my God, she stopped breathing, Veronica! I really think she stopped breathing. Did she swallow her tongue?"

Veronica scuttles up to us and puts her face next to Alice's, straining to hear the slightest sound of breath, feel any air on her cheek. She raises her eyes to meet mine. They're terror filled. "I don't think she is."

"Tilt her head back . . ." But I don't need to say anything else because Veronica jumps into action. She pushes me aside and lays Alice's head flat on the ground. She tilts it back like we learned in health class last year. She plugs Alice's nose and breathes two big breaths into her mouth. Then lifts her own head like she's been underwater and is coming up for air.

"Do we do the chest things?" I ask. "How do we know if we do the chest things?"

Her head is back down on Alice's mouth giving her two more breaths. I don't wait for an answer. There's no time. When she pulls her lips away, I put my hands together and press down on Alice's chest as hard as I can.

"One. Two. Three." Veronica and I chant out loud together.

And then we take a second to wait.

Nothing. There's only more blood draining out the back of her head and pooling around us. I've never seen so much blood.

"Come on, we have to keep trying." Veronica's voice is frantic.

Veronica breathes. I pound. I don't know how much time passes. Maybe seconds. Maybe minutes. Then suddenly Mrs. Wheeler's shrill scream cuts through the night.

"Veronica!"

"Mama!" Veronica matches her hysteria.

Krystal runs in front of Mrs. Wheeler, leading the way through the barn and to us at the other end. The front of her shirt is drenched in sweat like she just finished a meet. Sweat glistens on her forehead. Mrs. Wheeler thunders behind her in her long nightgown. They're both out of breath when they reach us. Mrs. Wheeler shoves Veronica and me away, kneeling beside Alice's body.

"Krystal, you run to the front of the driveway and wait for the paramedics," she orders in her thundering voice, and before the command is out of her mouth, Krystal is gone. "Veronica and Nichole, go open the gate so they can get their gear in."

Veronica and I jump up, scurrying away to do as we're told.

EIGHTEEN

KRYSTAL

The rooms in my home have never felt smaller as I pace the living room, but I can't sit still. It's been over an hour, and Eric still hasn't called me back since I left him a furious message about the incident Aiden caused on the unit tonight with Nichole. It takes every ounce of self-control I have not to go straight to the hospital and tear into Aiden.

I didn't get a chance to process anything that happened in my meeting with Eric before getting the call from Dr. McGowan that Aiden had gotten into Nichole's room and created a huge scene. How did he even get into her room? He's not on her visitor's list, and even if he was, patients have to be on level five before they get those types of room privileges. According to the nurses, he got onto the unit without raising anyone's suspicions because he was dressed in a gown and looked like a patient—except anyone who has spent time on the unit knows that most of the patients are in regular clothes. You're only in a hospital gown when you're first admitted or on level one like Nichole, with around-the-clock monitoring. You have to earn your clothes like everything else, so if Aiden was in his gown, then that would mean he was a new patient or a severely disturbed patient, and eyeballs should've been on him at all times. Not to mention the fact that he had bandages wrapped around his head, which should've been an immediate red flag. It really bothers me that it was so easy for him to get on the unit undetected.

Aiden claims he found her sleeping in her room. Her attendant had stepped away to use the restroom since Nichole was sleeping, and Aiden appeared within that window. Nobody knows what happened in the room, but according to Aiden, she became startled when he woke her and went into a panicked rage. But she didn't attack him. She went after herself, bashing her head against the wall. He ran to the nurses' station for help. When they got back to her room, they found her lying on the floor of her room, unconscious. Aiden said she must've knocked herself out.

But what if she didn't? What if he went up there to intentionally hurt her? Threaten her? Keep her quiet? Or something worse.

That's what everyone has to be thinking. If they weren't pointing their fingers at him before, they should be now. The questions swirl around each other, fighting for space in my head. I've grown to like Aiden over the years, even love him like a brother, but I wasn't always on Team Aiden.

Nichole met Aiden the summer after we graduated from college when Nichole was doing a six-week teacher training in Austin for developing a multicultural curriculum in low-income schools. I went straight to work after we graduated at a small law firm in Houston, so I stayed behind. It was the longest we'd ever been apart, and we made the joke that she'd probably find her husband while she was gone since I wouldn't be there to scare him away. She was convinced I just wanted her to be alone so I could have her all to myself, but that's never what it was about. None of the men Nichole chose were ever good enough for her. She always set her standards so low when it came to men and had been doing it since we were kids. It wasn't like I didn't want her to be with somebody else—I just wanted to make sure she made a good choice.

Aiden was in Austin for business at the same time, and she met him within days of arriving, at the coffee shop down the street from the house where she stayed during the training. We squeezed in phone calls whenever we could, and I listened to her prattle off stories about her new boyfriend without giving them much attention. Nichole doesn't know how to date. She never has. She's a serial monogamist, so when she said Aiden was the one, I never for one second believed that he might be because she said the same thing about everyone she was in a relationship with. They were all "the one" until they weren't.

She couldn't wait for me to meet him and arranged a get-together for us as soon as she got back to Houston. It's not like Aiden did anything wrong during our introductory dinner. Quite the opposite. He did everything right. He couldn't have been more of a perfect gentleman. They arrived before I did, and he rose from the table to greet me after Nichole pointed out who I was. He was just as handsome as she'd described, with his perfect smile, thick wavy hair, and muscular body from spending hours in the gym. He pulled my chair out for me and immediately called the server over to get me a drink. He listened attentively and asked questions that showed he cared, but there was something about him that didn't sit quite right with me, even though I couldn't put my finger on what.

Nichole thought it was because he was rich.

"But he's not rich—his family's rich," she said after she finally got me to admit that I wasn't his biggest fan, as if she didn't already know that's how I felt about him from our first meeting. "He broke away from the family business and went into business on his own. His family is huge, and they're super powerful where he's from. All he heard his entire life was how he was going to follow in his father's footsteps with the family business. That's all they ever told him he could be. Do you know what a risk that was, to step away from all of that? How brave he was to do something like that?"

It was one of the things she loved the most about him, and she shone with pride whenever she spoke about how he'd rejected the life of privilege he was raised in and set off on his own to make it in the world with barely anything in his bank account. It's a great story, except setting off on your own usually means starting from scratch and having to do lots of hustling to gain any kind of traction in the world. It doesn't mean having your first architectural company fully funded and bonded by an old family trust fund that you cashed out. But I let Nichole tell it that way because it was much more romantic, and all she'd ever wanted was to be swept off her feet by her Prince Charming.

So, I let her have her story, and it wasn't long before he swept me off my feet too. He courted me as much as he courted her, taking me along with them on so many of their dates. He figured out early on that it was more important to impress me than it was her. It wasn't so much the things he did for her but the way he did them. He treated her with such kindness and delicacy without her knowing that he was. There was respect in his tone whenever he spoke to her or about her. Whenever they were in a room together, his eyes adoringly followed her wherever she went. He anticipated her needs and did things without asking. I could see why she was smitten.

When he was ready to get engaged, he took me out for lunch and asked permission to marry her, like I was her father and he was asking for her hand in marriage. We went to a small café outside Houston where I liked to have tea and unwind after a long day. He barely touched his turkey sandwich and finally pushed it aside before turning all his attention on me.

"Look, Krystal, I love your sister. More than anyone or anything else in the world. You have to know that by now." His eyes searched mine imploringly. "I hope after all these years you can see that I've never wavered in my love or my devotion to her. That's not changing." He paused to gather himself. I'd never seen him cry, but tears welled in his eyes, and watching him struggle not to cry made it impossible for me not to get choked up too. "I want to marry Nichole and give her the best life. I want to make up for every awful and horrible thing that's ever happened to her. I don't want her to be sad for another day in her life if I have anything to say or do about it. So, that's why I'm here." He took a deep breath and brought his hands to rest on the table. "I want our marriage to be perfect from the beginning, and it won't be perfect unless she knows you support us. When I ask her to marry me, I want to be able to tell her that I have your blessing."

I gave it to him without a second thought, and I've never looked back. How could I have been so foolish?

My thoughts are interrupted by Eric's call, jolting me back to the present moment.

"What's going on, Krystal?" He doesn't waste any time.

"Aiden got onto the unit tonight, and somehow Nichole ended up unconscious on the floor." Fury lines every word, and I can't get them out fast enough. "He claims that she did it to herself, but I'm not so sure. Their rooms don't have cameras, and the attendant that was supposed to be watching her had stepped away to use the restroom, so there's no way to know what really happened."

"Are you serious? How did they even let something like that happen? I thought she was supposed to be under twenty-four-hour surveillance."

"She was—I mean, she is. I'm so mad I don't even know what to do."

"Well, I can tell you what we're going to do. The first thing we're going to do is file an emergency order of protection to keep him away from her."

"I thought about that, too, but don't we have to have solid proof that he's hurting her? Will this be enough?"

"Probably not, but it might be enough when we include the other incident that I found out about tonight. I was going to call you whether you called me or not. There might be some truth to your suspicions about Aiden hurting Nichole in the weeks leading up to the fire."

"What do you mean?"

"I ran a check through our system tonight, and the police were called to their house a few weeks before the fire."

"Are you serious?" I fume, trying to keep calm so I can think straight.

"It was twelve days before the fire, and the report is definitely there. A neighbor called 911 after he heard them screaming and yelling. According to the statement Aiden gave police, Nichole and him had an argument over dinner about something trivial that worked itself up into a huge deal. He told them that she'd gotten upset and locked herself in their bedroom during their fight and refused to come out. Nichole was still in their bedroom when they arrived and refused to come downstairs. They couldn't leave until they saw her and were able to prove that she was okay. I'm sure you know that domestic violence calls require one of the parties to be taken away, but both Nichole and Aiden swore to the officers that there wasn't domestic violence. The police report said Nichole appeared 'agitated and jumpy.' They suspected she was on drugs, which is why they'd left it alone, since nobody messes in Fischer family affairs."

"I can't believe this." I rub my temples. There's no way Aiden just forgot to mention the police were at their house. What else is he covering up? "I'm going up to the hospital first thing in the morning and asking him about all this."

"You might not want to do that if he's dangerous," Eric cautions.

I snort. "I'm not afraid of him. If he comes after me or tries anything, I'll just smash him in his burned face."

———

"How could you?" I scream. All the way down the hallway, I told myself I wasn't going to unload on Aiden, but seeing him in front of me makes me explode.

His eyes flare with anger. "How was I supposed to know she'd bash her head so hard on the wall that she'd knock herself out?"

"Don't lie to me!" I hiss through gritted teeth. "You've been hurting her all along."

He raises his arms in a peaceful gesture. "What are you talking about?"

"You know exactly what I'm talking about. How could you? After everything she's been through, Aiden, how could you?"

"I don't know what you're talking about, Krystal. I don't." He shakes his head back and forth, eyes wild. "I was afraid they wouldn't let me see her if I asked, and I had to see her. I wasn't taking a chance with anyone telling me no." He turns to the side and swings his legs over so he's sitting on the side of the bed. "All that drama, and I didn't get to even talk to her."

I put my hands on my hips and glare at him. "You're not going anywhere near her for a long time." And I mean it. Eric is filing the emergency order of protection as we speak.

"I didn't do anything. She freaked out on me. You've seen her do it," he shrieks in protest. "You know what she gets like."

"When were you going to tell me about the police coming to the house? You conveniently left that part out of the story when we talked yesterday."

There's no missing his shocked expression even with the bandages still covering his eyebrows.

"I meant to tell you about it. I really did. It's not like I left it out on purpose or was keeping it a secret. There's just so much going on. I didn't even think about it when we were talking about everything before." His eyes plead with mine for understanding.

"So, what happened?" I don't believe him, not even for a second, but I want to hear what he'll say.

"One of our neighbors heard her screaming, and they called 911. Believe me, I was going to call 911 myself if she didn't calm down. All I was thinking about when I was in front of her door was that if I couldn't get her to relax and come out of the room, then I was going to have to call the police. I was afraid about what she'd do to herself that night."

"Why didn't you break the door down?" That's what I would've done.

"She was terrified, Krystal. Absolutely scared out of her mind, and you don't understand the level of fear that takes over her. You think she loses it now? You should see what she's like when there's nobody to restrain her or any drugs to calm her down. I didn't want to push her over the edge. What if I kicked through the door and she jumped out the window or did something even crazier? At least when she was ranting, I knew she was okay and wasn't hurting herself."

"What set her off?"

He raises his shoulders and shakes his head like he's still bewildered by it. "I have no idea. I was in the kitchen getting a beer, and she let out this bloodcurdling scream. I dropped my beer on the floor. That's how much it shook me. I raced upstairs and pounded on the door, begging her to let me in, but of course she wouldn't. I kept banging and asking if she was okay, but all she wanted was for me to leave, to get away from the door. That's all she kept yelling every time I tried to say anything to her." His voice softens as he gets further along in the story. "The only way I got her to tell me she was okay and wasn't going to do anything to hurt herself was to promise that I would leave her alone. So, I pretended like I went down the stairs, but I sat on the landing the entire time and listened for the slightest sound signaling anything was wrong. I didn't know the police had been called until they banged on the front door. By then, she had finished carrying on."

"What did they do when they got there?"

"They said they needed to do a welfare check on her and to see whether or not she was okay. I gladly let them go upstairs and see if she was okay. Christ, I wanted them to check on her. One of the officers took me outside and stayed with me the entire time while his partners spoke with Nichole. I still don't think he believed my story that there wasn't some kind of domestic violence going on, so they needed to see for themselves."

"And it's the law," I interjected.

"That too." Aiden grins despite the seriousness of the situation. "They said they probably get a call at least every two weeks regarding a wife who has locked herself in a bedroom or bathroom during a fight with her husband and won't come out. One of the officers was even joking about it. He said wives freaking out and locking themselves up kept him employed."

"I'm glad you're amused, but I'm not amused by any of this." I want to slap the smile off his face. "Why didn't you let them know you needed help with her? Why didn't you tell them something was wrong?"

Anger flares in his eyes. "Haven't you been listening to anything that I've said? I was in denial, Krystal." He draws out the syllables in his words for dramatic effect. "I kept hoping that she'd snap out of it and it'd go away. Then we could go back to our regular lives and just pretend it never happened. That's all I wanted to do."

It's the only part of his story that might be true, because I know what it's like to bury terrible things. I'm good at shoving things down, too, and going on with life. After all, I've been doing it for over twenty years.

NINETEEN

NICHOLE

(THEN)

The air is electric, thick with the smell of blood. Krystal and I cling to each other while the paramedics go to work on Alice's body. I can't rip my gaze away. I know she's dead before they touch her. Know what the paramedic will say before he pronounces to his partner, "There's no heartbeat."

He starts pounding her chest like Mrs. Wheeler was still doing when they found us huddled outside the barn. The other one whips open the huge black bag he's carrying and starts pulling things out. Within seconds, he's sticking a tube down Alice's throat and puffing the bag that's attached to it while his partner pounds on her chest. They lift her body like she weighs nothing and place her on the red board.

Two more EMTs rush through the yard and hurry over to us. All the medical workers swarm her body, pushing us away like pesky barn flies. We stand on the outside of their circle, dazed.

"Girls, come," Mrs. Wheeler orders, but we can't tear ourselves away. She grabs Krystal's arm and yanks her back. "Hurry!" She looks over her shoulder, and I follow her gaze to two sheriffs coming through the yard.

Krystal, Veronica, and I follow Mrs. Wheeler like we're in a trance as she ushers us into the barn and into the milk room. She shuts the steel door behind us. The round cylinder machines hum as they process and sort the milk. Mrs. Wheeler wrangles the three of us up against the wall like an army sergeant. She points to the door. "Look, we don't have much time. The police are out there, and they're going to come looking for us any second and asking questions. We need to get a few things straight first. You—"

"Veronica pushed her out of the barn!" I blurt out.

"I barely touched her, Mama, I swear. I didn't mean for her to get hurt," Veronica cries. Her eyes are red rimmed from crying so hard. The front of her shirt is stained crimson with Alice's blood.

Mrs. Wheeler smacks her across the face, shocking us all. "Don't you ever say that again, do you understand me?"

Veronica raises her hand to her cheek, stunned. Tears well in her eyes. My insides shake. I grab Krystal's hand. Her palms are wet. Our hands stick together. Veronica is too shocked to say anything. Nobody on the wall moves.

Mrs. Wheeler is inches from Veronica's face and speaks through gritted teeth. "Alice fell during a game that you girls were playing and had a terrible accident."

"But, Mama, I—"

Mrs. Wheeler raises her hand like she's going to smack her again, and Veronica snaps her mouth closed. My heartbeat explodes in my chest. The hum of the machines swirls inside me. Krystal looks like she's going to throw up.

"Farm accidents happen all the time. Nobody will think anything differently as long as everyone sticks to the story." She shifts her gaze to me and Krystal. My knees buckle, and I lean against the wall for support. Mrs. Wheeler's eyes bulge out of her head in a way I've never seen, but she's not mad. She's something else. Scarier. "*Everyone* sticks to the story. You girls came up here to play, and Alice tripped while she was running. That's how she fell. That's what happened. Are we clear?"

Krystal starts shaking her head. "She tripped and fell all the way outside? Who does that? They're not going to believe that. Wouldn't she have stopped herself? We can't say that. They'll know we're lying."

Veronica jumps in with her agreement. "She's right. I'm telling you, that's not how it happened." Veronica's voice begs her to listen. "They were playing that stupid game. I told them I didn't want to play. They made me." Veronica points a shaking finger at us. "If only we—"

Mrs. Wheeler swoops in on her, gripping her jaw with one hand and squeezing in the same way Veronica grabbed Alice's throat before she threw her out of the barn. Veronica lets out a whimper. "Honey, I'm going to tell you what happened one more time, and then we're going to go out there and talk to the officers who are waiting for you girls. Are we clear?"

Krystal shakes her head. "It's not going to work. They'll know we're lying. We have to—"

Mrs. Wheeler drops Veronica and steps directly in front of Krystal, stopping her midsentence. "They'll know what we tell them. And that's all we tell them. Do you understand me?" Krystal gulps, nodding her consent. "Alice was a chubby, clumsy girl who'd never been on a farm before in her life. It makes perfect sense that she would be jumping around in the hayloft like an idiot. No one will dispute that. The four of you were having lots of fun during your sleepover and playing games in the barn when—"

"What games? Do we tell them truth or dare? Or something else?" I interrupt. I have to know the details of our lie if I'm going to be believable.

Mrs. Wheeler's forehead lines with annoyance, but before she can speak, there's a knock at the door.

"Ma'am? Are you in there with the girls? This is the Lafayette County Police."

———

Mrs. Wheeler, Krystal, and I are on our knees, furiously scrubbing Alice's blood from the ground. We work without speaking. Veronica's inside taking a shower. She wanted to stay and help clean, but Mrs. Wheeler made her go. Bleach burns my nose. The sound of the bristles against the concrete is punctuated by sniffles and hiccupping sobs from me and Krystal. But we have a job to do. We've got to get the blood off the floor. The harder we scrub, the bigger the circle grows, but we don't stop.

Alice is dead.

And Veronica killed her.

The same two thoughts run through my head, stuck on repeat. The medical examiner and coroner worked on Alice for almost an hour before they packaged her up and put her in the back of the ambulance. The four of us stood underneath the moonlight in our gravel driveway as the EMTs shut the double doors and latched them tightly. They moved slow. All their frantic movements from before were gone. Nobody got in the back of the ambulance with her. Because she wasn't there anymore. Only her body. And they weren't taking her to the hospital. She was going to the morgue.

Mrs. Wheeler hasn't said anything since Veronica went inside. Is it creepy in the house by herself? What if Alice haunts the farm? That's what I'd do if someone killed me over a stupid game.

Mrs. Wheeler hasn't shed a tear. Not this whole time. She didn't react at all when the coroner officially pronounced her dead. Even one of the EMTs had tears in his eyes. She's a kid. Kids aren't supposed to die. All of it felt like a dream until they brought out the white sheet and covered her body.

"Tonight isn't the last time you'll have to talk to the police about what happened," Mrs. Wheeler says without looking up or making eye contact with us. "They'll be back in the morning after they've spoken with Alice's parents, and they'll have more questions for you girls."

The officer asked Mrs. Wheeler if she wanted to call Alice's parents and give them the news about the accident—since that's what we're calling it even though Veronica shoved her on purpose—but Mrs. Wheeler opted out. She made them do it, which seems like being a bit of a chicken, but I wouldn't want to tell her parents either. She's their only kid. Their entire world. It makes me start crying again just thinking about what they're going through.

"We need to get clear about a few things just in case one of you decides to change your mind and tell the officers a cockeyed story about Veronica being responsible for tonight. You need to know what would happen next. First, I'll tell them that the two of you shoved Alice out of the barn, and I saw you do it. I'll explain that I lied about it because you threatened to hurt Veronica too. Take a moment to think about who they'd believe. A well-respected member of the community or two white trash girls whose parents don't even want them?" She pauses, making sure her threat has a chance to sink in. "Also, if I even get the slightest hint that anything like that might be happening, I'll call your social workers so fast that it'll make your head spin. I'll let them know that it's not working out for you here anymore and that I think it's best if they placed you in separate homes."

Her threats are a death sentence. We can't ever tell, because there's no way we can live without each other.

TWENTY

NICHOLE

(THEN)

I choke on the smell of burning flesh. Flames engulf dismembered hands, arms, legs. Black smoke covers blank faces. My eyes blister.

I can't see her, but she's coming for me.

I'm next.

My eyes snap open.

"Krystal!" I scream from my guts.

There's water between my legs. My shirt clings to me. I can't move. I'm frozen to the bed. There's another scream stuck in my throat, but it won't come out. And then Krystal's voice whispers softly in my ear while she strokes my hair. "I'm here. You're okay. It's just a dream. You're waking up."

But it's not a dream. It's a nightmare, and it's real. There's no escape. No relief.

Alice is dead, and I'm trapped in a house full of murdering liars. And I'm one of them. I might as well have shoved her out of the hayloft myself. We never should've snuck out, and we never should've let them come with us. What were we thinking? How could we have been so stupid? Krystal says we can't ask questions like that or the guilt will eat away at us until it destroys us. She says we have to keep moving, just putting one foot in front of the other, that eventually time will pass and it won't be so hard. Easy for her to say when she wasn't the one holding Alice when she took her last breath. She didn't have to watch the light leave her eyes or see her spirit leave her body and travel into the rafters. She didn't witness Mrs. Wheeler fling Alice off her when the paramedics arrived because she knew she was holding a carcass.

Every time I close my eyes and try to sleep, my brain takes me to hell. Literal hell, even though I've never stepped foot in a church because I don't believe in God. At least I didn't. That's why I know it's real. There is a lake of fire in my dreams and all these different people burning there. But that's not the worst part—it's the weeping and the wailing coming from their mouths as they scream for help, and I can do nothing to save them.

Sometimes I wake up there. But other times I don't. That's when Alice crawls out of the fiery water and comes after me. Her face is always burning, and her mouth gapes open like there's a silent scream stuck inside. She chases me around the lake while I scream.

No matter how I wake up, I'm always screaming at the top of my lungs.

It's been that way since the night it happened. Four days and no changes. Krystal sleeps with me, but it doesn't help. She can't keep the evil away. I wish that it did, but nothing's strong enough for the evil that's taken over this house.

The funeral is this morning, and Mrs. Wheeler is forcing us to go. She bought us all dresses. Brand new from Sears, because you can't find four black funeral dresses at Goodwill on such short notice. At least, that's what she said, but she knows all eyes will be on us, and she wants us to look our best. She might be able to lie without a tell, but I've studied how she works for years.

The police keep trying to talk to us, but I can't talk about it. So far there're two officers. A nice one and a mean one. I like the nice one. He's chubby and balding and shows me pictures of his twin baby boys. But he's supposed to make me like him. He's the good cop. His partner drills me with questions. Never cracking a smile. Obviously the bad one.

"How close were you and Alice?"

"What did the three of you talk about on the way home from school?"

"Was this your first sleepover?"

I can answer their questions right up until they get to the sneaking-out part. That's when I break. I start crying and can't stop. The harder I try to stop, the harder I cry. Then I can't even say her name.

Veronica barely speaks. She's locked herself in her room and hardly comes out. I've only seen her twice in four days. Mrs. Wheeler pretends not to notice, just like she pretends none of this is happening. She just carries her food to her on trays like she has the flu and leaves it outside her door.

Krystal is keeping things running. I don't know what I'd do without her. She's my rock. She's covering all my chores without complaining, because I can't function. All the light's been turned off in my world. I'm falling into a bottomless pit, swirling into soundless oblivion.

TWENTY-ONE

KRYSTAL

I race through the hospital corridors, continually scanning for Aiden. He never said anything about visiting Nichole again when I confronted him this morning, and I don't know how we're going to stop him from seeing her before the emergency order for protection goes through. Thankfully, Janice gave me a heads-up.

> Aiden determined to see Nichole today. Can't stop him. He's headed your way. Don't think it's a good idea . . .

> Totally understand. Will try to catch him before he gets here.

I spot Aiden just as he's coming through the emergency room reception area. He's impossible to miss in his hospital gown with his head covered in thick bandages, but nobody stops him as he moves through the sliding glass doors and into the valet parking garage. He walks like a man on a mission, and I hurry to catch him. I grab his unbandaged arm tenderly so I don't hurt him. He quickly jerks it away and keeps walking.

"I don't think this is a good idea, Aiden. She was really upset last night, and I think you should give her some time," I say, adding silently, *Enough time for the emergency order to get signed.*

"I don't care what you or anyone else thinks. She's my wife, and I have a right to see her," he says without turning around.

I grab his bicep and pull him backward. "Slow down. She's not going anywhere, and you're going to cross over into the cardio zone pretty quickly, which probably isn't the best idea, seeing as you just got off a ventilator." He's already breathing hard.

His slows his steps, and I jump at the opportunity to make him take it down another notch while my brain scrambles to come up with a plan to stop him. "She's probably not through with dinner yet, and they won't let you in the community room to see anyone until after dinner is cleared. Visitors aren't allowed in there during mealtimes."

He finally turns to look at me. "Really?"

"Really," I say forcing myself to maintain eye contact. Dinner was cleared over thirty minutes ago. "Look, Aiden. I get how badly you want to see her, but are you sure it's the best idea?"

He pulls himself away from me again. "Stop it, Krystal. You'd never let me talk you out of seeing her if she was in bad shape, so don't even try talking me out of it," he says like the matter is settled.

If I can't stop him from seeing her, then at least I can be with him to minimize the damage and make sure he's not alone with her. Maybe that's all I can do for now. I drop my arms to my sides and fall in step beside him. Our feet smack against the sidewalk together in staccato beats. His breath comes in short wheezing gasps. I cross my fingers, hoping he'll pass out before we get there, but it isn't long before Riverside East looms in front of us, and he quickens his pace. He enters the building and heads straight to the elevators, wasting no time checking into the main reception area. The elevator is on call, and we squeeze in just as the doors are about to close. A woman's phone buzzes with a call that she refuses to decline, and someone is sweating out booze from the night before. We're the first to get off.

Aiden makes a beeline for the nurses' desk. Two of the nurses are engaged in a conversation. They're animated and it looks serious, but he doesn't wait for a natural break in their conversation before interrupting them. "Excuse me."

Their conversation continues. Neither looks at him.

"Excuse me," he says even louder. I tug on his arm, but it does no good. "Can I see the visitor log? I'd like to sign in." He doesn't pretend not to be irritated.

"Who are you here to see?" The one with the pencil bun in her hair finally turns to look at him, annoyance written on all her features. She's not the least bit surprised by his appearance, which strikes me as odd, but then again, maybe they've seen everything on the unit, so nothing surprises them anymore.

"Nichole Fischer."

"Are you on her visitor list?"

"I'm her husband."

"Okay. Well, let me check to see if you're on her visitor list." She busies herself typing into the computer. Aiden taps impatiently on the desk with his unbandaged hand. Her forehead crinkles. "What did you say your name was?"

"Aiden Fischer. My wife is Nichole Fischer."

"I'm sorry, Aiden, but it doesn't look like you're on her list of visitors."

"How can that be?"

"I'm not sure." She shrugs, clearly not interested in giving him any favors after the way he approached her. "You'll have to speak with her doctor about that. Do you know which doctor has been assigned to her case?"

"Of course I know who her doctor is. What part of 'I'm her husband' don't you understand?" he snaps in a condescending and arrogant tone that I've never heard him use but immediately recognize as the one Nichole swears he uses in all their fights.

"Maybe we should just come back later," I say, trying to sound sympathetic, but I'm secretly glad they're turning him away.

He ignores me. "Call Dr. McGowan. I want to speak with him immediately."

"Dr. McGowan is in a meeting right now. I can take your number and have him call you."

Aiden's irritation radiates off him. "Look, I'm her husband and—"

"GET AWAY FROM HER!" Nichole's scream comes out of nowhere.

Our heads swivel to where Nichole is squared up in the middle of the hallway behind the nurses' station. She must've spotted us on her way to get her medication, or maybe she heard Aiden's loud voice from her seat in the community room. Before anyone has a chance to react, she races to the nurses' station and rounds the desk. I try to grab her as she hurls herself at Aiden, but I can't.

"What did you do with my husband?" Nichole screams as she starts beating her fists on Aiden's chest. "Give him back to me! Give him back to me!"

He tries to grab her wrists and stop her assault, but his wounded hands are useless against her. He grimaces in pain as she attacks him, smacking every part of his body she can connect with while he lets out wounded cries. I grab her and try to pull them apart, but she has superhuman strength now and flings me off her like it's nothing. The security team appears like magic, and Nichole senses their presence immediately. She shoves Aiden back and stands in front of him. Her fists are clenched at her sides, her face beet red.

"If you come near my sister again, I'll kill you, you sonofabitch, do you hear me?" Her eyes grow to hostile slits. "And this time, I'll make sure you die."

———

Dr. McGowan, Mr. Barnes, and I are gathered in the room where we met when they gave me the news about Nichole, except this time Detective Sparks isn't standing in the corner and Aiden is pacing the room instead. Detective Sparks's meeting with them happens later so that our meeting stays private. Eric advised against Detective Sparks being here because he's adamant about keeping a distinct line between Nichole's medical issues and her legal ones.

Dr. McGowan sits next to Mr. Barnes on the other side of the table like they did before, so I sit in the same spot too. I place my iPhone on the table faceup. Eric's face fills the screen. He has to be in court in an hour, so there was no way he'd make it back to the city in time if he were here in person. Nobody acted surprised when I told them I'd retained legal counsel on Nichole's behalf, not even Aiden.

"We've gone through an extensive amount of diagnostic testing and ruled out many differential diagnoses in regard to Nichole's health. As you know, it's taken us a while to arrive at a diagnosis we're comfortable with, but we finally have it, and that's what we'd like to talk about today." Dr. McGowan opens the meeting with a declaration of purpose.

I'm taken aback, and it takes me a few seconds to recover because I assumed we were meeting to discuss the incidents that happened between Aiden and Nichole in the last twenty-four hours. But this is the day I've been waiting for since Nichole was admitted. Her files are piled high on the table. Her diagnostic testing reports are splayed out next to them. Both doctors have their laptops open.

"Nichole is suffering from Capgras syndrome." He says it like it's two words—*cap grass*. "It's a delusional misidentification syndrome where the patient believes a loved one or familiar person has been taken over by an imposter. Most of the time when we see this disorder, it's in patients who are suffering from Parkinson's or Lewy body dementia. Dr. Bernstein has completed her full neurological exam, and both those illnesses have been ruled out. It's very uncommon to see the disorder manifesting by itself in the way we're seeing it with Nichole. We believe her disorder is rooted in psychodynamic conflicts because there aren't any neurological diseases to explain her psychosis."

"But you said she doesn't have Parkinson's or dementia, so I'm confused." Aiden stops his pacing to focus all his attention on Dr. McGowan. He hasn't sat down since we walked in the room. He's sweating profusely. His hospital gown clings to his chest.

"She doesn't have the neurological disorders typically associated with Capgras syndrome. She's in one of the rare patient groups where the cause is psychological rather than organic."

"How do you treat it?" I ask. That's really what I want to know. *Please tell me you can fix her,* I beg silently.

"Usually, a person with Capgras syndrome develops it as a defense mechanism to protect themselves or someone they love against information that might hurt them or their relationship in some way. You have to get to the root of what they're defending against in order to resolve it."

"That doesn't make any sense." Aiden looks annoyed by the psychological underpinnings of his explanation, like he is with anything in the therapy realm. It usually annoys me, but not this time since it sounds like mumbo jumbo to me too.

"Perhaps an example will help," Dr. McGowan says, sounding every part the college professor, but I don't mind. "One of the famous cases comes from a mother who lost three of her four children in a car accident. Afterward, she was convinced that her dead children had been abducted, and she organized search parties for them. She filed numerous missing person reports about it with the police department. In addition, she also believed that her surviving child had been replaced by someone else—a child who looked and acted like her daughter but who was really an imposter. She came under the care of the courts for refusing to provide proper care for her daughter. She created the delusion that her children were kidnapped because it provided the possibility of them still being alive and in the world somewhere rather than facing the debilitating loss of their deaths. Once she acknowledged her denial and worked through the grief, the delusion about her surviving child disappeared too."

"That's what we need to do? Figure out what freaked her out?" Aiden's speech is pressurized. "How are we supposed to do that?"

Dr. McGowan's calm despite Aiden's agitated state is impressive, but then I remember he's had years of practice. "I wish that it were that simple, but it's not. Separating the truth from the psychosis is the most difficult part. Sometimes it proves to be impossible."

"Then, she's just stuck?" Aiden asks.

"No, there're many things that we can do now that we have a diagnosis. It's going to allow us to properly define a course of treatment, and the first thing we're doing is taking her off all antipsychotic medication. I—"

"What?" I cut him off. He's spent endless hours harping on me about her medication and addressing all my concerns about it. He assured me the other day that they'd finally gotten it right.

Red creeps up his neck because he's embarrassed to eat his words, but he maintains his gaze on me. "It seems contradictory given the conversations we've had about how important the medication is for her recovery and stabilization, but that was before we put all the pieces together. Normally, these medications work very well with psychosis, and they're the gold standard treatment, but they're not nearly as effective in patients with Capgras syndrome. In fact, they can oftentimes exacerbate the symptoms and make things worse."

"So, we've been making her crazier than she already is?" I blurt without thinking.

Dr. McGowan goes to speak, but Mr. Barnes puts his hand on his arm to stop him. Eric might not be in the room, but his presence on the phone is enough for Mr. Barnes to worry about Dr. McGowan or anyone else inadvertently admitting guilt or responsibility for anything having to do with Nichole's condition.

"Patients' medication is changed according to their diagnostic needs. Nichole's diagnosis no longer warrants the continued use of anti-psychotics." Mr. Barnes states the hospital's position clearly, but lawsuits against the hospital are the least of my concerns.

"How long does it last?" Aiden asks. I wish he'd sit. His agitation only increases mine.

Mr. Barnes shifts his gaze to Dr. McGowan and gives him a brief nod, like he's granting him permission to speak.

"It can last anywhere from a couple days to years," Dr. McGowan answers.

"Years?" I ask, stunned.

"How's she ever going to change when I look like this?" Aiden points to his face and makes a circular motion. "They're taking all of this off tomorrow, and I'm going to look like a monster. She already thinks I'm one, and now I'm going to look like one too." His hysteria rises. "She's going to think I really am gone. It's not just going to be in her head."

Dr. McGowan nods in agreement. "That will make things difficult."

Aiden wrestles back tears, and despite everything that's happened, part of me can't help but feel sorry for him. What if he's telling the truth about what happened? If Nichole really believed he was an imposter, she would've done anything to save herself from him, especially if she thought he'd taken her husband away. It sounds far fetched, but if what they're saying is true, it's entirely possible.

Mr. Barnes shifts in his seat, clearly uncomfortable with the intensity of emotions. He clears his throat. "Well, the silver lining in all of this is that she's unlikely to do jail time. Her diagnosis will certainly impact the charges filed against her, given her mental illness. Most likely they'll transfer her to a correctional psychiatric facility soon until they've deemed her fit to return to society."

"Oh, I'm not pressing charges," Aiden interjects before he can go any further.

"Whether or not you want to file charges is irrelevant. The state lodged attempted murder and arson charges against her this afternoon," Mr. Barnes says.

The floor vanishes underneath me. My stomach drops.

Eric's voice leaps to attention on my phone and comes through crystal clear. "Formal charges have been filed?"

"Yes, the family was very insistent that charges be brought against Nichole." Mr. Barnes rubs his chin and refuses to look at the phone.

I'm too stunned to speak. Part of me has been holding on to hope that charges wouldn't be filed against her. That once she got better, we could go on with our lives, and eventually it would all seem like a bad dream. But Mr. Barnes's words have just stripped that hope away.

Aiden slaps his hands on the table, startling us all. "My family? Are you saying my family was the one pushing for charges?"

"Your father has been placing multiple calls to the district attorney's office every day since the fire," Mr. Barnes says, looking almost as displeased about it as Aiden.

"Dammit!" Aiden yells as he shoves a chair and sends it flying into the table. I grab his arm to tug him down onto the seat, but he steps away. He clenches his fists like he's looking for something to hit. "I told them not to. My mom has always hated Nichole, but I made her swear to stay out of this. How could she do that?"

Because she was determined to make someone pay for hurting her son. Doesn't he get that? People like the Fischers don't do well when you mess with their lives, and I never should've underestimated them.

TWENTY-TWO

NICHOLE

(THEN)

We should've just gone home after the funeral. Why did we have to come here? We trail behind Mrs. Wheeler and Veronica into the Greers' house. Most of the town is crammed in their house, even though they've only lived here for a couple months. Nobody's had a chance to really get to know them yet, but everyone's pretending like they're super close. Our town loves a good tragedy, and it's been a long time since we've had one, so nobody's missing a minute of this.

The screened-in porch entrance leads right into the living room. The bathroom and small galley kitchen are to the right side. Their small house is packed to overflowing. Krystal and I have been glued together all day, and she stiffens next to me when she spots Whitney and her friends crowding around the fireplace in the living room. Whitney never even said hello to Alice the entire time she was at school. None of them did, but their eyes are all red and watery, and they're all holding tissue like they're not sure how they'll go on living without her. We make a sharp turn to avoid them and plunge into the crowds in the dining room.

Groups of people are huddled together, speaking in hushed whispers with their heads down. Nobody's eyes rise to meet us, and I breathe a sigh of relief that we might go unnoticed. I find us a spot on two of the folding chairs set up in the corner.

"How long do you think she'll make us stay?" I whisper, taking in the dining room.

Alice described this room, and it's exactly like she said—gleaming with order and sterility. The sliding glass doors open onto a small wooden deck overlooking the backyard, which is perfectly manicured except for the lonely swing set in the center. She talked about that, too; said her parents were so out of touch with her that they'd gotten her a new swing set when they moved in even though she was way too old for one. The dining room chairs are precisely spaced along the table, and there is not a plant, book, or personal effect in sight. There is no sign of life whatsoever. She said it was like living in a postcard. She wasn't wrong.

Is this what it's going to be like now? Every day filled with the spirit of someone who I knew for less than eight hours? I did the math last night while I lay there in bed not sleeping after my nightmares woke me up. Eight hours. That's how long she lasted on the farm.

I hear her screams as she plummeted out of the barn in the same way Krystal says she hears the pigs. I never understood what she meant all these years. Now I do. It's not just her screams. I see the blood pooled around her head and hear the way it gurgled as it came out of her mouth at the end. Nothing I tell myself or anything I do keeps the images away. They're burned into my brain forever.

Krystal peeked at her in the coffin. She said she didn't want the picture of her lying dead on the concrete to be the last one she had of her, but I couldn't bring myself to look. Krystal told me they had her painted up with so much makeup that she barely looked like herself. Mrs. Wheeler and Veronica paused behind us to pay their last respects or whatever it is you're supposed to do at open-casket funerals, but I rushed Krystal along. We kept our heads down as we walked past Alice's mom and dad in the procession line too. They were too grief stricken to recognize anyone. And I was glad. Not because I wanted them to be so sad, but I can't have a conversation with them about Alice. I just can't.

I'm afraid if I open my mouth, the truth will come gushing out, and once it does, I won't be able to stop. I don't know what Mrs. Wheeler will do if that happens. Would she really send one of us away?

She hasn't said anything to us about it since it happened. Not a word. She whistled while she made breakfast this morning like we weren't going to the funeral of the girl who died on our farm. I always thought Veronica was the one I needed to be scared of, but maybe I've had it wrong all along.

TWENTY-THREE

KRYSTAL

Eric stands to greet me when I walk into the Belmont police station reception area. He's in perfectly pressed pants with a collared shirt and matching tie like he just stepped out of a *GQ* magazine. Flashbacks to my Goodwill clothes pass through me, and I'm instantly self-conscious but quickly remind myself that I'm wearing a Milano blouse. "Can I get you anything?"

"No thanks, I'm good," I say, tucking my shirt into the back of my pants and straightening the front of it. "How was traffic?"

"It was decent. Not too bad," he says, reclaiming his seat. "I let the receptionist know we're here." The receptionist is protected behind a Plexiglas window, even though Belmont has the lowest crime rate in Goodhue County. Her head is bent as she scrolls through her phone.

He starts going on about the weather, but all I can do is think about how different Nichole was this morning. The shift in her was noticeable and dramatic from the moment I walked into the community room. Her body wasn't hanging on her like a deflated balloon. She'd been filled with air again, and it showed in the way she held her head up. Not like she was completely upright or anything, but her shoulders weren't hunched over like she was carrying a backpack filled with rocks anymore. Our visit was short, because in addition to being off her medication, she's also going to start all the programming and therapy on the unit. It's going to be the best thing for her to have some structure and routine. Most importantly, it will keep her safe from Aiden, since the judge denied the order of protection last night on the grounds that there wasn't enough evidence that he posed an imminent threat. Maybe he's right. I'm so conflicted about Aiden.

Yesterday's meeting changed everything. Between her new diagnosis and the charges filed against her, I'm at a total loss. I have no idea what to do now or which direction to go. Do I put my focus on finding out what really happened that night or on keeping her out of jail? I just want to bring her home with me, because sending her to a forensic psychiatric unit sounds even worse than jail.

The door opens beside Eric and me, bringing us to our feet again. Detective Sparks holds the door wide. "Good afternoon," he says, giving us a tired smile like the one I gave Eric when I arrived. "Let's head this way and get started."

The stubble on his chin has grown into a small beard, and there are bags underneath his eyes that weren't there the last time I saw him. He's been in the trenches too. He must have other cases going on besides Nichole's. Gratitude washes over me that I chose family law rather than criminal, because I couldn't do what he does every day. There's no way I could live like this. We follow him in silence to an office a few doors down the hallway. He opens the door, revealing a small interview room with three chairs and a cheap desk.

"Take a seat where you're comfortable," Detective Sparks instructs, as if there're multiple options. He grabs the only wheeled office chair in the room and leaves Eric and me with the beat-up aluminum ones.

There aren't any windows, and claustrophobia engulfs me as we seal ourselves into the tiny space. We're cut off from the rest of the world underneath the harsh fluorescent lighting that only draws attention to the grimy yellow walls in desperate need of a fresh paint job.

There's nothing hanging on the walls to soothe us. A no-smoking sign posted on the back of the door is the only visual distraction. It's probably been there since the eighties. Detective Sparks sits against the wall facing the door, which means I have to sit with my back to the door, and the thought of it makes my stomach churn. I quickly reposition a chair to have a sideways view of the door while Eric takes a seat on the other one.

"I'm glad both of you could join me this morning, and I know your time is precious, so why don't we just get started with things?" Detective Sparks begins as he flips open a file on his desk. "We've been able to review all the footage from the police officer's body camera the night of the fire." He skips right over the fact that attempted murder and felony arson charges have been filed against Nichole. He reads aloud: "Suspect was singing 'Ding Dong, the Witch Is Dead,' from *The Wizard of Oz*." He places his hands on top of the report and looks at me. "Are you familiar with that song?"

I'm not sure how to respond. Thankfully, I don't have to because Eric responds for me.

"I'm fairly certain most people in this country are familiar with those lyrics."

Detective Sparks doesn't shift his eyes from me. "Yes, of course, but I'm wondering, Krystal"—he pauses, giving me a long, pointed stare—"whether or not the song is significant to Nichole in some way. Are you aware of any special meaning the song might have?"

I shake my head. Keep my expression neutral.

Detective Sparks tilts his head while he skims the report, like he's mulling something over. I gulp, wiping my sweaty palms on my pants. He waits way too long before he speaks again, doing his best to make sure we're uncomfortable. I'm crawling out of my skin, but Eric's perfectly relaxed. "I noticed that the judge denied your emergency order of protection." He says it like he's trying to shock us with the information, but it's no surprise that he knows about the request.

Eric doesn't falter. "Yes, and it's unfortunate, because we believe Aiden poses a significant threat to Nichole's safety and well-being."

"Funny, Aiden's family feels the same way about Nichole," Detective Sparks responds.

"With all due respect, there's some pretty strong evidence that she had every reason to be afraid of Aiden. Even though she told police she was fine when they showed up to do a welfare check a few weeks ago, you and I both know that domestic violence victims lie to protect their abusers. It takes them a long time to stop. And please, let's not forget that she ended up unconscious two nights ago after he'd been in her room." I've never been so grateful for Eric, as he speaks with total confidence against Detective Sparks's implications about Nichole. "It's pretty telling that anytime somebody gets hurt, they're the only two people in the room, and only one of them can ever talk about it. I'm interested to hear Nichole's side of the story once she's stabilized on her medication and more coherent."

I wish I could high-five him. Instead I give him a knowing smile, but he's not focused on me, anyway. His eyes are on Detective Sparks.

Detective Sparks shrugs like the information means nothing to him. "Maybe, except Nichole's the only one in the pair that has a pretty big reason to want to hurt the other party."

"Besides being a possible domestic violence victim?" Eric looks miffed.

"Let me put it this way: Nichole's the only one who has a motive we can prove," Detective Sparks says.

"Meaning?" Eric cocks his head to the side. I lean forward in my seat, hanging on his every word despite myself. He's got us exactly where he wants us.

"Jealousy," Detective Sparks replies matter-of-factly.

"What are you talking about?" I ask, unable to hold myself back anymore.

Detective Sparks turns to me. "You didn't know Aiden was a playboy?"

"A playboy?" I hold back the urge to laugh. That's what he's got? "Who even says that anymore?" I don't wait for a response before continuing. "But yes, I know that Aiden used to get around. He had lots of girlfriends, and none of them were happy when he settled down to get married. He told Nichole all about it." Aiden fooled around a lot when he was younger, but Nichole didn't care about his number. That was before her. She didn't care about the women he'd been with any more than he did about the men in her past, even though her number could fit on one hand.

"I'm not talking about when he was younger. I'm talking about now."

His words drop like lead in my gut. "What do you mean *now?*"

"Exactly what *now* implies. Present tense," Detective Sparks says.

"How do you know for sure? What's going on?" People say all sorts of things in small towns, and rumors spread like a pandemic—the juicier the better.

"For starters, his company paid out three different sexual harassment suits filed against him over the last twelve years." There's no mistaking the judgment in his voice.

All the air feels like it's leaving my lungs. Aiden's been married to Nichole for every one of those years. The world tilts like I might fall off.

"Against him specifically or his company?" Eric asks.

"He's the person named in the suit. They paid all three women off, and the settlement details are locked up in nondisclosure agreements, but it happened." As an afterthought to me, he adds, "I'm sorry."

I struggle to make sense of what he's telling me. It's the last thing I want to be true. My feelings tumble over each other. How could Aiden do that to her? She trusted him. They built a life together. He promised to never hurt her.

"There's a lot more than that, though . . ." He gives me a second to prepare for what's coming next, but I'm not sure I can handle more news. "There's a pretty standard 'don't ask, don't tell' policy in place at his office and with his colleagues about his ongoing relationships with other women."

My heart pounds inside my chest. Is this how Nichole felt? There's a swirling abyss underneath my feet threatening to suck me in. I focus on my breathing.

"Are you okay?" Detective Sparks asks.

"I am," I manage to squeak out. "Yes, I'm okay. I just . . . I didn't have any idea."

"Do you think Nichole knew?"

I can't imagine that she knew and didn't tell me, because her pain would be impossible to contain or hide. But I do think she found out, because the only thing I want to do right now is set everything on fire that he's ever touched.

TWENTY-FOUR

NICHOLE

(THEN)

I told Krystal the police were going to separate us, but she tried convincing me they'd interview us together. That's what she wanted to believe, but there was no way that was happening. There's nobody in the room with me besides the detective. It's just me and him—Detective Carl Woods—but he's Jonah's dad to me.

Jonah's one of the best artists at school, and his dad always shows up at the school days in advance to help him set up for the art fair. He looks like a totally average dad then in his jeans and T-shirt, but I've never seen him like this. He's wearing dress pants and a suit jacket like he came from church or somewhere else important. He's over six feet, but he's got that weird stoop people get when they're ashamed of being tall so they're always trying to shrink themselves. He's wearing a black turtleneck underneath his gray suit. Makes no sense to me since it's over eighty degrees outside. I broke a sweat coming in from the truck, but Mrs. Wheeler refused to come inside. She's parked in the shade at the very back of the parking lot with all the windows down.

Krystal and I walked into the police station together, and they separated us right away. I don't know why they bothered. It's not like we haven't been together 24/7 since the accident happened and had plenty of time to get our story straight. I've slipped into calling it an accident. I didn't mean to. Not even a little. But that's what everyone around me calls it. Nobody's going around the house calling it what it was—murder. Except Krystal says it's not that either. She says murder is intentional, and there's no way Veronica intended to kill Alice when she shoved her.

Maybe she didn't mean to kill her, but she definitely intended to hurt her. Just so happens she hurt her enough to kill her. There's accidental murder too. That's what they should charge her with.

But they aren't going to charge her with anything. Not if Mrs. Wheeler has anything to say about it, and she's running this show. She made sure her and Veronica met with Detective Carl before we did. She took the entire day off yesterday and put me and Krystal in charge of the farm so that she could be with Veronica during her interview with him. Who knows what she said about us. That's what makes me so nervous. She thinks we're too naive to see what she's doing, but I know exactly what she's up to. She's setting things up for us to take the fall for this if the police start getting suspicious about anything.

Detective Carl is taking forever to get started. He's been rummaging through his top drawer for over two minutes. I've been watching the clock. He might be doing this on purpose. Isn't there supposed to be a parent with me? And then I remember—like I've been doing since I was seven—I don't have a parent. Not a real one, anyway. Not one that cares about you or shows up for you at important things like this.

That hasn't stopped me from wanting to get ahold of my mom, though. I've been begging Krystal to call her and see if she'll let us come stay with her, because I have to get out of here. Any place is better than this.

"Please, Krystal, can we call my mom? I can't take this." I tried again yesterday while we were gathering the eggs and Veronica and Mrs. Wheeler were at the police station. It would've been the perfect time to sneak onto the phone and call her. We're not allowed to use the phone without Mrs. Wheeler's permission, and she has a special code to dial out, but we guessed it years ago. We could've called her and been gone before they got home. "Let's go stay with her. At least we'll have a roof over our heads, and we won't be on the streets."

She gave me a pointed look. "We might be safer on the streets."

"You don't know that. She might've stopped." I defended her even though she doesn't deserve it.

A few years ago, Krystal broke the news to me that my mom was a prostitute. She figured it out when we were younger but never told me because she didn't want to hurt my feelings, but she didn't have any choice when my mom started coming around again in seventh grade. I'd never questioned why I had so many uncles, but once Krystal pointed things out, everything became clear—like when I found out what really happened to the pigs. All the clues were there: how I hadn't been allowed to answer the phone and all the strange messages men had left on the answering machine asking if different women were available for the night. Nobody ever came around during the day, and when they came calling at night, they called her different names—Candy, Ginger, or Jasmine. I was a kid, so I thought she was playing a weird grown-up game that I didn't know anything about.

Things didn't end well with my mom that summer. Even though Krystal knew what she did and gave me the heads-up, neither of us imagined that the only reason my mom had come back around was because I was old enough for the family business. I had to knee one of my uncles in the balls and jab him in the rib cage because he wouldn't take no for an answer. That was my last visit. I haven't seen her since.

Krystal shook her head. "I'm not going from one bad situation into one that's worse."

She's always so smart. Sometimes I wish she wasn't.

"How have you been handling all this?" Detective Carl asks, jarring me into the current nightmare.

How am I supposed to answer that? If I say good, then I look like a heartless person, but if I say bad, then he'll ask me more questions I don't want to answer. I settle on saying nothing and give him a nervous shrug, because I don't know what else to do. I might throw up. What if I throw up? I quickly scan the room and spot his trash can next to the bookshelf. That's where I'll go if I puke. I can make it.

"I'm sorry for your loss," he says, like the officer who separated Krystal and me said too. He has the same concerned expression.

It's such a strange thing to say because I barely knew Alice, but I've lost everything. Does he know that? Everything from my life before is gone. Dropped out from underneath me. I'm floating. There's no ground.

"I know this has got to be uncomfortable, so I want to make it as painless as possible for you. Anytime a child dies, there's an automatic investigation, even if we know it was from natural causes or an accident. We have to do this even if a child dies from cancer, so I just want you to know this is totally normal and you haven't done anything wrong. It's standard protocol." He leans forward in his chair with his hands on the desk, trying to ease my nervousness.

"You're a liar," a female voice interrupts him.

Is she talking to me? To him?

I scan the room, looking for the source of the voice. There's nobody but us. Maybe it was someone being questioned in the room next to us. These walls must be really thin. What if they can hear our conversation too?

"I know you hear me."

Dread twists my guts and works its way through my veins. Detective Carl keeps talking, but his sound is turned off. The hair on my arms bristles. A chill runs down my spine. I can't see her, but she's in this room. She's come out of the lake of fire just like I told Krystal she would. My pulse pounds in my chest.

"Honey, are you okay?" Detective Carl asks. His voice is so kind that the truth almost comes tumbling out of me.

I clear my throat. There's no phlegm. Just fingers pressing against my windpipe. I can't blame her for being mad. I'd be mad too.

"I'm okay." It comes out strangled, deep. Not like me.

He opens up his desk and pulls out a Diet Coke. He's probably got a bottle of whiskey in there, too, but he can't give me that. He opens the can and slides it across the desk. I take a sip and clutch it on my lap, grateful to have something in my hands.

"You saw what she did to me." This time there's no mistaking she's speaking to me or who she is, even though her voice doesn't sound like it did when she was alive. She sounds older and meaner. No more bubbliness.

I should be surprised, but I'm not—I've been waiting for this moment. If someone shoved me out of a barn, I'd haunt them, too, until they brought my killer to justice. Even though I'm not surprised, I'm still terrified. All I want to do is run out of the room as fast as I can.

Detective Carl studies my face as he talks. "We can skip all the other stuff and just get right down to what happened that night so you can get out of here quickly. How does that sound?"

I gulp, struggling to breathe around the suffocating fear, and nod for him to go on, even though every part of me wants to tell him to stop. But there's no way out of this. I just have to get it over with so I can get out of here.

"Do you remember what time it was when you girls went outside?" He grabs a pen and reaches for the yellow legal pad on his desk.

"Ten fifteen."

"You're sure?"

"Yes, Mrs. Wheeler is always in her bedroom at nine. Lights out at nine thirty."

He raises his eyebrows. "Every night?"

"Every night."

"Do you think you could walk me through what happened?" He taps his pen on the notebook.

Sweat drips down my back. Can he see my heart thumping in my chest? What if I screw up the answers? My heartbeat rings loudly in my ears. I want to cover them, but I'll look like an idiot if I do. I have to keep it together. Contain the storm inside me. Krystal and I rehearsed this.

I let out a deep breath. "We got a bottle of gin from Scott at school on Friday and—"

He holds his hand up to stop me. "*We* meaning who?"

"Me and Krystal."

"Which Scott?"

"Vaye," I say, realizing as soon as I give up his last name that I just ratted him out to the police. He's never going to get us booze again and will be really mad if he finds out I told on him. I should've seen that one coming. I have to focus.

"Okay, so the two of you had the bottle on Friday. Go on."

"We just got outside, and we were going to the barn when we ran into Veronica and Alice. They'd snuck out, too, but we weren't planning on hanging out together or anything like that. It just happened that way." We should've just said no, forgotten the whole idea, and gone back inside. What were we thinking saying yes? "Alice really wanted to hang out in the barn with us, and she begged Veronica to go. That's how we all ended up in the hayloft together."

"Whose idea was it to go in the hayloft?"

"What do you mean whose idea?"

"Why the hayloft? Why not another one of the buildings that might not have been so hot? It was really hot that night, wasn't it?" I nod, remembering how the heat made my thoughts even thicker. "So, why there? You could've found much cooler spots."

"We always go in the hayloft."

"How come?"

"Because Veronica—" I almost spill the beans again, but this time I catch myself. "We just like having a huge area to ourselves."

"Does Mrs. Wheeler allow you girls to go up there?"

Mrs. Wheeler doesn't care about what we do as long as we fulfill our responsibilities. Plus, she's busy from sunrise until sunset, so she doesn't have time to worry about every little thing we do. But I can't say that to him.

"She's fine with it," I respond instead.

"Take me through what happened while you were up there."

Here we are—the big lie part. Up until now I haven't had to lie. I've never gotten this far, and nobody's pushed me past here. I don't want to lie or talk about what happened, but I just have to get through it once, and then I never have to do it again.

"We played some games and—"

"Drinking games?"

I nod before continuing. "Yes, but it was a lot of just talking and laughing too." Flashes of Alice's smile as she spun around the barn with Krystal belting out Shania Twain cut in. I shove them out like I do every time they come. It hurts to remember. "Mostly we played truth or dare."

"The four of you?" His eyes pierce my soul. I break away from his gaze and stare out the windows behind him. Part of my soul strains to leave, to travel out the window and into the sun, where I can breathe for real.

"Yes."

He waits like there's more to say, and there's so much more I should say, but I can't. "Can you tell me about when Alice fell?"

"Yeah, Nichole. Tell him."

I thought she was gone.

I automatically turn my head to the side, to the sound of her voice.

"Don't look at me! He's going to start getting suspicious. He'll think you're a freak."

I sit up straighter in my chair and tuck my hair behind my ears, trying to look normal even though my mind is racing in a thousand different directions. "It all happened really fast. One minute we were running around playing, and they were over by the hayloft door—"

"They?"

171

"Alice, Krystal, and Veronica."

He scribbles away for a few seconds. "Where were you? I thought you were there when it happened?"

I dig my nails into the palm of my hand. I hate this, but I have to keep going.

"I was. I just wasn't right in front of the door." Now it sounds like I'm trying to put the accident off on them, and that's not what I want to do.

He studies me for a second before asking his next question. "What'd you see?"

Alice is quiet, but her breath is hot on the back of my neck. I watch Detective Carl for any recognition, and there's none. He doesn't see her.

"They were in front of me, so I didn't see much except the running and playing around. Then Alice tripped."

"She tripped?" He doesn't hide his skepticism.

I nod. The taste of bile rises in my throat.

"Did she trip on something?"

This time I shake my head.

He leans in across the table. "So, she tripped on her own feet and fell all the way out of the door?"

Another nod. I don't have words. I can't open my mouth. I'll puke.

"And she just, 'Whah!'"—he makes a spread-eagle movement like he's a flailing superhero—"and went flying through the hayloft door?" His eyebrows arch in disbelief.

One more nod. We've got to be getting close. The end has to be near. Almost there, and then I never have to do this again. Krystal said they'd only make me tell it once. I can do anything once.

"See, Nichole, that's where I'm having a little bit of trouble. Maybe you could help me understand something." He scratches his chin. His forehead wrinkles. "If she tripped and pitched herself forward out the door, it's only a few stories to the ground, so she'd fall straight down. You'd expect to find her facedown on her stomach, but that's not how the paramedics found her. She was lying on her back. How did she trip if her back was to the door?"

"We moved her," I blurt without thinking.

"Hmph." He rummages through the papers on his desk until he finds what he's looking for. "This is the paramedics' report, and it says here that you told the paramedics you didn't move Alice. That you were 'too afraid because you didn't want to hurt her.'" He makes air quotes while reading my part. "Are you sure you moved her?"

"Everything happened so fast," I stammer. I twist my hands on my lap. "Maybe we didn't. Maybe I'm just getting confused."

The room spins. Tilts. I grip the edge of my seat like it's a ride and I might fall off if I don't.

"Was she running backward?"

"No."

"The forensic team came back the next day, and all the blood had been cleaned up. Did you help with that?" The kindness in his eyes is gone.

"Was I not supposed to? Did we do something wrong?" I don't like where this is going.

"You didn't do anything wrong. I just want to know if you helped clean it up."

"Me and Krystal did. It was a huge mess." That only grew bigger and wider the harder we scrubbed. Blood spreads like oil paint when you clean it with water. "Mrs. Wheeler told us to help, so we did."

"Do you always do what Mrs. Wheeler tells you to?" He raises his eyebrows.

"Yes."

"Did she tell you to do anything else that night?"

I freeze. I'm pretty sure you can go to jail for lying, but I'm not scared of going to jail. I'm scared of going to hell. I haven't only just seen what it looks like—I've smelled it too. I strain my ears for Alice's voice, but she's gone. Will she be back?

Every lying word takes effort, but I spit the last ones out. "No, we didn't talk about anything. We just cleaned."

TWENTY-FIVE

KRYSTAL

I came straight to the hospital as soon as the daily activities ended, because I couldn't go another minute without talking to Nichole. I tried burying myself in work after my meeting with Detective Sparks but couldn't focus on anything. How could I, after finding out Aiden cheated on Nichole for their entire marriage? Probably the whole time they were together. Was everything he said a lie? I can't stop replaying our lives together, searching for any clue or sign that I missed—anything hinting at infidelity or a double life—but I keep coming up empty handed. They seemed like they had a perfect marriage.

I left my office and drove around in circles for hours, then walked down by the river. I was hoping to clear my head, but nothing worked. Detective Sparks has no idea if Nichole knew or recently found out about Aiden's history of affairs and inappropriate sexual behavior at work. As far as he can tell from the interviews he's conducted with Aiden's colleagues and friends, all of them kept it a closely guarded secret. It seems like staying quiet about his indiscretions was an unspoken job requirement no matter what position you held. But Detective Sparks is betting just like me that finding out about it is what flipped her. It makes the most sense.

There's no way Nichole's psychosis happened on its own or unprovoked. She started hearing Alice's voice when she was under extreme strain, and finding out the love of your life isn't who he said he was doesn't just shake up your world—it annihilates it. I've seen it happen to hundreds of women I've represented over the years. Lots of them go into mind-numbing depression after they find out about their husband's betrayal, and it takes them a long time to climb out of that hole. Maybe she found out about Aiden's cheating and was so devastated that she couldn't get out of bed. That's what happened after Alice's death. She didn't leave her bed for days. She just lay there like a limp, lifeless doll. It would explain why she didn't leave her house or go outside for a week. It also explains why she never reached out to me. That's bothered me since the beginning, but the last time she got into this kind of trouble, she didn't reach out to me either. The only reason I knew about her struggle was because we shared a bedroom, and there was no way for her to hide it from me.

The difference between other women and Nichole is that she brought a demon with her out of that dark place. It wasn't long afterward that she started hearing Alice's voice. Is someone talking to her now? Controlling and manipulating her in the same way Alice did? She's always referring to "they" whenever she talks about Aiden or is in one of her paranoid states, but she never says who "they" are. I just hope it's not Alice. I don't know what I'll do if she's back. I barely saved Nichole from her last time.

What if she's too far gone for me to reach into her psyche and pull her back into reality like I did before? That's the question that terrifies me the most and won't leave. I try shoving it back down again while I wait for her to get back on the unit. Thankfully, I don't have to wait long.

Within a few minutes, she walks into the community room with the other patients, and she looks even better than she did this morning. Her face is back to its usual pale and not the pasty gray that it's been—like she's got cancer or some other terrible disease. Her eyes are the most startling, though. They're clear and crisp like she's inside herself again. Those drugs were poison.

"Hi," she says, giving me a small smile.

Derek slides a chair out for her before taking a seat at the table behind us, trying to give us as much privacy as possible.

"How were all the groups and activities you went to today?" I ask in the same way a mother asks their child about school when they get home.

"Exhausting," she says, slumping forward in her seat.

It's our first real exchange since the accident, and I want to throw my arms around her and swing her around the room to celebrate, but I can't come on too strong. I don't want to scare her back inside herself, so I keep myself in check.

"I want to talk to you about something," I say, not wanting to waste a minute of her lucidity.

She lowers her head and drops her gaze low, barely moving her lips when she talks, like we used to do when we were kids and didn't want anyone to overhear. She's still a master. "I want to talk to you too." She clutches my hand. Her nails dig into me. "It's about Aiden . . ." Her eyes skirt the room. She twists her body to look behind her, making sure he's not coming into the room or at the nurses' station. I hold my breath, hoping this time it'll be different, that her thoughts will be grounded in reality. She's so alert, almost coherent.

"Okay, what about Aiden?" I prompt after the seconds stretch into minutes and she still hasn't gone on.

She makes another sweep of the room before speaking. "He's not who you think he is."

Hope falls like a heavy rock into the pit of my stomach. For a second, she seemed like she was taking her first steps toward getting better. "Nichole, we've been through this. Aiden—"

She grabs my arm and pulls me closer, smashing my body against her side. "I'm serious. I'm starting to remember things."

All thoughts drop from my head. Nothing from this afternoon matters.

"From that night?"

She nods. "Yes, I think so . . . I don't know. None of it makes sense." She flings a terrified glance over her shoulder, still not sure she's safe. "I guess I just have a few memories. At least, I think they're memories. They're little flashes. I think I'm remembering, but it feels like I'm dreaming . . . maybe I'm dreaming. I don't know. It's so confusing." She drops my hand and rubs her wounded forearms. The scars create a jagged ladder running up to her elbows.

I can't give her time to lose her grip and fall backward. I've never pushed, and I still won't push hard, but she needs some pressure to keep going. I reach out and take one of her hands in mine. I knead her fingers, doing my best to relax the tension making them stiff. "It's okay. Just tell me what you remember."

She lets out a long, shaky breath. "Aiden screaming at me. Lots of angry screaming. His face is in mine. He's just yelling and yelling at me. I can't make him stop. He—"

"You see his face?"

She nods.

"Not just hear his voice?"

"Yes."

Relief floods my body.

"What's he saying?"

"I can't tell. I can't hear it. But he's just so mad. And I don't know what to do. I'm just scared of him. So scared . . ." Her voice trails off, and her face crumples like she's going to cry. I squeeze her hand. Rub her back.

"It's okay," I reassure her for what feels like the thousandth time. Her terror is palpable through her shirt. I've only seen her like this one other time. "You're safe now. Nobody can hurt you here."

"And then there's a girl too. Well, not a girl—she's a woman."

My stomach free-falls, mouth instantly dry.

"What did you just say?" I ask, hoping she misspoke. Maybe I didn't hear her right.

"There's a woman. I see her too."

My heartbeat thuds in my chest. The blood rushes through my ears in a swooshing sound. I take Nichole's other hand in mine, holding them both on my lap, terrified for the answer to the question that comes next, but I have to know, because that changes everything and confirms my worst fear.

"Is it Alice? Is she back?"

TWENTY-SIX

NICHOLE

(THEN)

"What are you doing out there?" Krystal calls to me from our bedroom window, trying to keep her voice down. Her hair is piled high in a towel on top of her head. She doesn't have to whisper any more than I had to go out the window tonight. I could've used the front door, because as long as we don't tell the truth about what happened to Alice, Mrs. Wheeler doesn't care what we do anymore. Everything's changed around here.

The four of us have stopped speaking to each other in the house unless it's to say *pass the butter* or *can you grab the milk from the refrigerator*. We don't pretend anymore or talk just because we don't want to sit in silence. I got up in the middle of dinner tonight and carried my plate into our bedroom. That's against about ten different house rules, starting with *no food in the bedrooms* and *you must ask to be excused from the table*, but Mrs. Wheeler didn't do anything to stop me. Krystal was minutes behind me with a goofy grin on her face.

"Oh my God! She didn't even know what to say after you left. She got this surprised reaction when you first took off, but then this

weird indifference came over her face, and she went back to her food."
Krystal's plate was almost empty but she'd brought it with her just to
see if she could get away with it too. "That totally came from nowhere.
What made you just get up all of a sudden?"

Alice.

That's the answer I wanted to give her, but I was too scared. Just like
I am now to tell her I came outside to see if I could still hear Alice. She's
only spoken inside so far. I was hoping maybe she was only an inside
voice like the ones they used to tell us to use in elementary school, but
she's not. She's an outside voice too. An everywhere kind, and I don't
know what to do.

What if Krystal doesn't believe me? What if she thinks I'm crazy?
That's all Alice kept whispering tonight—"*Don't say a word to anyone
about me*"—but I've never had a secret from Krystal before. Not one.
It feels icky on my insides.

"I just needed some fresh air," I answer Krystal in my regular voice
before too much time passes and she starts getting suspicious.

She jumps up on the window ledge and swings her legs through the
window in one swift movement. She plops onto the ground and walks
over to join me behind the rosebushes. She's dressed in the Mickey
Mouse T-shirt she sleeps in every night. His picture is so faded there're
only pieces of the image left.

"What's going on?" she asks. "You've been weird since we left the
police station."

I didn't speak on the drive home or during chores. It's hard to speak
when all you're doing is listening to see if you'll hear it again—terrified
you will.

"I can't stay here anymore. I have to get out. I really want to call
my mom."

She sighs. "We've been through this. It's too dangerous. Besides,
you don't even know where she's staying. She might not be in this state."
She speaks to me like I'm a toddler, and I don't like it.

"So what? At least we can try to find her. I'll make her take us both even if she says no, and then we can do all the stuff we've talked about with emancipation. It'll be just like we planned except we'll be doing it there instead of here. We'll get jobs and go to community college at night." The plan sounds better and better as I talk. "Most community colleges have track teams, and we can try out. There's no way we won't make the team. I'm sure you'll get recognized right away and probably still get a scholarship to a good school once they see how good you are. We can do what we planned. I can't wait, Krystal. We have to go."

"I'm still not sure."

"Why do you get the final say?" I put my hands on my hips. Sometimes she makes me furious. I've switched sides like she's been begging me to do for the past year, but now that she thinks it's a bad idea, we're not going to do it. That's not fair.

"It's not about having the final say. It's about being smart—"

I cut her off. "So, I'm dumb?"

"That's not what I'm saying. You know I don't think you're dumb. But think about it for a second. Filing emancipation paperwork is going to draw more attention to us, which is the last thing we want. We're trying to be invisible and keep the focus off of us. Detective Carl doesn't know we've been planning and talking about this for almost two years. It will look like we suddenly filed paperwork giving us the right to legally run away. Don't you see how bad that would look for us?"

"Yes, but I don't care. We didn't do anything wrong! This"—I gesture to the space around us—"is what we're doing wrong. Lying. Sitting around rehearsing the story we're going to tell people when they ask us questions. Please, I want to go to my mom's."

That's all I could think about when we left Detective Carl's office— out. Just get out.

"There's got to be another option," Krystal says, crossing her arms on her chest.

She knows as well as I do that there's not. My mom is it unless we want to live on the streets. Social services lost contact with Krystal's mom three years ago, and she's never known her dad. I'll live on the streets if we have to, but at least my mom's might be a little safer and we'd have a bathroom.

She plops down on the grass and pats the spot next to her. I sit beside her cross-legged, and the solid ground underneath me feels good. "I get all that, but it's not why you went out the window while I was in the shower, Nichole. We never go out the window unless we're sneaking out. I freaked out when I saw it open because I thought someone came in and grabbed you, but then I spotted you out here. What's up for real?"

I pull my knees up to my chest. I was putting my clothes away in our bedroom after my shower when someone called my name. I held my breath, hoping it was Krystal as I opened our bedroom door to see what she wanted, but it wasn't her. She was singing in the shower. The hallway was empty. I closed the door and stepped back in our room. The world swirled underneath my feet like it did in Detective Carl's office. It felt like I'd been hanging upside down for hours.

"I know you can hear me."

I clutched the shirt I was folding to my chest and twirled around the room, searching for Alice. My eyes bounced from the window to the bed to the desk. I wanted to move, but I was frozen.

"Where are you? Why won't you let me see you?" I asked, keeping my voice low.

She giggled.

"It's more fun this way, don't you think?"

"Why are you doing this to me?" I cried.

"Because of what you did to me."

"But I didn't do it! It wasn't me. Please leave me alone. I'm sorry. I'm so sorry, but I didn't do it." I started crying.

"Doesn't matter. You should've done something."

"I couldn't stop her. I didn't know she was going to do it. I swear I didn't." I sobbed while I talked. "It happened so fast, and I wasn't even close to you guys. Don't you remember that? I would've grabbed you if I could've. Tried to save you. I really would've. Please, leave me alone." Where was she? Not being able to see her made me feel crazy. "You can't stop Veronica, okay? You don't know her. Something's broken inside her. I don't know what it is or how it got broke, but you can't fix it. I tried. But that's not my fault. Please, that's not my fault. You have to leave me alone. I never would've hurt you."

The air stilled as I waited for her to talk. She was still there. I couldn't see her, but I sensed her in the same way I sensed deer when they were close in the woods. A few more seconds passed, and my legs loosened up so that I could move again. I didn't wait for her to respond or do anything else. The window was the quickest way out of the room, so I tugged it open and hurtled my way through. I bolted across the lawn like someone was chasing me and didn't stop until I got to the rosebushes. My heart's still pounding.

"Nichole?" Krystal calls me back into the present, and I collide with my dilemma.

Will Alice be mad if I tell Krystal? I don't want to make her any madder than she already is. But I can't lie to Krystal either. We don't lie to each other. That's our rule. Number one on the top of our list that we made when we were eight. Number two was never hurt each other on purpose.

I drop my voice to a whisper, even though there's nobody around for miles. "I have something to tell you, but you have to keep it a secret."

She nods.

"Promise? You can't ever tell anyone. Ever."

"I won't tell anyone, Nichole. I promise."

TWENTY-SEVEN

KRYSTAL

"It's not Alice." Nichole shakes her head. She unwinds the leather bracelet she made in occupational therapy from her wrist and twists it around her finger. "At least, I don't think it is."

We don't speak about Alice. We left her behind when we ran away from Mrs. Wheeler's and haven't spoken of her since that first night alone in the hotel room. When we were eight, we wrote down a set of rules to govern our lives. They were the rules for how we'd function to meet our goals, and we thought they'd last forever, but we were too young to know that adulthood requires different rules, so you have to make up new rules to fit your new world. We stayed up half the night creating ours. Not talking about Alice was somewhere in the top five, since there was no way we were taking her with us on our fresh start.

"How do you know it's not her?" My voice is barely above a whisper. Alice's name snaps me back to age seventeen. Memories violently push their way to the surface in the way they do after they've been brought to light after so many years buried in the darkness. Alive Alice liked me, but Dead Alice hated me almost as much as she hated Veronica.

Nichole was so scared to tell me about Alice, and I was proud of how I handled it that first night. I gave her a hug and told her that I was there for her no matter what. It made sense that she thought she heard Alice's voice, and I shared how Alice's face flashed through my brain when I was least expecting it and that I had nightmares too. Mine were just different. Hers had her being chased around a lake of fire, and mine were stuck on repeat with the image of Alice's horrified face as Veronica shoved her out of the hayloft. So, I got what Nichole was going through. I thought we were going through the same thing and that things would get better over time.

But we weren't going through the same thing, and things didn't get better over time. My intrusive images of Alice weren't the same as Nichole hearing her voice. I knew the pictures of Alice's face that flashed through my mind unbidden and refused to leave weren't real. Nichole really believed she heard Alice speak. She thought she was an invisible ghost.

I would wake in the middle of the night to find Nichole sitting on her bed talking animatedly to Alice even though nobody was there. She developed weird tics because she wanted to look whenever Alice said something to her but constantly fought the urge so she wouldn't appear weird. Alice made her do things to prove her loyalty, like stealing food from the dinner table or hiding Veronica's favorite clothes. It wasn't long before Nichole pulled away from me because Alice told her I didn't understand their relationship.

"The woman I'm seeing is pretty," Nichole says, as if that settles everything since Alice wasn't exactly a good-looking kid.

Except some of the most unattractive teenagers grow into the most beautiful adults. Nichole didn't have to look any farther than the mirror to confirm that fact. She wasn't ugly by any stretch of the imagination when we were kids, but it took her a long time to grow into her features and become a woman who turns heads. But I don't want to challenge her or make her second-guess herself because she's finally talking, and I don't want her to stop.

"Maybe Alice grew up to be a beautiful woman," I say as lightly as possible, even though dead people don't age.

"Okay, well, the woman has green eyes just like me, and remember—Alice's eyes were brown?" Nichole twists her hands on her lap, still anxiously working the bracelet around her fingers.

I shake my head. I did my best to blot out those parts. I haven't thought about Alice or pictured her face in years. I work hard at staying in the present moment and not traveling back in time, especially to periods that were so awful and painful. That's the only way we moved forward.

Nichole turns to me, her face anxious and pale. "I'm so confused, Krystal. Nothing makes sense."

Her eyes take in the community room like it's the first time she's really noticed where she is. The room is in disarray because it's impossible to keep it orderly when the patients are continually flipping out and creating chaos. Hilda wanders the perimeter spitting on the floor every few feet and muttering to herself. Jackson, the youngest on the unit, sits huddled in the corner pulling chunks of his hair out because he's convinced aliens have stuck probes in his head. The two rail-thin anorexics sit at a table playing Scrabble, their board cluttered with food words. The blue plastic chairs are filled with clusters of other patients whose stories I don't know and, frankly, don't want to.

"What's happening to me?" she asks, taking another sweep of the room. Like me, she clearly feels out of place in this bizarre land.

I do my best to channel Dr. McGowan, keeping all emotion from my voice and sticking to the facts. "You're having a hard time separating what's real and what's not real. You're believing things that aren't true." She scrunches up her face the way she does when she's listening really hard and trying to understand the material, just like she used to do in math class. "It's not your fault, Nichole. None of this is your fault. You didn't do anything to cause this. There're lots of reasons people get this way, and the doctors are doing everything they can to fix you."

She locks eyes with me, registering exactly what I'm saying. "Did my brain break like before?"

She doesn't have to explain which before; there's only one.

I nod. Admitting the truth to myself at the same time that I'm admitting it to her.

Her eyes grow wide. "Do you think it has something to do with the woman?"

"I'm not sure." I've wandered through the world of her delusions with her before. It was like a fun house museum with double mirrors and sliding glass doors, and I dread going there with her again, but I'm not sure we have any other choice if we're going to get to the bottom of things.

Things stir around us. The energy rises. The patients' voices grow louder and more animated. I glance at the clock: 6:45 p.m. Almost medication time. The change shifts Nichole's state too. She starts jiggling her legs underneath the table.

"I can't tell if I'm sleeping or awake, Krystal. I think I'm sleeping, then I think I'm awake, then I'm like no, I'm asleep—I'm dreaming. I tell myself, 'Wake up, Nichole. Get up—it's time to wake up.' Remember how I used to say that sophomore year to get me through stats class?" Her voice is pressured and hurried, like it could be snatched away from her at any moment so she's got to get everything out before it does. "I just want to know what's going on—to be inside myself again—but I'm outside me and I can't remember. I'm trying so hard. I really am. Like maybe if I focus enough, then I'll figure out what's happening. But I can't. My mind leaves. It just goes, and I can't control it. And then there's Aiden. I'm so scared of him. But I love Aiden. Why am I so scared of him?" She peeks behind her like someone is sneaking up on her. Her agitation is palpable. Her hands never stop moving. She scrapes at the wounds on her forearms. "What about the woman? Does she need my help? She looks scared too."

"Take a deep breath and slow down," I say, even though she's way past the point where deep breathing would be helpful, but I have to ground her before she spirals any further down. "You don't need to figure everything out right now, okay? It's going to take a while for you to feel normal again, and you have to give yourself that time. Don't push yourself so hard. And the reason it feels like you're waking up is because you are, in a way. You've basically been in a drug-induced stupor for around a week. They had you doped up on so much medication at first it was disgusting."

She can't hide her shock and surprise. "A week? I've been here that long?"

I nod.

"How did I get here?" She keeps stealing glances at the other patients. I can tell it's as unsettling to her as it was to me during my initial visits on the unit.

"You don't remember?"

She shakes her head.

"There was a fire at your house, and when the firefighters showed up, you basically attacked them. The police officers came next, and you jumped on one of their backs like you did to Jesse Alberts in fourth grade after he stole your snack money." I can't tell her everything yet. It's too overwhelming. I've got to back her away from the edge, not toward it.

"How did my house start on fire? Did it burn down?" Her eyes are wide with fear. She searches my face for understanding.

"Your house is okay. It's still standing. There's a lot of smoke damage, but beyond that, I think it will be fine." I take a long, deliberate breath and let it out slowly. "It looks like you started the fire."

Her mouth drops open. She sits straight up in her chair. "Why would I do that?" Her forehead wrinkles as she grapples with the information.

"I wish I had an answer, but we don't know. That's what we're trying to figure out."

"Why would I do that?" she asks again, like she didn't hear what I said. She shoves her chair back and stands. Agitation takes over her expression and moves into her body. I quickly pull her back down to the chair.

"Listen, honey, just sit down, okay. This is a lot to take in." She does what I say, moving robotically into her chair.

"I just . . . I just don't understand." She shakes her head. Her eyes are fixed in a thousand-yard stare.

I put my arm around her and pull her rigid body next to mine. "This is a lot for you to take in all at once, and I know that's hard, but you're back from whatever dark place you were in. That's a good thing. We're going to get you better, okay? And we're going to get through this just like we get through every other difficult thing in our lives, sweetie." Her body slowly relaxes against mine as my words work like soothing balm to sunburned skin on her psyche.

TWENTY-EIGHT

NICHOLE

(THEN)

"Leave me alone, go away!" I yell, running out of the barn and away from Krystal. I don't want her anywhere near me. It's barely a month since Alice died, and she acts like it never happened—like we're just supposed to go on with our lives. She's no better than Veronica and Mrs. Wheeler. "Get away from me!" I holler again, but she easily catches me. She tugs on my arm and pulls me back.

"Listen to me. Stop, talk to me. Come on," she cries. "Don't shut me out. I don't know what I'm doing. What the right thing to say is. I've—"

I spin around to face her. "You say you believe me. That's what you say." Rage surges through me as I try to catch my breath. I've never been so mad at her. "How can you not be on my side?"

She grabs my other arm, twisting me toward her and forcing me to stop. "I'm always on your side. You know that."

I shrug her off me and turn away, walking in the direction of the house. I don't want to go back inside yet, but I don't want to be in that barn with her anymore either. Alice told me she'd do this. She said she'd stop believing me. She said she'd turn on us. I hate that she's right. I hate it. Angry tears burn my eyes. I've never felt so betrayed, and it only makes it worse that she was right.

"*I told you,*" Alice whispers in my ear.

Shut up, I think in response.

She's so immature. Like a toddler. She and Veronica should've been friends. They're perfect for each other.

Krystal grabs me from behind, pulling me hard this time. "Stop, Nichole. Just stop."

"You said that it was okay that I heard Alice's voice. That there was nothing wrong with it because of what happened. Remember that? Remember what you said, Krystal?" I glare at her.

"Yes, but that was before . . . before . . ."

"Before what?" I step closer to her. She steps away, but this time I'm the one not letting her get away. "You said you wanted to talk about it. Let's talk." I put my hands on my hips.

"It's just that . . ." She takes a deep, shuddering breath. "It's been weeks. Almost a month, and I think things should've started mellowing out. But nothing's better. You're still the same."

"You're saying I should get over it?" That's what the rest of them have done. They get up every day and go on with their lives like everything is totally back to normal. Nothing is okay. It's never going to be again.

"I'm not saying anything like that, but all your grades are dropping, and you're skipping school. You've never skipped school." There are tears in her voice, but I don't care.

I shove my finger in her face. "I knew you were still mad about that. You told me you weren't mad."

Last week I walked out of math class because Alice was yelling so loudly that I thought my head would explode. I couldn't hear anything else. Nothing. That's what she does now if I ignore her. She screams at me like a tyrant until I give her my undivided attention. Everyone told

Krystal about it afterward because apparently I put my hands over my ears and bolted out of the room like someone was chasing me, but they all like to tell stories. They're always blowing things out of proportion. It wasn't even like that. I just had to get out of there, so I did.

"It's not about skipping school. It's just about how much you're changing. You're doing things you don't ever do. You talk to yourself—I mean, Alice—all the time. I don't think you know how often you're doing it, Nichole." Her eyes fill with concern. "It's scary how you get into it with her."

That's why she's so freaked out. Me and Alice got into a fight while I was draining the hoses, and Krystal walked in on us. You would've thought she walked in on my having sex with someone by the way she reacted. She looked at me like she didn't know who I was.

"What are you doing?" she'd asked.

"Nothing." I'd tried playing it off like I didn't just have my finger in Alice's invisible face, yelling so hard spit flung from my mouth.

"That wasn't nothing, Nichole. That was something." Her eyes were filled with fear. Like I was a stranger.

"Leave me alone," I shouted and pushed her aside.

She's wearing the same expression that she did in the barn.

"What if you talked to one of the school guidance counselors about what's going on?" she asks. "They always say we can come to them with anything, and it's completely confidential. I'll even come with you if you want. We can talk to her together so it doesn't seem so weird."

"Why would I talk to the counselor? Aren't we trying to avoid talking to people?"

"She's scared, Nichole."

"She doesn't understand."

"Nobody understands."

"I'm the only one that gets you. I already told you that."

I ignore Alice and focus on Krystal.

"Come on, Nichole, please quit being so difficult. I'm just trying to help you."

"Help? I'm not the one that needs help. Alice was the one that needed help, but we didn't help her, did we? And these people?" I shake my fist at the house. My body trembles with rage. "They need help too. Little Miss Veronica is the devil. Notice how she's just moved on like it's nothing? Nothing. Why can't Alice torture *her*? She's the one who did it. Did you know that's what we fight about? That's what we're always fighting about. You know that? Oh, but you don't know that because we don't talk about it anymore. You're just as bad as they are."

"This is what I mean. You're not you anymore. It's scaring me." She starts to cry, and she rarely cries. Usually that makes me stop, but I can't. Something inside of me has been unleashed.

"I'm scaring you?" I want to shake her, make her understand. "I'm not going crazy, Krystal!"

"I didn't say you were crazy—I just said you needed help."

"Voices are inside your head—inside!" I jab my fingers to my temple. "'The voices in her head told her to do it.' How many times do people say that? How many?" She takes a step back. I take one toward her. She's not getting away. "Tell me how many?"

She holds up her hands to protect her face like my words are going to hurt her. "Please, Nichole. Don't. Not again."

"No, you think I'm crazy even though you won't admit it. You might as well just admit it and stop pretending." I take another step closer to her. Our chests almost touch. Our noses are within inches of each other. "Everyone always says the voices in their head made them do it. But she's not in my head, Krystal—Alice's voice isn't in my head. It's here. It's everywhere. Why can't you understand?" My fists clench at my sides. I want to shake her. Make her see the light. "That's what you don't get. She's outside of me. She's not in my head." I stab my temple again to drive the point home.

"Listen to me, Nichole. Listen." She puts a hand on each of my cheeks and looks me dead in the eyes. She's never been so serious. "If she was a ghost, then I would hear her, too, but I don't. You're the only one that does. That means she's not real."

"So now you're jealous of me?"

She springs back, dropping her hands from my face. "What? You can't be serious. That might be the stupidest thing you've ever said. I'm jealous because she doesn't talk to me? You really do need help." She points to the house. "Go ahead. I'm going back to the barn."

She turns on her heel and leaves me standing alone in the driveway.

I told you she wouldn't understand.

———

"NONONONONONONONONONO," I scream, shaking my head wildly.

Alice finally has me where she wants me—alone and without Krystal's interference in our life. Krystal has barely talked to me since our fight last week, but Alice won't shut up. I press my fingers into my eyes as hard as I can to blot out the images of her burning face. Pink and white specks dance in front of my lids. Her breath is in my face. Rancid and hot.

She's never going to stop. She won't stop until Veronica pays for what she did to her, but Veronica won't listen to me. She never listens. I hate her, but I won't hurt her.

"I can't. I can't." I sob as the shower beats down on the empty tub while I sit on the toilet. It's the only way no one hears us. She said no one can hear us. But if no one can hear us, no one can help us.

She whispers in my ear, *"You think my face is bad? Wait until you see what I'll do to your sister if you don't do what I say."*

"Shut up. Shut up. Shut up," I yell, covering my ears with both hands.

But she won't shut up. She never shuts up.

She laughs. She's laughing in my face. She's laughing in my ears. She's laughing all around me.

Sing the Krystal song. My Krystal song.

"Hush, little baby, don't say a word. Mama's gonna buy you a mockingbird—"

"Don't test me, Nichole—"

I plaster my hands on my ears, singing louder. "And if that mockingbird don't sing, Mama's gonna buy you a diamond ring—"

"Your mama's not going to buy you anything."

"And if that mockingbird don't sing, Mama's gonna buy you a diamond ring . . ."

I rock and sing. Rock and sing. Drowning out the sound of her voice.

TWENTY-NINE

KRYSTAL

I creep down the hospital corridor, keeping my eyes peeled for anyone from Aiden's family. Aiden texted me last night that he was being discharged today, so one of them has to be here to take him home, and I'm not taking a chance with running into any of them. I'm still angry that they pushed so hard to bring charges against Nichole, and I don't know what I'll do if one of them tries to confront me today.

I round the corner and step into his room. All the cards and flowers that had filled his room and covered his walls since his arrival are gone. Marlene kept his room decorated so that there was something happy and inspiring no matter where you looked, but he's taken all that down. It's stripped bare. He stands with his back to me, and a surge of anger shoots through my body at the sight of him. He's a filthy cheater of the worst kind.

He turns around at the sound of my footsteps, and I stagger backward when I see his face. With everything going on, I forgot they took his bandages off yesterday. His eager blue eyes stare out at me from bright pink eyelids that look like they've been flipped inside out. His head is misshapen and shaved on one side. Nasty burns in various stages of awfulness cover the left side of his face. There're blisters and huge welts like a really bad sunburn, but his right side is worse. Parts of that skin are blackened like a burned marshmallow. His appearance sucks the words and the rage out of me.

"Hey!" he says in a voice full of eagerness and desperation. "What's going on? Why haven't you been returning any of my texts?"

"It's . . . I've just, you know, been really busy with everything going on." I stumble over my words, trying not to look at his face or his eyes peering at me like those of a little boy longing for acceptance. His skin looks so painful. There's a fleshy open hole in the side of his cheek packed with gauze.

He follows my gaze to his wounded cheek. "A piece of the carpet melted to my cheek. The doctors said it was still attached in the emergency room, and they had to—"

I put my hand up to stop him. I don't want to hear the gory details. "I'm good. That's enough."

"It's pretty bad, huh?" His face crumples.

"It's not your best look, that's for sure," I joke, despite how angry I was minutes ago.

"I'm thinking I might shave the other side of my head just so that it matches, you know?" he responds, forcing a smile, but tears prick his eyes.

I nod. Everything I'd planned to say since last night is gone. He turns around to zip the duffel bag on top of his bed, and I take a huge gulping breath, trying to regain my center. "Are you going to stay with your parents?"

His back stiffens at the mention of them, and he whips back around. "Absolutely not. I haven't spoken to them since I found out they forced the DA to file charges against Nichole. I'm staying at the Old Road Inn so I can be close to Nichole."

The Old Road Inn is the only hotel in Belmont, and nobody stays there. They've cleaned it up over the years, but it's still a dump, and nothing good happens there—especially at night. Out-of-towners make the thirty-minute drive to the city. Any other time I would've offered him my guest room, but I can't bring myself to do it. I take a deep breath.

"I know all about the other women, Aiden." It comes out soft and filled with sadness, nothing like I'd expected.

The life drains from his body. He leans back on the bed. "I knew it was only a matter of time before you found out." He hangs his head low, staring at his shoes while he speaks. "You have to understand that it has nothing to do with Nichole. You know how much I love her. She's my world."

My anger flares instantly. "Nothing to do with Nichole? You're married to her!"

"Yes, but that's different. It's not even the same thing." His voice wavers like he's going to cry. "You have to let me explain myself."

"What's there to explain? You're a cheater. No explanation changes that, and you know it. All you had to do was let people know from the very beginning that you are a cheating scum and your wife found out about it. You could've—"

He jumps in. "No, that's not what happened."

"You didn't cheat on Nichole?"

He looks away.

"Exactly."

"Just hear me out, okay?" His voice is thick with emotion. He doesn't wait for me to answer. "It's true that I have sex with other women, and I'm sorry. Not just for the sex but for keeping it a secret." His expression fills with deep regret, but I don't feel sorry for him. Not even a little bit.

There's no denying I've kept quiet about Nichole's past, but I did it to protect her. Disclosing her breakdown before would've meant dredging up Alice's death, and there's no doubt in my mind that Mrs. Wheeler would follow up on her threats, even though so much time has passed. There's no statute of limitations on murder, and I couldn't take that chance, however remote it might be. Our deception isn't the same thing, since I'm pretty sure he's only been lying to protect himself.

"I'm not the one you should be apologizing to," I snap.

"Being faithful has been a problem for a long time." Shame contorts his mangled face. "It started when I was a teenager and never stopped. I've tried to quit so many times. I can't even tell you how many times I swore I was done, but that part of me has nothing to do with Nichole. I—"

"Except you're married to her." She's not here to defend herself, so I have to.

"I know, and it was a huge mistake."

"A mistake? It might be a mistake the first time, but after that it's a choice and one you made over and over again."

"But it never feels like a choice. You don't understand. It's a twisted compulsion that I don't have any control over."

I move my neck back and forth, trying to release the tension in my body. As mad as I am at him, I also want to know what happened. "How many women were there?"

He balks. "Um . . . I mean, I don't know. I've never really counted."

"Give me your best estimate, then." I refuse to let him off the hook.

"Maybe twenty?" he says softly, dropping his gaze to the floor and lowering his head in shame.

"Twenty women?" I don't even try to hide my surprise at his number.

He nods, still refusing to make eye contact.

"When? I mean, how? How do you even find the time for that?" I still can't wrap my brain around his number.

His face bears the weight of his guilt and his secrets. "I've always had this sex-crazed side of me since I was a teenager. It's like this weird compulsion that comes over me and won't leave me alone until I give in and feed it." He takes a deep, shuddering breath. "I thought it would stop after I married Nichole, and for a while it did, but then it came back, and when that darkness comes over me, I don't know how to stop it. I can't help myself, and I feel like the biggest piece of shit afterward. Every time I do it, I tell myself I will never, ever do it again." He finally raises his eyes to meet mine. "I love Nichole with every fiber of my being. She's the most important thing to me."

"You can't love someone like that and cheat on them."

He shakes his head wildly. "But it's not that simple or that black and white."

"Yes, it is, Aiden. In cases like this, it's very black and white."

"It's just sex. That's all it is. Nothing more. I'm a cheater, but it doesn't mean that I don't love Nichole. That part of my life is completely separate from our life together."

I want to slap his wounded face. "Do you know how ridiculous you sound?"

"Sex and love are two different things. Those women? They mean nothing to me. Absolutely nothing. Half the time I don't even know their names." His eyes beg for understanding, but all his excuses just make him sound more like a pig.

But what did I expect? He's a Fischer, and people like the Fischers think they can get away with anything. The normal rules of life don't apply to them. Aiden has always been a part of the "goldens." That's what Nichole and I used to call Ben and Whitney back in the day. Small-town life doesn't vary even if you change states. Just like them, Aiden was born with a golden ticket in his hands and every sense of entitlement that goes with it.

There's no sense in arguing with him. Besides, none of that helps Nichole, and she's the one I really care about. "What did Nichole do when she found out?"

"What do you mean? She doesn't know about any of it." His face goes white. "Can you imagine what that would do to her?"

The new information throttles me.

"Are you sure?"

He ferociously shakes his head. "Absolutely. She had no idea."

"What if she found out and didn't tell you that she found out?"

"There's no way. Do you really think she could've kept that to herself?"

Everything spins and blurs, like my mind is on a Tilt-A-Whirl. How is that possible? If Nichole didn't find out about his cheating, then what caused her breakdown?

Aiden rushes to me and takes both my hands in his. "You're not going to tell her, are you? Please, Krystal, you can't tell her. Not now."

"I don't know what I'm going to do." Nothing adds up. There are too many holes. Too many pieces that don't fit in the puzzle.

"Please, Krystal." He squeezes my hands. His eyes fill with tears again. "I can't live without her, and she can't live without me either. This would devastate her. It'd wreck any chance I have of her coming back to me." He drops one of my hands and points to his face. "Look at this. I don't even know how I'm going to get her to recognize me when I look like a monster. And if she finds out the things I did, I'll lose her forever."

Tears spill down his cheeks. He flinches and lets out a yelp as the salt in the tears stings his wounds. He goes into the bathroom and grabs a handful of towels to blot his face but quickly changes his mind and doesn't bring them up to his skin. We wait in silence while the tears air-dry.

"I've learned my lesson. I swear. I'm done. Never again, you have my word." His face is serious. His jaw set in a straight line. "Haven't I been punished enough?"

"I don't know what to do. I have to go. I just have to go." I can't look at his face. Part of me can't help but think he's right. He's scarred for life.

"Please don't go." He reaches for my arm, but I'm already gone.

———

I sit in my living room, staring at my laptop on the coffee table like I've been doing for the last hour, but the screen has long gone black. I couldn't bring myself to talk to Nichole about Aiden today. More of her was back, but barely: only little pieces. It's like she's peeking out from behind a curtain, and if I overwhelm her, I'm afraid it'll snap shut. I pet Hobbes while I think, wishing I had someone to process all this with, but Nichole's the only person I ever go to when things are tough. She's my person.

A knock at my front door startles me. Nobody buzzed from the lobby downstairs, and I'm not expecting anyone. I get up and peer through the peephole. Aiden stands outside. Someone must've let him in. I hate when other tenants do that. I should've known he'd show up here. He's been texting me nonstop since I left him in his room earlier, but I never responded. I didn't know what to say because I still don't know what I'm going to do. I reluctantly open the door and motion him inside.

He lets out a deep sigh of relief. "Thanks for letting me in. I had to talk to you." He walks into the living room, but he doesn't sit. He paces back and forth in the small space.

It's the strangest feeling being alone with him in my house. Not that we've never been alone in my house before, because we have. Lots of times. It's just that Nichole was always in the other room or about to walk in the door at any given moment. Hobbes immediately darts off to hide underneath the bookshelf upstairs, where he'll stay until Aiden leaves. He hates visitors. The awkwardness stretches out between Aiden and me.

"Do you want a glass of wine?" I ask. It's a Wednesday night, and I rarely drink on weekdays because I don't want to risk a morning head-ache, but I can't get through this conversation without a glass of wine. I'm not sure Aiden can either.

He's sweating a lot again, and his putrid smell fills my condo as he trails after me into the kitchen. I open a bottle of prosecco and pour us each a glass. He looks grateful as he takes it from me and slides onto one of the barstools at the island. It's a relief having him sit still.

"Cheers." He raises his glass with his good hand.

I raise mine without saying anything, then take a sip while he drains half his glass.

"Sorry I don't have whiskey," I say. He's a whiskey drinker, but I don't drink anything except wine, so that's what I have in the house. I only stock up when I'm having people over, but I can't remember the last time I had someone over besides Nichole.

"I don't mind at all," he says as he takes another drink, and I follow suit, the familiar sweetness coating my throat. I slide onto the other barstool next to him.

We stare at the stainless-steel refrigerator across from us. The front of it is covered with tacky magnets from all the places Nichole and I have traveled over the years. We took our first real vacation during our freshman year in college. We went to Pensacola and were so broke once we got there that we couldn't afford any real souvenirs, so we had a competition to see who could find the tackiest magnet to take back and put on our dorm refrigerator. The tradition stuck, and over the years, no matter where we go, we bring home the ugliest one we can find.

The top spot is currently held by the Vegas shot glass with ice-cube boobs that we got two years ago when Aiden insisted on taking Nichole and me to Vegas for the weekend. He couldn't believe we'd never been, since it was one of his favorite places, and was determined to give us the best time even though we didn't want to go. He promised to show us the city in a way nobody else could. His eyes travel through the souvenirs, too, stepping back in time. My phone vibrates in my pocket.

He traces his fingertips on top of the wineglass. "Did you tell her?"

That's the big question filling the room. The only reason he really came to see me.

"No." He reaches to hug me, but I push him back. "Don't."

"Thank you, Krystal. Oh my God, thank you so much. You have no idea how happy I am to hear that," he gushes, his excitement spilling over.

"Not telling her wasn't because of you. Believe me, it had nothing to do with you," I snap. "I didn't tell her because she even seemed better today than she was yesterday. She's starting to have moments of lucidity. Being off the meds is working magic, and I think all the groups on the unit are helping her too. I didn't want to set her back. That's all."

I don't want him to get any ideas that I'm aligned with him. That couldn't be further from the truth. I don't know what I'm going to do about telling Nichole, but I do know what I'm going to do with him. He's done. After tonight, we don't need to have another conversation.

"Look, Aiden, I think it's in her best interest if you just leave her alone for a while. Give her time to heal." My phone buzzes again in my pocket, and this time I pull it out to check. I've missed two calls from Detective Sparks. He left me a voice message on the last one. Just as I'm about to speak again, my phone lights up with another call from him. He's never called me so many times in a row. My gut clenches, and my heart speeds up. "Can you give me a second? I have to take this call," I say without giving Aiden a chance to answer.

I get up and make my way down the hallway to my bedroom while Detective Sparks leaves another message. My nerves jump wildly as I shut the door behind me and put the phone to my ear to listen to his first voice mail.

"Hey, Krystal. This is Detective Sparks. I need to talk to you about Aiden. Some serious issues have come up with him in the investigation. I need you to give me a call as soon as possible, okay? As soon as possible." There's an urgency in his voice that's never been there before.

I immediately call him back, and he answers before the end of the second ring.

He doesn't bother saying hello. "Krystal? Are you with Aiden?"

"What?" His question takes me by surprise. Who told him Aiden was here?

"Are you with Aiden?"

"Um . . . you can't just—"

He interrupts me. "Krystal, I don't have time for this. Neither do you." He's frantic, hurried. It sounds like he's driving. "Aiden has been discharged from the hospital, and he's supposed to be staying at the Old Road Inn, but when we went there to talk to him, he wasn't there. I thought he might be with you. I—"

This time I'm the one to interrupt. "Why are you so worried about Aiden?"

"Listen, Krystal. I need you to trust me on this, okay? You just have to trust me. Can you do that?"

"I mean, I guess, yes, but what are you talking about?"

"Where are you?"

"I'm at my house."

"Is he there with you?"

"He just stopped by. He hasn't been here long," I add in case that matters.

"There's a strong possibility that Nichole has a good reason to be afraid of Aiden." He clears his throat. "Aiden might be a murderer, and if he's in your house, then I need you to get out of there now. Or get him out. Whatever you have to do, just stay away from him until we can bring him in for questioning."

He's talking too fast. He needs to slow down. I can't keep up. My knees go weak. I stumble backward onto my bed, taking a seat on the edge to steady myself. "What? I don't understand . . ."

"We've been looking into Aiden's affairs with other women, and today we learned that Aiden was having an affair with Marie Davenport." He says it like I should know who he's talking about, but my mind draws a blank.

"Who?"

"Marie Davenport. The woman from Cambria who was found murdered in the Walmart parking lot three weeks ago?"

His description immediately jars my memory. I didn't remember the name, but I remember the story. It was brutal. The poor woman had been stabbed twice in the stomach and bled out next to her car in the middle of a parking lot without anyone noticing anything. They found her body next to her bags of groceries, a puddle of spilled milk at her feet. Her car was parked too far away and out of the sight of any security cameras in the parking lot for anyone to see the attack. They didn't have any good leads on her killer, and the news anchors ran nightly stories for an entire week warning women to carry Mace whenever they were alone at night or by themselves.

Suddenly, I'm instantly aware of Aiden's presence in my house. That I'm not alone.

"Are they sure?" I whisper as I strain to hear if he's still in the kitchen or if he's moved to somewhere else in the house.

"That he killed her or that he was having an affair with her?"

"Both."

"He was definitely having an affair with her, and he was with her the night she died. He's on hotel cameras going in and out of her room. He might've been the last person to see her alive."

He's still talking fast. He hasn't slowed down. He needs to slow down.

"We discovered the connection between them this morning, and we considered the possibility that Nichole might have been involved, but all that went out the window when we learned that he has a history of violence against women. We subpoenaed all his business accounts, and they arrived yesterday. We found a large payment made to a personal account last year and traced the account to a woman in Maryland. Aiden met her on an anonymous-affair website, and she filed a police report against him after he allegedly choked her when she threatened to tell Nichole about their relationship. I spoke with her this evening, and she sounds like a credible witness. Everything she says checked out too. She dropped the charges and her threats after Aiden paid her twenty-five thousand dollars to keep quiet about it all. I've got a copy of the check deposit from her bank on my passenger seat."

My tongue sticks to the roof of my mouth. I can't swallow. He wouldn't. He couldn't. But up until yesterday morning, I would've bet my life on his being faithful to Nichole. My eyes are fixed on my bedroom door. I didn't lock it. I never lock it. I should get up and lock it.

"Krystal? Are you still there?"

Detective Sparks's voice reminds me that I'm still on the phone.

"Yes," I whisper into the phone, not because I think Aiden will hear me but because I'm too terrified to talk.

"You need to get him out of there, Krystal. He's dangerous."

Just then Aiden's voice calls out from down the hallway. "Hey, Krystal?"

"I have to go." I end the call without waiting for a response.

I stuff my phone into my back pocket like Aiden might come through the door at any second and I don't want him to know I've been talking to Detective Sparks. My eyes scan the room for a weapon, coming to land on my lamp. I jump to get it, then quickly stop myself. What am I doing? This is Aiden we're talking about.

In the next instant I realize I don't know anything about him. His affairs change everything, and he might as well be an alien. If he could live that kind of a double life, then he's capable of anything, right? Does that include murder? A brutal murder? What if it does? Oh my God, what if it does?

"Krystal?" Aiden calls again. His footsteps are coming down the hallway. "Is everything okay? Did something happen with Nichole?"

"Everything's fine. I'm in the bathroom!" I yell, trying to make myself sound farther away so that I can buy myself time to think. "It was just an emergency with one of my clients, but Mark is taking care of it." Everything is spinning. Nichole started losing touch with reality

207

a few days after Marie Davenport was stabbed. Was it because she found out Aiden killed her? I cover my mouth with my hand. I keep trying to swallow, but there's no spit. I can't breathe. These walls are paper thin. What if he heard me talking to Detective Sparks? What if he knows that I know?

I just have to go out there and ask him to leave. He can't be here. Not a second longer.

I force myself to move into the bathroom. I stick my head underneath the faucet and take a huge drink. I don't look in the mirror as I splash cold water on my face. I pull open my cabinet drawers and rummage through them, looking for something sharp. My only option is my nail tweezers. They're not much, but they'll hurt if I stab his eyes with them. I dry my face on the towel and take another three deep breaths to steady my racing heart.

I crack my bedroom door and peek out. There's a clear view all the way through to the living room and the front door. He's standing at the end of the hallway with his back turned to me, swaying side to side like he's trying to rock himself.

What am I doing? Aiden's not a murderer. But that doesn't stop me from gripping the tweezers in my hand as I walk down the hallway toward him. I stop halfway, keeping plenty of distance between us.

"I think it's time for you to leave." It takes great control to keep my tone even and calm.

He turns around immediately at the sound of my voice. He takes a step toward me, then stops.

"Are you okay?" he asks. "You look pale."

"I'm fine. Just tired." I don't break my gaze. Don't let him smell the fear. "It's been such a long day, and I really need to go to bed."

He stares at me, and I force myself to maintain eye contact. "Can we talk tomorrow?"

"Sure," I say quickly, nodding my agreement, hoping he doesn't see through me, but I can't read him. His eyes are tunnels without leads to follow. He settles something within himself and straightens up, heading to the door. My knees tremble while I walk. I follow behind him to the door like I always do so nothing seems unusual. He just needs to get out of my house.

"Thanks again for not telling Nichole."

I nod and open the door for him without saying a word. He throws a backward glance at me before heading out, and I force a smile. I turn the dead bolt as soon as he's gone and punch in my security code. I insisted on having my own security system in my unit even though the building already has one. I let out a huge sigh of relief as I lock myself inside, because the other thing I know about people like Aiden is that they don't do well when they're caught.

Dr. McGowan has said again and again that there's always a part of psychosis that's grounded in truth, and all I can think about as I stare at the locks on my door is that Nichole called Aiden a murderer. Maybe she's been right all along. It wouldn't be the first time she's tried to make a murderer pay for their sins.

THIRTY

NICHOLE

(THEN)

I straddle Veronica on the bed, gripping the pillow with both hands and smashing it over her face. Her screams are muffled as she kicks and flails her arms wildly, struggling against me. She's way stronger than I imagined, but she's no match for me. I wrestle with her body like I do the young bucks and press my forearm to her chest to keep her down.

Alice giggles and claps behind me. *"She can't breathe! She's totally suffocating!"*

Veronica scratches and claws at me, connecting with any part of my body she can reach. I try to block the blows, but some of them connect. Landing on my face, my chest, my arms. It's a struggle keeping her down. She twists and turns, bucking her hips and throwing me off balance. I stumble, loosening my hold. The pillow slips off her face.

"Mama!" Her scream is raspy, desperate. She tries to scramble off the bed, but I shove her back down.

"Stop it!" I yell, sobbing at the same time. I grab the pillow and fight against her as I try to press it on her again.

She moves her head side to side, making it difficult. "Please, Nichole, please, I'm sorry."

"Finish it."

I grab her hair with one hand, snapping her head back on the bed while my other hand grips the pillow.

"Do it!"

I let out a sob as I smush the pillow on her again, but I don't have a choice. Tears stream down my face. Snot bubbles from my nose. Veronica kicks her legs at me. Her arms flail everywhere, swatting at me, but I don't let go. I can't let go. One of her fists connects with my face, but I hold tight.

"What are you doing?" Krystal's voice cuts into the room. She grabs me from behind and throws me off Veronica. I stumble backward, crashing into the nightstand next to her bed. The lamp topples to the floor.

Veronica rolls off the bed and collapses on the floor, choking and gasping for breath. She gags and dry heaves onto the carpet. She does it again.

Krystal steps over her and grabs me, yanking me off the floor. She puts her hands on my shoulders and shakes me. "What are you doing, Nichole? What the hell are you doing?"

I can hardly speak through my heaving sobs. "Alice told me to do it. I didn't want to do it, Krystal. I swear. I didn't want to. But she said she'd hurt you if I didn't. I couldn't let her hurt you."

She releases me and steps back like she's in a trance. Something strange comes over her eyes. She kneels down next to Veronica and puts her arm around her.

"Are you okay?" she asks.

Veronica points a shaking finger at me. "Crazy bitch."

"Krystal? Please? Krystal? You have to understand. She said she'd hurt you if I didn't make Veronica pay. She said she had to pay. Please, I didn't have a choice." I grab her arm, and she flinches, pulling away from me like I'm going to hurt her, but I'd never hurt Krystal. Never. She doesn't understand. Why doesn't she understand? This was all for her. I had to keep her safe from Alice. "I was trying to protect you. I just wanted to protect you."

Mrs. Wheeler flings open the door and thunders into the room. She takes in the scene in one quick swoop before rushing over to help Veronica on the floor.

"What's going on in here?" she demands, as she brings Veronica next to her.

"She tried to kill me, Mama. She tried to suffocate me with a pillow," Veronica says breathlessly. Tears stream down her face. The front of her white nightgown is drenched in sweat.

"It almost worked. Next time it's going to."

"Shut up; be quiet," I hiss out of the corner of my mouth.

"You do what I say now. I'm the boss, remember? Do I have to remind you what happens if you don't?"

Mrs. Wheeler whips around to look at me. "Who are you talking to?"

I freeze. Don't speak. Don't move. Don't let anything come out.

She turns to Krystal, pointing to me. "Who is she talking to?"

Krystal frantically shakes her head. "Nothing. Don't worry about it. She wasn't talking to anybody."

Mrs. Wheeler gets up and takes a step in my direction.

"Ugly fat mama whore. Say it."

I cover my ears with both hands.

"SAY IT!"

"What's wrong with you?" Mrs. Wheeler asks, towering over me and peering at me with bulging angry eyes.

"Bug-eyes Beetlejuice." Alice giggles.

I hate her giggle more than her voice.

"Stop!" My scream shatters the air. Krystal rushes to my side, putting her body between mine and Mrs. Wheeler's.

"What's wrong with her?" Mrs. Wheeler points her question to Krystal.

Bugs are moving on my insides. Crawling inside and out of me like I'm dead grass. I need to move. Run. Run until it's done. Make her say she's sorry. That's all she wants. But I can't give her what she wants. Not until the nighttime passes.

"She's crazy! That's what's wrong with her!" Veronica yells, rising to her feet. "She came into my room, Mama! She came all the way into my room and tried to kill me while you were sleeping. She's a sick monster. Something's wrong with her. She was talking to Alice. She was. I heard her."

"Did you try to kill my baby?" Mrs. Wheeler's eyes are slits as she locks eyes with Krystal.

Krystal stands trembling in front of me.

"Not Krystal, Mama. Just Nichole. Krystal tried to save me."

Mrs. Wheeler flings Krystal aside. "You're gone, you little monster." She smacks me hard across the face. Krystal catches me as I stumble backward from the impact. "Tonight is the last night you spend under my roof."

THIRTY-ONE

KRYSTAL

Adrenaline and caffeine fuel me as I hold back the urge to sprint down the hospital corridor to the elevator. It's before eight, but Eric called and got permission for me to be on the unit this early to talk to Nichole. He also made sure that Aiden isn't allowed anywhere near her, and all the staff have been put on alert in case he tries to sneak onto the unit. Eric is in court all day, and it couldn't be worse timing given all that's happening, but he promised his partner would be available to help with any issues that come up. Detective Sparks and the investigators are bringing Aiden in for questioning today.

And not about Nichole.

Aiden is officially a person of interest in Marie Davenport's murder. I scoured the internet last night for information connecting the two of them but came up empty handed. I found her social media accounts, but they were all set to private, so the information was limited to her profile pics and basic information. The profile pics were useless since they weren't of her face, and all her page would tell me was that she was divorced and lived in northern Texas. She was a manager at an IT company and, from what I could gather, kept mostly to herself and traveled a lot. She was in Westchester on business. I couldn't find anything about her that the news hadn't already discovered and reported.

Aiden texted me nonstop until after three in the morning even though I never responded.

> Thank you so much for not telling Nichole today. Seriously, it meant a lot to me.

> I hope you're feeling better.

> We'll get through this.

And the one that made my skin crawl:

> #familyforever

That's when I turned his notifications off.

I went through all my texts and phone history last night to see if there was anything I missed the first time around. Nichole and I FaceTimed the day of Marie Davenport's murder, and Nichole seemed perfectly fine. She was going to the doctor's office and having lunch afterward with one of her students who was home from college on summer break. She even invited me to join, but I was too busy preparing for trial. She never would've done that if something was wrong. There were no signs of anything amiss, and I know what to look for. It took me years to stop watching her like a hawk for any sign of her mental health slipping. Just because we agreed not to talk about Alice ever again didn't mean I didn't examine Nichole for the slightest indication that she'd popped back into Nichole's life. There's no way she'd known about Aiden and Marie. The break had to have happened after. Did she find out Aiden was having an affair or that he was a murderer? Could it have been both?

Nichole is in the community room waiting for me when I get onto the unit, and she gets up at the sight of me. She gives me a huge hug when I reach her. Her body feels stronger against mine.

"You look pretty awful," she says, and it's the first time she's noticed anything about me since she got to the hospital. It's so good to slowly be getting her back.

"I didn't sleep at all last night."

I jumped at every sound, convinced every creak or strange noise was Aiden breaking into my condo. It didn't make any logical sense, since my condo is on the second floor and he'd have to get buzzed in at the lobby first or scale the building to get to me, but it didn't stop the fear. I tossed and turned for hours before finally giving up on the idea of sleep at three.

We take our seats at the table. Her eyes flit around the room. I nod a quick hello to Derek before turning my attention back to Nichole. I'll be happy when she gets rid of her shadow. Dr. McGowan said it should be soon. Maybe even today.

I pull my chair closer to hers so that he can't overhear. "Are you remembering anything else?"

"A little bit, but not really. Nothing is in order or together. It's hard to explain." Her forehead lines with concentration like she's admonishing herself to think harder but coming up short. She shifts in her chair to face me. "I think I might remember parts about the night of the fire, though. Like I remember the smoke and how hard it was to breathe. And coughing. Lots of coughing." She pauses for a second, her eyes scanning the room to make sure nobody is listening. "And there's this strange image I kept seeing while I was falling asleep last night of me pushing the desk in the entryway in front of our bedroom door. Isn't that weird?"

My stomach rolls. Part of me is still holding out hope that it's all a mistake despite how the facts are lining up. Her happily ever after was partly mine, too, and it's all been stripped away. "The desk was pushed against the bedroom door to keep Aiden inside." There's no use keeping the truth from her.

Her eyes grow wide with horror. "Did I try to kill him?"

"I think you did," I say, as the full reality crashes over us like a heavy wave.

She brings her hand up to her mouth. "Oh my God. Why would I do that?"

Because Aiden is a disgusting pig and an entitled man that hurts women to get them to behave—but I can't say that. It will crush her. Eventually, the full story will come out, but now isn't the time. One step at a time.

"I don't know. There's not anything else you remember?" Her memory is delicate, and I don't want to plant any false ideas.

Confusion wrinkles her expression as she tries to pull memories from somewhere deep in her brain and put the pieces together. "No, just the yelling and the screaming that I was telling you about yesterday."

The other patients start filing into the room, and a cafeteria worker arrives with the breakfast cart. The rustle of activity throws off her concentration for a second.

"You need to eat," I remind her, feeling silly for bringing up food at a time like this, but she's going to need her strength to get through this. "We can talk while you eat."

She gets her tray and brings it to the table. She sets it down in front of her but doesn't take any of the covers off the food. She takes a small sip of the orange juice. I reach over and uncover her main plate. There are two pancakes, scrambled eggs, and a small fruit bowl, but she turns her nose up at it and puts the cover back on.

"And you're sure Aiden didn't hurt you?"

Her eyes get that faraway look in them again, and I want to crawl inside her head to see what's there. Pull out the important parts and put together the pieces of her fractured psyche.

"I don't think so," she says, like she's not sure. "I guess he could have, though. Anything could've happened." Her lower lip quivers. She looks like she's going to break into tears at any second. "What's going to happen to me?"

"You're going to do like you've always done," I say with determination. "You're going to get through this and rebuild a new life. A different life. A better one."

The tears flood her cheeks. "But this was my new life. I loved my life."

My heart breaks for her all over again. I take her into my arms and hold her against me. She cries silently on my chest, and I don't let her go until the tears pass. We sit staring at her food once she's finished, trying to wrap our brains around what to do next, but I don't have a plan. I've never not had a plan.

———

A hand grips my shoulder from behind as I open my car door in the hospital parking lot. I turn around, coming face to face with Aiden. I smash into the door behind me, flattening myself against it, but I'm trapped.

"Get away from me before I scream," I say, frantically looking around to see if anyone is close. Where are the parking lot cameras? Are they getting this?

Something hard presses into my side. "No, you're not. You're going to get in the car and not say a word."

He's got a gun. Aiden has a gun.

My bowels almost release onto the concrete. Blood rushes through my head. My pulse pounds. Scream. Yell. Kick. Do something—anything. I'm frozen to my spot.

"Get in," he hisses, pushing the gun against me to move me into the car.

My head spins. Someone has to be watching. It's broad daylight. *Help me.* I want to yell, but the words can't get past my lips.

"Don't make this any more difficult than it needs to be. I don't want to hurt you, Krystal." His voice is even, calm.

I'm shaking so hard my teeth chatter. I can't feel my legs.

He gives me a shove, and I stumble into the driver's seat.

"Give me your keys," he orders. I've never heard him speak like this before.

My keys? Don't give him my keys. Where are they? He grabs my wrist and forces my fingers open, revealing the fob in my hand. He takes it from my palm.

"Move over. I'm driving," he says, like we're going on one of our Sunday-afternoon drives in the country.

I scramble over to the passenger side while he slides into the driver's seat. I grab the handle and ram my shoulder against my door, trying to get away, but he's locked it with the fob.

He grabs my arm and yanks me back. "Don't even think about it. Please, don't be difficult, Krystal."

"Don't be difficult? You have a gun!" I shriek, finding my voice at last. Terror pulses through every word.

"Would you be in this car with me otherwise?" he asks as he puts the car into reverse and pulls out of the parking lot. He keeps his eyes focused on the road. One hand grips the wheel. The other hand holds the gun on his thigh.

I can't take my eyes off it. When did Aiden get a gun? My heart races. Pulse pounds. Everything moves in slow motion as we make our way onto the street. I want to yell or scream for help, but the gun keeps me quiet and in my place. Everything I've ever been taught about self-defense or what to do in this situation flies out of my head.

"Where are we going? Where are you taking me?" I cry, sounding like a little girl.

He says nothing. His eyes remain on the road. He's in the same clothes he was wearing when he left my house last night, which means he's probably been up all night. He works his jaw like a meth addict on a binge. His face is clammy with sweat. His dank smell fills the car, mixing with the scent of my fear.

He takes a left out of the hospital complex and proceeds down Fifth Avenue until he gets to the second light. A right would take him in the direction of my house, but he makes another left instead.

"Aiden, stop. Where are we going? Where are you taking me?" I ask again, like maybe he didn't hear me the first time, but he ignores me the second time too.

Could I jump out of the car? Should I pitch myself out the next time he stops? What if I break the window? We're moving down the street like nothing is wrong, and I want to bang on the windows for someone to help me, but I can't take the chance. He's already killed one woman.

"Whatever you're doing, Aiden, you don't have to do it. There are other ways," I say, starting to cry. "Please, let's just talk about it."

He shakes his head. "I tried talking to you last night, but you wouldn't listen. This is the only way to get you to listen."

I ferociously shake my head. "No, that's not true. I want to hear what you have to say. You didn't have to do this. You don't have to do this."

He lets out a sinister laugh. "Don't treat me like I'm dumb."

I break into heaving sobs. I can't help myself. They come in huge hiccuping waves. My entire body trembles. I want to throw up.

We drive on in silence. It doesn't take me long to figure out we're headed toward his and Nichole's house. He makes the turns down the necessary blocks until he pulls up in front of their two-story colonial. The yellow police tape still encircles the property.

"Here's how it's going to go." He shuts the car off and turns to me. "You're going to get out of this car without saying a word and come with me into the house. If you scream or do anything"—he lifts the gun from his thigh—"I'm pulling the trigger."

He opens the door, and I'm shaking so hard I can barely walk up the driveway. He puts his arm around me and helps me to the house like I'm sick or hurt and too weak to make it on my own. I should bite his arm. Kick out his legs. Scratch his eyes out.

But I do nothing because of the gun. All I can think about is the gun. He tucked it into the back of the waistband of his jeans like he's been packing for years. Who is this man?

He moves my body into the house. I don't dare look over my shoulders, but I'm hoping their busybody neighbor, Edith, is watching out of her living room window. They've complained about her since they moved in because she's in everyone's business. Please let her be peeking through the windows now. This doesn't look normal. It can't look normal. Please let her call the police.

Dread fills me as Aiden closes the front door behind him and blocks it with his body. Their house is as familiar to me as mine, but now it's like walking onto another planet. Nothing feels familiar. Most of the furniture has been removed since I was here. The pungent smell of sulfur fills my nostrils and turns my stomach. It's everywhere, clinging to me as I try to breathe.

"I hope you know that I didn't want to do this, but you didn't leave me any other choice."

Anger burns my insides. How dare he make this about me?

"You always have a choice," I snap.

"Let's go upstairs." He motions to the stairs, but I refuse to move. I'm not going anywhere with him.

"Why are you doing this, Aiden?"

He ignores my question and pushes me to the stairs. "Move."

"Aiden, please, no," I cry, terrified that if I go up those stairs I'll never come back down. "Please. It's me."

"I'm not going to hurt you. I was never going to hurt you. I just needed to get you here. It was the only way I could talk to you, make you see what needs to be done."

I don't believe him. If that were the case, then why is he still holding on to me so tightly? Why is the barrel of the gun pressed against my back?

"Then, let me go," I say.

He shakes his head. "I can't do that."

"You can, Aiden. This doesn't have to get any worse."

"You don't understand, Krystal."

"Then make me understand."

"Okay, but you have to come upstairs. I need to show you something, and then I'll tell you everything, but you have to come upstairs." He shoves me forward. "Don't make this hard."

His presence looms behind me as we go upstairs. I could kick him backward, send him flying down the stairs, but I would still have to hurdle him and make it out the door without him catching me. He's in much better shape, and I don't stand a chance at beating him to the door even if I do catch him off guard and send him flying down the stairs. I trudge up as cold fear settles into the pit of my stomach.

The smell of smoke grows stronger and stronger as we reach the landing. The door to their master bedroom is gone, and I see right through into the charred remains. He doesn't take us into the bedroom but moves us down the hallway on the left to the guest bedroom—the one I sleep in whenever I stay overnight. I picked out the platform bed frame and the Anthropologie drapes. He throws me into the bedroom and slams the door behind me before I have a chance to react. He grunts as he moves something in front of the door to lock me inside.

I race to the windows and scan outside, still not giving up hope that Edith spotted us and called the police because we looked suspicious.

"Help! Help!" I beat on the window with my fists.

The street is silent and empty below me. Everyone's tucked inside their houses, but it won't be long until someone walks down the sidewalk. Their neighborhood is always filled with joggers and people taking walks since their community is so beautiful. I keep scanning the street for any sign of life.

Aiden returns within seconds. He grabs me and pulls me away from the window. "What are you doing?" he asks, like it isn't obvious. I glare at him. He's holding a beat-up cardboard box that he hands to me. "Here."

I don't want to take it, but I don't have a choice.

"Open it," he says as I stand holding it like it's a bomb that might go off any second. I shake my head. "Do it."

His eyes bore into me as I lift the top flaps, my hands shaking with fear. The inside is filled with old notebook papers and newspaper clippings. All of them are worn and wrinkled. I raise my eyes to meet his.

"Just look through it," he says, and then purses his lips in a straight line.

I slowly walk to the bed and set the box on it, never taking my eyes off him. I pull out the newspaper clipping on top of the pile. The edges are torn. The print is faded and blurry, but there's no mistaking the headline:

16-Year-Old Vernon Girl Dies in Farm Accident

My stomach leaps into my throat.

"I know all about you two," he says as I raise my eyes to meet his.

THIRTY-TWO

NICHOLE

(THEN)

Krystal jiggles my arm, and I snap awake. She puts her fingers to her lips and points to the window. She hands me the clothes I wore yesterday.

"Hurry," she mouths.

I quietly move out of bed and take my clothes from her. I slip out of my pajamas and into my jeans. She hands me my backpack when I'm done. Hers is strapped to her back. She's serious and focused as she tugs open our bedroom window and motions for me to go first. I hop through easily, and she tumbles out next. She pulls the window down when she's through, clicking it shut behind her.

"Hey, you just—" But my words stop as I realize what's happening. We're not going back inside, so it doesn't matter that she just locked us out. She gives me a knowing look before taking off across the grass. I hurry along after her, shooting glances over my shoulder to see if Veronica or Mrs. Wheeler is following us, straining for the sound of Alice waking up. She's still sleeping. Thank God. I enjoy the moments when she's not yammering in my ear.

"Where are we going?" I whisper as we make our way across the yard.

She doesn't look at me or answer. Just marches down to the driveway and heads to Mrs. Wheeler's red Ford truck. My eyes widen in shock and surprise. We've never stolen the truck. We've talked about it plenty of times, but we've never done it. We've been hot-wiring tractors for years, though, so hopefully all the practice pays off. She opens the driver's side door and tosses her backpack inside the cab. I chuck mine in with hers. I'm expecting to crouch next to the steering column and twist the wires together since I'm better at hot-wiring than her, but Krystal pulls the keys out of her jean shorts pocket. She holds them up in front of me.

"You got the keys?" I ask.

She nods. "But we're not starting the truck until we get to the road. I don't want them to hear it and wake up before we're out of here."

"Then, what are we going to do?"

"We're going to put it in neutral and push it."

"Ourselves?"

She nods.

"All the way down the driveway?"

She nods again.

Our driveway is almost a quarter mile long. That's like pushing a truck three football fields. I don't know how we're going to do it with only the two of us, since someone needs to steer while the other pushes and the truck is super heavy, but I step inside the driver's seat anyway because I don't want to waste time. Krystal moves to the front of the truck and places both her hands on the hood. She braces herself, ready to push.

I adjust the wheel so it's easier to keep the truck on the driveway and moving backward in a straight line. I press my foot on the clutch and shift the truck into neutral. With one hand on the wheel and the other on the door to keep it open, I step out of the pickup to help push. I nod at Krystal, and together we shove it backward. The truck makes a small lurch, then starts slowly rolling backward. Thankfully, our driveway is on a slope.

Our pace is painstakingly slow. I have to keep getting back in the truck to straighten the wheel and keep it in neutral. We're covered in sweat within minutes. Krystal's forehead is lined with exertion. We're nearing the end of the driveway and almost ready to get in when Veronica steps out of the shadows.

"What are you doing?" she demands, even though it's obvious.

I freeze in place. My hands clutch the wheel. I lock eyes with Krystal. Her eyes are terror filled. We almost made it. Hope sinks in my chest.

Veronica places her hands on her hips and shakes her head. "You're not going anywhere."

"We're leaving," Krystal says at the same time as me.

Veronica shakes her head. "Absolutely not. I'm telling Mama that you're leaving and stealing the truck."

"Go ahead," I say, pointing to the house in the distance. "By the time you get there, we'll be long gone."

I'm not sure about that. She's a slow runner, and we'll be in the truck driving by then, but Mrs. Wheeler will call the police. We won't get far if that happens.

Before I have time to think, Krystal rushes around the truck and jumps in on the passenger side. She grabs me and pulls me into the truck with her. She sticks the key in the ignition while I slam my door.

"Drive!" Krystal yells.

I put the truck in first gear and turn the key. The engine roars to life. Veronica runs to the back of the truck and stands in the middle of the driveway, blocking our path. She spreads her arms out wide, making herself as big as possible.

"What do I do? What do I do?" I ask, frantically looking in the rearview mirror filled with Veronica's face and outstretched arms.

"Just go!"

I twist the steering wheel, making a sharp right and whipping it around. Veronica grabs the tailgate and jumps in the truck bed. She holds on to the sides as I make the full circle and peel out onto the driveway. I make a quick right at the end of it. My hands clutch the wheel, and I slam the gas pedal to the floor. The truck thunders down the gravel road.

"What are we going to do, Krystal?" I shriek, flicking on the headlights before I hit anything.

"Shit! Shit! Shit!" Krystal punches the dashboard.

"Push her out. Get out there and push her out."

"I'm not pushing her out!" I yell.

"I didn't tell you to push her out," Krystal cries, but I'm not talking to her.

Gravel crunches underneath our tires as we pass the Pattersons' farm. I swerve to avoid a raccoon, narrowly missing the ditch before pitching us back onto the road. Shadows dance across the headlights.

"Where am I going? What am I doing?" I scream as we fly down the road.

"Turn left!" Krystal screeches.

Veronica stands in the back, gripping onto the cab with one hand as she tries to work the rear windows to slide them open so that she can crawl in with us.

"She's trying to get inside!"

"Just turn!" Krystal yells.

"Push her out. Push her out. Push her out."

"STOP IT!" I scream, slamming on the brakes, making the truck skid and fishtail wildly. Veronica's body hurtles over the windshield, crashes onto the hood, and tumbles onto the road as we come to a screeching halt.

"Agh!" Krystal howls.

"Ohmigod, ohmigod, ohmigod." I pound the steering wheel with my hands.

But Krystal's frozen in place. She's gotten us this far, but she's stuck. I fling open the metal door and step outside the truck. Dust from the gravel is kicked up everywhere. My headlights shine down the empty road. Veronica's facedown on the road, arms straight out in front of her. I walk slowly toward her. Shouldn't she be moaning or crying out?

"Please don't let her be dead. Please don't let her be dead," I whisper, waiting for Alice to yell in my ear, but she's silent.

I kneel next to her.

"Veronica?" Her body is still, motionless. I wiggle her shoulder. "Veronica?" I say it louder.

Nothing.

I gingerly take her head and turn it to the side, terrified to look, but I have to help her. The skin on her right cheek is stripped raw, the dark-pink flesh pitted with dirt. Gravel is shoved up her nose. Her lower lip is gone. Blood drains from both ears, but it's her eyes that send ice-cold shock through my body. I know the look in her eyes—it's the same one in Alice's the night she died.

Krystal steps into the light. Her eyes are wide and panicked. She reads the fear in my face. Her breath comes in ragged bursts. She crouches next to me, feeling along Veronica's neck for a pulse.

I put my hand up to my mouth. "What did I do?" I burst into an anguished sob. "What did I do?" I clutch my stomach, doubled over.

Krystal jumps to her feet. "Nothing. You didn't do anything, Nichole. She's still breathing."

I drop to my knees and put my fingers on her neck in the same way Krystal just did. There's a faint pulse underneath my fingertips. "We have to get her help." My eyes scan the darkness. The truck engine roars behind us.

"We have to get out of here," Krystal says, eyes wide.

"But we can't do that. She needs help. She might die if we leave her here." My head is spinning. There's a ringing in my ears that won't stop. My heartbeat pounds in my chest.

"We can't stay, Nichole. Nobody is ever going to believe that this was an accident. Another accident in such a short time? Think about it. They'll pin Alice's death on us. Mrs. Wheeler will make sure of it, and she'll make them think we tried to kill Veronica too. You know she will. She's probably already called the police, and if she hasn't, she's going to as soon as she finds out we stole the truck. She'll never believe us. Nobody will."

The mention of Mrs. Wheeler fills me with new terror and adrenaline. She could be right behind us on the ATV. What if she brings the shotgun?

"Krystal, go. Get out of here." I point to the driver's seat in the truck. "We'll get her off the road together, and then you leave. Run away from this place. I'll wait for help to come."

"What? No." She shakes her head like a mad dog. "I won't leave you here. Absolutely not. You're coming with me."

"I don't want anybody else to die. Please. Just go." I clutch my sides as my shoulders shake with sobs. "There's been enough pain. No more."

Krystal puts her arm around my shoulders. "Exactly—no more. It's over, and we're leaving. We're going to get Veronica off the road, and then we're going to get back inside the cab and drive. We're going to drive until we can't drive any further. And this?" She makes a swooping motion behind her. "It's done. It's over. Do you hear me, Nichole? It's over."

I'm crying so hard I can barely breathe. I just want it to be over. All of it. *Please let it be over.* I'm sobbing too hard to talk, so I nod my consent instead.

Krystal locks eyes with me, and we work together without speaking like we've done thousands of times over the years. Every second matters. Our thoughts meld into one as Krystal grabs Veronica's ankles, and I move to take both her wrists but stop short because one of them is definitely broken. It's bent, and a bone protrudes through the skin. Bile rises in my throat, and I swallow it down. I take one of her wrists and grab the other arm by her elbow.

"One. Two. Three," Krystal counts down, and we lift her mangled body off the gravel. She swings in our hands, deadweight. We almost drop her.

We carry her across the road in shuffling steps and over to the shoulder. We walk a few paces into the ditch, making sure she's far enough away from the road so that there's no chance of a car hitting her but not in the ditch where nobody can see her, before Krystal nods at me to lay her down. I'm careful and cautious as we lower her body to the ground so we don't hurt her any more than she already is. Her body is twisted and crumpled like a deer that's been hit by a car. She stirs, and her eyelids flutter like she might be waking up. There's no time to think or second-guess our decision. Krystal and I bolt to the truck, scrambling to get back inside. She jumps into the driver's seat, and I jump in on the passenger side. She shifts the truck into gear, and we peel out, gravel flying behind us.

I keep my eyes forward. I don't look back.

THIRTY-THREE

KRYSTAL

"What is this?" I ask when I finally get the courage to speak.

"Keep looking." Aiden crosses his arms on his chest like he has all day to wait. "See for yourself."

I rummage through the box, pulling out letter after letter addressed to Alice. All of them are handwritten in Nichole's loopy scrawl that I'd recognize anywhere. They date all the way back to our days in Gulfport, Mississippi. I have to skim read them because there're so many that it'd take hours to get through them all. The messages are almost identical in each one, no matter what the time stamp on top is.

> I'm so sorry that you had to die. Please forgive me.
>
> I would do anything to go back and save you. There are so many things I would've done differently that night.
>
> You were too young to die. You had your entire life ahead of you. I'd give mine up so that you could have yours if there was a way. I promise you that. I'm so sorry.

She goes through every detail of that awful night every time she writes her a letter, like the retelling of it will somehow end in a different outcome. There's a card for every birthday Alice would've had—more than twenty of them—and she puts each one in an envelope with an address and a stamp, like someday she'll mail them and they'll find their way to heaven. There are even a few letters to Alice's parents. My hand goes to my mouth as I delve into her unrelenting pain and sorrow. She goes to incredible lengths describing her guilt and how it eats away at her; that she'll never truly be happy despite the smile she wears on her face for everyone else to see. Tears fall unbidden down my cheeks.

"I had no idea," I say through my tears, finally looking up even though I haven't gotten through half of what's inside the box. How did she keep her pain from me all these years? Was she ever happy? Were any of the moments we shared together real?

"I had the same reaction." Aiden's eyes are wet too. "I found it a few years ago when I was moving offices in the house. She hid it in one of the cabinets in the back of the file closet. That's actually where it still is."

"What did she say when you talked to her about it?" My brain scrambles to make sense of what I've just read, everything that's just happened, why he's showing it to me now.

"That's the thing. I never told her I found it."

"You didn't?"

"I figured if she wanted me to know, then she would've told me about it, and it just seemed so incredibly personal, you know? It was like I had read her diary, and I didn't want to be that guy. Besides, we all have our secrets. She had hers, and I had mine." The mention of his secret darkens his face and his mood. He walks over to the bed, and I flinch, scurrying to the other end, still afraid of him. He takes the gun out of the back of his waistband and hands it to me like a peace offering. "Here."

I eye him quizzically, like he's baiting me in some way, but I can't figure out why or for what. Nothing makes sense. I take the gun from him even though I don't want to touch it. I'm terrified of guns. I've never touched one, even though Mrs. Wheeler had a .22-caliber shotgun on the farm that she used to shoot any wandering rodent that came in the yard.

"Clear the chamber," he orders.

"I have no idea how to use a gun."

He takes the gun back from me. He points the muzzle to the ground and places his hand on the grip of the gun without putting his finger on the trigger. He presses a button on the side, and the magazine pops out. He hands the magazine to me. Relief moves throughout my entire body now that it's not loaded, and as I look at the magazine, I discover that it never was.

"There're no bullets inside," I say in shock and surprise.

"I'm a cheater, but I'm not a murderer." He tosses the gun on the bed and raises his hands in a peaceful gesture. "I told you I couldn't hurt you, and I meant it, Krystal. In the same way that I could never hurt Nichole. But you didn't leave me any other choice. Detective Sparks told me he spoke to you about me being a suspect in Marie's murder and that he'd warned you to stay away from me, so I knew you'd never come with me on your own. This was the only way I could get you here and to understand what needs to be done."

"There're always choices, even if you don't like them." My sadness rockets to anger in seconds. "And what are you talking about? There's nothing that needs to be done. You've done enough. More than enough."

"Just hear me out, okay?" He doesn't wait for me to answer, knowing full well that if he does, I might get up and walk out of the room, never coming back. "We have to work as a team if we're going to help Nichole."

"What do you mean?" What else does he know? Is there more that Nichole hid from me? From him?

"Can I trust you? I mean really trust you?" His eyes probe mine.

"Trust me?" I snort. "Are you kidding me?"

"I'm serious. Anything I did to Nichole, I did to protect her. Every single thing was to keep her safe. It might not look like it, but it was."

"What did you do?" My stomach rolls. I don't know if I can handle any more news.

"I didn't kill Marie Davenport, no matter what it looks like or what the investigators are saying. You have to believe me on that." His eyes are desperate, pleading.

I'm not sure what I believe. He's a liar. Nichole's a liar. And I'm one too. We all are.

"Somehow Nichole found out about Marie even though I always cover my tracks. I—"

"Wait," I interrupt him. "Was she a one-night stand or someone you were seeing for a while?"

Our conversation about the details of his affair got derailed by Detective Sparks's call last night, and we never got to this part.

"I don't have relationships with other women. Only sex." He shakes his head like he's disgusted by the insinuation that he had a mistress.

I can't believe that insults him. Like just having sex is okay, but having a relationship crosses some invisible line of faithfulness? I shove my anger down and focus on what's important. "So how long?"

"A couple years."

That sounds like a relationship to me, but I don't say that to him. "How'd you meet her?"

"Is all this really important?"

"Yes, Aiden. Every detail is important, especially considering she's dead." I glare at him, annoyed and angry that he'd give me any kind of attitude after he just used a gun to force me into his house.

"Well, I don't usually hook up with anyone that I work with since it makes things so messy, but I made an exception for her." His burned face lines with regret.

It's the first hint of emotion he's shown over the fact that the woman he was sleeping with is dead, but I'm not sure if it's over her or because he got caught and screwed up his entire life. How was I so blind to how selfish he is?

"I don't know how Nichole found out about her, but she did. I never in a million years would've thought Nichole was capable of snapping like she did, but you never know how people are going to react to things. I wouldn't have believed it myself if I didn't see the condition she came home in that night." He shakes his head like he still can't believe it.

"The condition she came home in that night?" Alarm bells go off inside me. "What night?"

He looks me square in the eye. "The night Marie Davenport died."

All the air is sucked from the room. There's a long silence while we stare at each other, waiting for the other person to make the next move. I let out a shuddering breath before finally asking the only question that really matters.

"What happened that night?" I want to get up and run out before he answers, but I'm glued to the bed. Every awful truth has to come out.

"I came home around seven, and Nichole was gone. I hadn't heard from her all day, and I texted her about dinner, but she never responded. You know how she is about dinner, so I knew something weird was happening, but I didn't think it was that big of a deal. Sometimes she forgets to tell me things. It wasn't until nine o'clock rolled around and I still hadn't heard from her that I started getting nervous. That's when I started blowing up her phone, but she didn't respond to any of my texts or voice mails. Her phone just went straight to voice mail. I even texted you to see if she was with you, remember?"

I nod. I saw those exchanges last night when I went through my phone again. I didn't think anything of it at the time because it wasn't unusual for him to text me looking for Nichole, since she was always letting her phone die.

"I moved into panic mode when she wasn't home by eleven and was debating whether or not I should call the police when she stumbled through the door around midnight. She was half-crazed and covered in blood. Her hands. Her face. Her clothes. Even her shoes. All she kept saying was that she didn't mean to do it. She was shaking and pacing all over the house, clawing at her skin like she wanted to rip it off. I kept asking her what she'd done, but she wouldn't answer me. Not at first. She just kept crying and crying. I suppose she was in shock too. Then, she started screaming that we needed to go to the police and tell them what she'd done. That she'd killed Marie. She kept saying it was an accident—just like Alice."

The enormity of his disclosure pummels me like I've been punched in the chest. I press both hands to the mattress because it feels like I'll fall off if I don't hold myself in place. Everything spins, then stills. Goes fuzzy, then becomes laser focused.

"You're saying Nichole killed Marie Davenport?"

"That's exactly what I'm saying."

My blood runs cold.

"Shut up—that's not true. No. Just no." I leap from the bed, pacing the room back and forth, shaking my head over and over again.

"Just sit back down." He motions to the bed, but I won't sit. I can't sit. I need to move. Run. Get away from here. From him. From this. From the story coming out of his mouth. But he won't stop. "She kept saying that she stabbed Marie, but she didn't mean to kill her. Just punish her for ruining her life. Honestly, I don't know what happened in the moment between the two of them in the parking lot, but I do know that Nichole stabbed her."

I whip around to face him. "How do you know that for sure?"

"She used our kitchen knife. It was still in her purse."

"Oh my God. Oh my God." My mind races in a hundred different directions.

"So, that's why you have to help me." He grabs my arms, standing in front of me. His eyes have never been so serious. "We have to protect her, Krystal. It's what I've been doing all along."

"What do you mean?" I can't comprehend what he's saying. It won't fit in my head.

"She snapped when she found out I betrayed her, and who could blame her after what I'd done?" His shoulders hang low with the weight of his shame. "She didn't deserve to be punished from my crimes. So, I got her calmed down enough to get into the bath, and I cleaned her up. The first thing I did was get rid of all the evidence. I took the knife and—"

I raise both hands. "Stop right there. Don't tell me any more about what you did to the evidence. I don't want to know." Is he telling the truth? What if this is just another one of his dirty tricks? A way to shift the blame away from him and onto Nichole?

"Right, right." He nods. "I suppose the less you know about those details, the better. Anyway, I told her that I'd take care of everything, and that's when I decided that I had to protect her no matter what."

"How in the world did you protect her? She's been locked in a psych ward for over a week, and she's being charged with attempted murder and arson. Her brain might be permanently broken. That hardly seems like protecting her."

"Don't you see? That's exactly what I wanted to happen. It was all part of my plan. I made her crazy. Granted, I had no idea that she would get as sick as she did or turn against me. I didn't expect that. Definitely never imagined that she'd try to burn our house down with me in it." He lets out a bitter laugh. "I never saw that one coming."

"I don't understand. You made her sick? You did this to her?"

He nods, looking pleased with himself. There's not an ounce of shame or regret on his face. "I started giving her Benadryl that night and increased the dosage over the next couple of days. I—"

"But she's allergic to Benadryl," I interrupt before quickly realizing that's exactly why he gave it to her.

He was with us in Hawaii when she broke out in hives from something in the water. She'd never had any kind of allergic reaction before, so we gave her two Benadryls to calm the itching. It cleared up her hives, but it was like we'd given her a line of coke. She wouldn't stop talking in this high-pressured way, and all her movements were spastic. She kept saying it felt like bugs were crawling all over her body. He called her primary doctor back home, and he determined Nichole was having a rare allergic reaction to Benadryl. He told us to monitor her through the night and to take her to the clinic in the morning if she wasn't better. At her follow-up once she got home, her doctor warned her to refrain from any antihistamine use because it could trigger a similar allergic reaction and result in worse hallucinations and mania.

"Why would you do that?" Horror rises up the lower part of my stomach and moves into my throat.

"Because, Krystal, it's like I told you. It was only a matter of time before the police made the connections between our lives, and I couldn't let her go to jail. I just couldn't, not on account of me. It never would've happened if she hadn't found out about me. I had to help her, and there are very few ways to get away with murder once you've been caught, but the insanity defense is always a strong contender."

I walk over to the window, dazed. My brain swings between adrenalized denial and overwhelming sadness. Edith sits on her front porch, scanning the neighborhood for any sign of trouble, but I don't need help anymore. Nichole does.

"All of the stuff I told you about her being terrified of me and locking herself in her room? I didn't make that up. It was true. All of it. But I swear, Krystal, I only did it to keep her out of prison. I just couldn't stand the thought of her being locked up after everything she's been through and having to live with the fact that my stupid actions put her there."

I slowly turn around. "I still don't understand. Even if the police found out about your affair, it's not like they'd immediately jump to one of you murdering her, especially if there's no proof."

He hurries over to me. "But there is. That's the thing."

"What else is there?"

"The car," he announces like I should've already known. "There was as much blood in the car as there was on her. I did everything I could to clean it, but do you know how hard it is to clean up blood?" Sadly, I do, and it only takes him a second to realize it too. "You have to help me figure out what to do about the car."

I blink, confused. "You used a gun to get me into your house so that you could talk me into . . . what? Getting rid of her car?"

He nods, as if that should be clear and there's nothing wrong with what he's done. There's so much wrong with what he's done I don't even know where to start. Not to mention that I'm not even sure I believe him about Nichole. Is he trying to cover up his tracks or hers?

"And just what exactly did you have in mind?" And why can't he just do it himself? Why do I have to be involved? His logic doesn't add up.

"I thought maybe you could take it. You know, just get it out of here," he says, like it's that simple.

"Are you serious? And do what?"

"I don't know. That's what we've got to figure out. We've got to make sure all our bases are covered. Whatever we have to do to protect her."

"Protect her or protect you?"

He recoils like I've slapped him. "Are you for real?"

"I'm sorry if I'm having a hard time believing that my sister, who was racked with guilt for over twenty years about an accidental death, would turn around and murder her husband's mistress." I cock my head to the side. "Doesn't really make sense, does it?"

"Oh my God, you still think I killed her." He clenches his fists at his side.

The only thing I have to go on is his word, and that doesn't mean anything to me anymore. I need to talk to the only person whose word I truly trust. Pain squeezes my chest as the realization hits me that it's no longer true. Nichole hid her most intimate parts from me.

"I was afraid you might say that. I was hoping it wouldn't come to this." He points to the box sitting on the bed. "Listen to me, Krystal, and listen to me carefully. If you don't help me and work with me on this, I'm taking this box and everything that's inside it to the police. What do you think the state bar will think when they find out you've been covering up a murder since you were seventeen? Or that you left another girl practically dead on the side of the road?" I quickly snatch the box from the bed and hug it close to me. He raises his eyebrows and sneers. "You think I need what's in there to prove my case? I already made copies of the most important stuff, especially how you made Nichole keep everything quiet."

"I don't care if you tell the police. Go ahead. I'll take my chances." I can't stay in this room with him a minute longer. I move to leave, and he grabs my arm, spinning me around.

"Where are you going?" he demands.

"Where do you think I'm going? I need to talk to Nichole."

"You can't tell her any of this." His fingers dig into me. "It'll ruin everything."

"Get off me," I say, jerking my arm away. "Give me my keys."

"Krystal, please. I'm sorry. Don't leave. We have to talk about this." He quickly rearranges his face to look soft and kind, putting on the right mask to get what he wants.

"I don't have anything left to say to you. Now, give me my keys." Rage surges through me at everything he's done, all that's happened. I've had enough.

He reaches into the pocket of his jeans and pulls them out, but he doesn't give them to me. "We can't let her go to jail. Think about what that will do to her. Please, we have to protect her. You can't tell her anything. Not what I did—not what she did. None of it."

"Give me my keys," I say through gritted teeth, balancing the box on my hip.

He reluctantly drops them into my hand and follows me out the bedroom door.

"Please, Krystal. Please." He sounds like a wounded puppy. He looks like one too.

I throw an angry glance over my shoulder at him. "Maybe it's time we stopped interfering in Nichole's life and started letting her make decisions for herself."

THIRTY-FOUR

NICHOLE

(THEN)

My eyes burn as I watch the sun peek over the horizon. We've been driving all night. Neither of us has our license, but we've got lots of practice driving the truck. The inside of the cab smells like the farm. There's no air-conditioning, so my legs stick to the seats. I'm scared to move or do anything in case I wake Alice. That's what it feels like—that she's sleeping and at any minute she's going to wake up and start yelling at me again. She hasn't said a word since we left Veronica on the side of the road. Krystal won't let me drive. She insists on doing it herself. I think she's afraid Alice is going to come back, too, but maybe she's going to be silent now that she finally got what she wanted.

I'm not sure which scares me more—Alice, Mrs. Wheeler, or the police—since I'm pretty sure they're all searching for us by now. We're going to ditch the truck once we hit the Missouri state line. Krystal's eyes are glued on the road in front of us, but mine stay on the road behind us. I don't know what we'll do if we see police lights. Pull over and stop? Tell the truth? What happens then?

We carried on like blubbering idiots for the first twenty minutes. I kept screaming at Krystal to turn around, but she refused.

"Turn around! We have to go back!" I must've screamed ten times until she finally whipped the truck over to the side of the road.

She pointed at me from the driver's seat, and her voice was tight, like she was doing everything she could not to yell at me. "We're not going back, Nichole. Do you hear me? Not ever."

"What if she dies, Krystal?" My body trembled with my voice. "What if she dies, and I killed her? I don't want to be like Veronica."

She put the truck in park and flung open her door before hurrying over to my side of the cab and flinging my door open. She gripped my shoulders. "Listen to me: You are not anything like Veronica. You are a kind and wonderful person who cares about everyone, even people that are awful and mean to you. Veronica jumped in the truck on her own. You didn't make her get in, and you definitely didn't mean for her to get hurt. If there was any way to make it right—to make any of this right—we would, but there's not. There's just not, no matter how much you want there to be."

"But what if Alice comes back? What if she never leaves me alone?" Pain leaks out of me like a bad smell.

"Your brain broke, Nichole. You bent your brain until it snapped. Just for a second. But that's all it was. It wasn't permanent. Your brain is going to heal itself just like your ankle did in sixth grade. Do you hear me?"

I couldn't speak around the lump of emotions in my throat.

"We're leaving Mrs. Wheeler and that disgusting farm behind us. Along with Veronica and all her twisted games. Any part of it is done. Over." She shook me twice. "Whatever happened to you never has to happen again. Do you hear me, Nichole?"

Tears spilled down my cheeks. I nodded through my tears. I wanted it to be over.

"I'm going to get back into the truck, and then we're going to drive until we can't drive anymore. We're going to find a new place and a new home, and it's going to be just ours. Just ours and nobody else's. You and me, like we always planned. Doesn't that sound good?"

I fell into her chest, and she wrapped her arms around me as the pain came in waves. I could've stayed in her arms forever, but we had to get back on the road before someone caught up with us.

I want to believe in her promises of a new beginning so badly, but I'm not sure I deserve it. Is it possible after everything that's happened? All I've done? I'm terrified Alice will follow me everywhere like a hungry wolf circling its prey. Any other animal would've been put out of its misery, but not me. I've got to walk around like a wounded dog, and I'm scared I won't be able to do it.

———

I smooth the bedspread a final time and glance around the hotel room, double-checking I didn't miss anything. The room looks tidy and clean despite the cigarette stains on the carpet and the water spots on the ceiling, but I can't do anything about that. The door locks behind me as I grab my housekeeping cart and move to the next room.

It's been exactly thirty days since we ran away from Mrs. Wheeler's farm. I know, because I keep track of every single one. We spent the first week on the road driving south. We didn't have a map. No directions. Just south. We kept going south. Once we ditched the truck, we hopped a Greyhound bus until the rolling cornfields gave way to the green country of Illinois littered with small towns with cute names. I didn't stop feeling like we were being chased until we made it through Tennessee. We rode as far south as we could go until we reached Gulfport, Mississippi, and saw the ocean for the first time. But it's not the good ocean. The bottom is filled with sludge and oil, but we didn't know that, and even if we had, it probably wouldn't have stopped us from jumping in.

I've never been to Las Vegas, but everyone calls this place a miniature Vegas because of all the casinos lining the coast and jutting out into the ocean. There's a sex shop between every casino, and they stay just as busy. All the casinos are attached to hotels, so it was easy to get a housekeeping job. Nobody even asked for our ID.

Every week Krystal goes to the library to see if there're any reports on us or Veronica. We have the internet at work, but she says it's anonymous at the library because nothing she looks up can be traced. I could barely breathe the first time she looked for an obituary on Veronica, and I've never been more relieved in my life for a search to turn up empty. Krystal keeps checking the local newspapers and media outlets just to make sure she doesn't miss an announcement about her, but there's never any mention of her or an accident. I can't help but wonder how long she lay there on the side of the road before someone found her. Sometimes I worry nobody ever found her, but Krystal assures me if that was the case, it'd be all over the papers and the news because Mrs. Wheeler would've done everything to find her. She's probably right.

There's never any mention of us either. We disappeared, and no one even noticed or cared. It's like we never existed, but I guess that's what happens when you're nobody's children. Krystal says she's going down to the courthouse after we turn eighteen and making sure our juvenile records are sealed. She wants to go to law school, and she needs to make sure there's nothing on our record. She's determined to make a new start.

Our apartment is run down and dingy, but we didn't have many options, and I'm just grateful for any place to stay. There aren't too many people who will rent to two seventeen-year-old girls without an ID, even though we told them we were eighteen. We had to practically beg to get into this one, and if the landlord wasn't so desperate for money, we wouldn't be living here. Our fake IDs should arrive by the end of the week and were easier to get than we'd imagined. We even got to use our own pictures, even though neither of us looks like ourselves anymore. I still can't believe Krystal cut her hair. She's blonde now, and I finally got rid of my red hair, but I look funny with black. Someday when we know we're safe and far enough away from any chance of our past catching up with us, we'll go back to how we used to look.

We've been pillaging Goodwill and other people's throwaways. Krystal used to go dumpster diving with her mom back when she lived with her, and it didn't take long for me to follow in her footsteps. It grossed me out at first because of other people's icky germs being all over the stuff, but it hasn't been that bad. We've actually found some decent stuff.

Our apartment is filled with plastic chairs, and neither of us has a bed, but it's ours and we're safe. The first thing we did when we got our first paychecks was to buy multiple locks for the door. We have two dead bolts and an upper sliding-chain lock. It's a weird feeling being safe in my own house. It doesn't matter what it looks like. Nobody can touch it, and nobody can touch us.

Our jobs as housekeepers are at the Pacific Edge Motel. We spend our days cleaning people's rooms, and we waitress at night in the casino restaurant. By the time we get home, we're so exhausted that we just crash. Only to get up and do it all over again. We used up all the money we'd saved over the years on the deposit and first month's rent of our apartment, but we're determined to build up our nest egg again.

I'm just trying to get through each day. The days are easier. Nights are more difficult because that's when Alice finds her way to me in my dreams. I wake up every morning with the blankets twisted in knots and my shirt soaked in sweat. There's so much space in my head without all the chatter, and sometimes the emptiness scares me. I'm constantly straining my ears for her voice. I'm scared to get my hopes up that she might be gone for good and in the next instant overwhelmed with guilt because of everything that happened.

Krystal says it'll get easier and easier as the days go on. I hope she's right. She usually is. I just have to keep putting one foot in front of the other until I've walked far enough away from all the evil. I keep telling myself that brains are like bones, and they can be fixed.

Sometimes when I wake up in the middle of the night from my nightmares, I write Alice letters. Krystal would be horrified if she found out, so I hide them in a box at the back of the closet. She wants to put it all behind us and pretend like it never happened, but I can't. I've tried. Even though we didn't push her out the door, her blood is still on my hands, and no matter how hard I scrub, it'll never come off.

But I'll keep moving forward. That's what I do, and maybe someday I'll be as strong as Krystal, so I won't see her face every night before I fall asleep or have my stomach turn to mush at the smell of cheap gin. I know Krystal thinks I went crazy, and maybe I did, but I'm pretty sure a part of me will always be haunted by Alice's ghost.

THIRTY-FIVE

KRYSTAL

I stare at the private Facebook profile of Marie Davenport on my computer screen, racking my brain for where to search next. My first instinct when I left Aiden's was to go to the hospital and talk to Nichole. But halfway there, I turned around and came home.

I'm convinced one of them killed Marie Davenport. I just don't know which one. Aiden's story doesn't add up. There's no way someone like Nichole just snapped and killed her husband's mistress in cold-blooded revenge like Aiden's trying to get me to believe. I've seen her lose her mind before, and it wasn't like that. Nichole didn't snap into madness—she slid. If what Aiden says about making her sick is true, then she was mentally fit at the time of the murder, which makes no logical sense and brings me back to square one, which is why I'm so obsessed with Marie Davenport. Somehow I just know that she's the one holding the key to all this.

So far, I haven't found much information about her online, not even an obituary. I find that a little odd. It's not a legal requirement to file an obituary, but I don't know any family that doesn't. What kind of a family wouldn't do that?

A very disturbed one.

And then it hits me—maybe Marie Davenport wasn't her real name. What if she changed it in the same way Nichole and I did when we were nineteen so we'd have the same last names and there wasn't any chance our past could follow us into our future?

I immediately log on to the Department of Records and Vital Statistics. I type in my password as fast as I can and wait for the site to load. It's always so slow. I use the database all the time when I'm trying to track people down in divorce proceedings, especially when I'm searching for deadbeat dads behind on child support. Changing your name is one of the oldest tricks in the book, and I can't believe I'm just now thinking of it. My heart speeds up with anticipation like it does every time I'm on the right path.

A search of the entire state of Texas reveals nothing. There's no marriage certificate or name change that includes a Marie Davenport within her age range, but I'm not deterred. It would've been too easy to just get it on the first try. I spend the next hour digging into other states and plowing through the results, still finding nothing. I work my way through the middle of the country, heading toward the Midwest, and that's when my stomach starts twisting in knots and heat rises in my chest. A sense of impending doom settles over me. My hands are clammy as I type *Iowa* into the search bar. I slowly scroll through the results on the first page.

Nothing.

I click on the second page. Her name is at the top:

Marie Davenport 2/12/2009 Marie Wheeler (former)

My pulse throbs in my temples as I pull up the full report revealing a marriage between Luke Davenport and Marie Wheeler on 1/23/2009. The next result knocks every wisp of air from my lungs:

Marie Wheeler 8/4/2002 Veronica Wheeler (former)

I shove my chair back from the table. My emotions won't translate into language. All I can do is stare at the screen. The blinking cursor. The missing link. The doubt in my mind over who killed Marie Davenport vanishes instantly, but there's no way Nichole did this on her own or unprovoked. Alice has to be back. What if she's never been gone?

I've never forgotten how she snaked her way into every crevice of Nichole's brain until it splintered or how she used Nichole's love for me to get Nichole to do what she wanted. I've lived with the fear of her coming back. I didn't let it control me or hinder me, but it's always been there in the far corner of my mind. Was she there in the recesses of Nichole's mind in the same way that she was in mine? Just waiting for the proper cues to be called back to life?

Nichole never saw herself as mentally ill. Alice was as real to her as I was, and the only thing Alice ever wanted was for Veronica to be punished for her sins. Nichole said Alice left her alone after she hit Veronica with the truck, and I believed her, but what if she never did? She clearly still dreamed about her and wrote her letters—did she hear her voice too?

I'd thought she was cured, but was that only because of how much I wanted her to be? I just kept telling her that if she acted normal, eventually she'd feel normal again. That her brain needed to rest, and once it had, she'd be better. I was convinced that enough time away from the farm would make her better and that my love and support would be enough to hold her up until she could stand on her own two feet again. Guilt pummels me in waves for failing her.

There's no way Aiden knows about the connection, or he would've said something to me about it earlier. He probably would've used it as another way to bribe me into doing what he wanted. How did Veronica find him? Was it a coincidence, or has she been looking for us all these years? I never gave her existence a second thought after I felt confident that she'd survived the accident. I buried her memory in my consciousness like they buried Mrs. Wheeler's stillborn babies in the backyard.

What did Nichole find out first? Was it the affair or Marie's identity? And why didn't she tell me? It feels like such a huge betrayal. Pain seeps into my chest. I'm walking on the edge of an abyss with nothing to hold on to. My emotions are still numb from disbelief.

I slowly rise from the table and eye the box of letters sitting next to my computer. I have so many questions fighting for space in my head but no answers. There's only one person who has them. I grab the box from the table, tuck it underneath my arm, and head out the door to find Nichole.

———

Nichole and I huddle alone together in one of the small therapy rooms on the unit even though she's still not off one-to-one supervision, but I wasn't having this conversation with anyone else present. Not Dr. McGowan, not Eric, and definitely not Detective Sparks. This is between me and her.

Eric's partner is keeping guard outside the door. I called him, and he got permission for me to speak to Nichole without an aide or anyone else present. Somehow, he arranged it with Dr. McGowan, probably because Dr. McGowan knows we're dealing with something much bigger than Nichole's mental illness, but they have no idea what we're really facing. They're still hot on Aiden's trail.

Ever since Nichole walked into the room, I can't stop staring at her hands and trying to picture them plunging a knife into Veronica's stomach. Not just once, but twice. That's the part that's the most disturbing. After she'd done it once, she pulled it out and did it again. There's no way she could do that without Alice controlling her. What did she threaten her with this time? Was it me? One of her kids at school? Nichole would do anything if it meant keeping one of her kids unharmed.

She eyes the room nervously. "What's going on?"

I keep my expression neutral as I pull out the box from underneath the table and slide it in front of her. Her mouth drops open in shock and surprise.

"How did . . . I mean . . . what? Is . . ." She looks at me with stunned amazement.

"I got it from Aiden."

"Aiden?" she asks like it doesn't compute.

I nod.

"He knows?"

I nod again. I wait for a response. Seconds pass that feel like minutes before she speaks again.

"I'm sorry, Krystal," she says with her lower lip quivering. "I tried to get over it. I really did. I tried so hard, but I'm not like you." She shifts her eyes to the box on the table and wrings her hands together on her lap. Those hands. The ones capable of doing things I never imagined, even though I'd seen them put a pillow over someone's face. "I just couldn't go on with my life like it never happened. I had to find a way to get it out. I never sent any of the letters. I promise."

"Why didn't you tell me?" It's hard to get the question out around the waves of conflicting emotions ricocheting through me. It's been that way since I left my house. I jump from horror to fear to guilt, then spiral into sadness and grief before flipping back to horror.

She yanks her head up. "Tell you? How many times did I try talking to you about it? How many? And you know what you always said?" Her eyes are lit with a challenge. I expected a lot of emotional reactions from her when I showed her the box, but anger wasn't one of them. "'You have to let it go, Nichole. We have to move forward. You can't move forward if you're always looking behind you.'" She mimics my voice almost perfectly. Not in a mocking way but in a way that allows me to see myself from her perspective like I never have before, and I plummet into shame. "I don't know how you do it. I think about Alice every day. Every. Single. Day."

"I had no idea you felt this way," I say softly, doing my best not to cry.

"We're not any better than Mrs. Wheeler and Veronica. We never have been. We might as well have pushed Alice out of the barn ourselves. Who's more guilty, Krystal? The one who hurts someone or the one who watches someone get hurt and does nothing? We're no different from them. Don't you see that?" Her eyes fill with righteous indignation.

"We were kids, Nichole. What were we supposed to do?" I fire back.

"The right thing." Her face crumples, and her voice fills with so much pain I could reach out and touch it, hold it in my hand. She sinks back in her chair.

"We did the best we could, given the circumstances," I say in our defense. "You were a mess. An absolute mess. And we lived with monsters. Did you forget that?"

She shakes her head. She's not willing to let herself off the hook. "We should've done more."

"We did everything we could. It was an awful situation," I say, and not because I'm trying to make her feel better but because it's the truth. She acts like we had so many different options to choose from, but none of our choices were good or ones we would've chosen for ourselves, but we had to pick one.

"That's easy for you to say because you got to make all the decisions. You decided everything. I never got a say. Never." She peers at me through wounded eyes filled with the pain of decades-old wounds.

"I'm sorry." I don't know what else to say. Remorse burns my cheeks.

She pulls her knees up to her chest and wraps her arms around them. Her unblinking stare fixes on the box in front of her. Dread rises in my chest at what I have to do next, but there's no turning back.

"When Aiden gave me the box, he told me everything about Marie Davenport," I announce and then wait. There's no sign of recognition. Her expression doesn't change. Her posture stays the same.

"Marie Davenport?" Her face is blank.

"He was having an affair with her."

She recoils in disbelief. "Aiden was having an affair?"

"He was." I study her carefully. Did she really not know? I hate having to be the one to do this to her, but I hate the seed of doubt planted in my mind about everything she says even more. I take both her hands in mine. "I'm so sorry." I give her a minute for my words to register, but she still sits unmoving, flat and emotionless like she's in shock. "But that's not the most important part."

"There's more?" she asks in a tiny voice, like she's terrified to know the answer.

"Marie Davenport was killed. They found her body in the Walmart parking lot. It was all over the news. Do you remember anything about it?"

"You mean like seeing it on the news?" Her eyes are innocent and wide.

But those eyes lie to me. They always have whenever it came to Alice. She wanted Nichole all to herself.

"Yes, on the news, but more than that—do you remember anything about her? Knowing her? Meeting her?"

She shakes her head, wrinkling her forehead in confusion.

I pause and take a deep breath, trying to steady myself. This is the hardest part.

"Aiden says you were the one who killed her."

She snaps back in her chair like she's been smacked. Her entire body goes rigid. She blinks rapidly like she's trying to digest what I've said but can't get there. She covers her mouth with her hands. "I . . . I don't understand. What are you talking about?"

"You came home the night she died covered in blood and babbling incoherently." I repeat Aiden's version of the events, wondering if that's how it really happened or if there's more to the story.

All the color drains from her face.

"No. No. No. Why would I do that? That doesn't make any sense. I—no. Just no." Her features curl in revulsion.

"Because Marie Davenport was really Veronica Wheeler."

She leaps from her chair. "What are you talking about? What did you say?"

"I said that Marie Davenport was really Veronica Wheeler."

She races to the other side of the room and plasters herself against the wall. Her eyes blaze with panic and dart around the room. "Get away from me!" She points a shaking finger at me. The veins bulge in her neck. "They got you too. Oh my God, they've got you too." She runs to the door and beats on it with her fists. "Please, help. Let me out of this room."

I rush to her, grabbing her and pulling her back just as Eric's partner whips open the door. I hold Nichole's shaking body against me as she struggles to get free.

"We're fine. She's just upset," I say, trying to push the door shut. His eyes fill with bewilderment and disbelief. "We're fine. Really, we're okay." I motion for him to go away, and I smash the door in his face before he has a chance to say or do anything else.

Nichole breaks loose and runs to the other side of the room, then backs up against the brick wall. Her eyes roam the small space, searching for a place to hide. I stand with my back against the door, holding it shut in case anyone tries to get inside. I have to calm her down before security hears her throwing a fit and comes to restrain her.

"Nichole, listen to me. Just listen to me," I say breathlessly, keeping my voice even and as nonthreatening as possible. "It's me. Krystal. Your sister. It's really me, and I would never lie to you or do anything to hurt you." I point to her chair at the table. "Please, just sit down and we can talk about this, okay?"

She shakes her head like she's trying to clear it. "No. No. No." She brings her hands to her ears.

I hold my hands up in a peaceful gesture and start singing the song we sang together when we were little girls and one of us was scared or couldn't fall asleep at night. "Hush, little baby, don't say a word . . ." I pause, waiting for her to sing her part or tell me I'm still completely tone deaf. She doesn't sing, but she slowly drops her hands from her ears. "Hush, little baby, don't say a word . . . come on, Nikki. You can do it. You know what comes next."

"Mama's gonna buy you a mockingbird," she stammers.

"Good. Good." I smile. "And if that mockingbird don't sing . . ."

She lets out a shaky breath. "Mama's gonna buy you a diamond ring."

We sing another round, and some of the tension leaves her body. I take a cautious step toward her. "It's just you and me. Nobody else. There's nothing to be scared of. Can we just sit down?"

I take a seat first, and she takes a minute to consider it before following me to the table. She starts rocking slowly in her chair.

"Aiden was having an affair?"

I nod.

"With Veronica?" she asks, like she doesn't want it to be true.

"He was," I admit, even though I don't want it to be true any more than she does.

The horror of the realization fills her face and moves its way into her body like a disease. She lets out a small whimper before putting her face into her hands and breaking down in heaving sobs. Her cries are guttural, like an animal being tortured. I instinctively move to comfort her because that's my job—I take care of her no matter what—but she shoves my arm away.

"Leave me alone." She's crying so hard she can barely talk.

She's always been my center of gravity. The force that keeps me on this earth, and her rejection hurts me to my core. I feel the separation in my bones. She shakes with sobs, hunched over on her chair, arms crossed on her stomach. I sit on my hands to keep from reaching out to her. Her pain bleeds my insides. Minutes pass before she can speak.

She lifts her head to look at me. Her nose runny, eyes raw and red. "Are you sure?"

"Yes, Aiden and the police told me about the affair. He doesn't know who Marie really was, though. I only found out this afternoon." I speak slowly and purposefully. "Marie is Veronica's middle name. She changed her name to that first. I'm not sure why. Maybe to start fresh in college? Anyway, Davenport was her married name, and she never switched back after her divorce."

"And I killed her?" Her voice is barely above a whisper.

"Aiden says that you came home that night covered in blood and confessed. You had a bloody knife in your purse, and there was blood all over your car."

"That's not possible. I wouldn't. I couldn't," she says, but she knows that she almost did twenty years ago and would've finished the job if I hadn't stopped her. Her fingernails scrape at the scarred welts on her forearms that match the ones healing on her face. I instinctively grab her arms and pull them away from her, setting them on her lap and placing mine on top of hers.

"There's more." I want to stop, but I have to keep going. She deserves the full story. "Aiden helped cover it up. He got rid of the knife and tried to clean up the car as best he could. He says he gave you Benadryl to make you lose touch with reality and mess up your brain."

There's a long pause as she mulls it over.

"I don't understand." Her voice is a whimper. Tears flow unchecked down both cheeks.

I recite his reasoning nearly verbatim to when he gave it to me. "He knew the investigation into Marie's death would eventually lead to him and then to you, so he wanted to keep you sick. If you were sick, then you couldn't be held accountable for your actions. He never expected you to turn against him, but you did. That's why you tried to burn your house down."

She brings both hands to her face. "But I don't remember. Wouldn't I remember something like that?"

"You don't remember anything?"

She shakes her head.

"He asked me to take the car off his hands and get rid of it. It's the only other piece of evidence linking you to her murder. I was—"

She shoves the table so hard it slams against the wall, and she jumps up, knocking over her chair. "No, not again. No more lies, Krystal, no more lies." She moans like she's in pain as her eyes roam the room, but there's nowhere to run, no place to hide. "I don't care if I go to jail or prison. Not this time. I can't lie. Not again. Please."

A wave of knowing floods over me, and I get up before stepping cautiously toward her. "Then, you don't have to."

She stops in her tracks. "I can tell the truth?"

I'm not keeping her out of prison by protecting her. I never was. And neither is Aiden if what he says is the truth. She's lived behind bars for decades and will never live in peace until she gets the punishment she thinks she deserves for her crimes. She's been waiting for it for over twenty years.

"You can do whatever you think is best," I say, conceding defeat. I've always thought I knew what was best for her. Every decision that I made, I made from that vantage point, like a mother to her child, because that's what you do when you don't have any real parents. You take care of each other.

"I just want it to be over, Krystal." Her voice cracks with emotion. Her body trembles.

"Then, let's let it be over."

I walk back to the table and take a seat in the chair. I turn her chair upright and bring it next to mine. She slowly walks over to the table and sits down. She hugs herself next to me. Every part of my being wants to reach out and hold her, pull her close to me, but taking care of her almost killed her, and I want her to live.

"What are we going to do?" she asks.

"The only thing we can do. The thing you've been wanting to do for twenty years—we tell the truth and let the police work things out." They always say the truth will set you free, but maybe it has to destroy you first.

I take my phone out of my pocket and pull up Detective Sparks's number. I set it on the table and put it on speaker while it connects. Nichole and I stare at each other as we wait for him to pick up, knowing that we are about to cross over an invisible line that once we get over, we never get to come back.

"Hello?" his familiar voice answers.

"Hi, Detective Sparks, it's Krystal Benson." I clear my throat. "I'm here with Nichole, and we have something to tell you."

THIRTY-SIX

NICHOLE

THREE WEEKS AGO

Those aren't my hands on the wheel. They can't be. They're attached to my body, but a force outside me has taken them over. Sweat pours from my armpits, drips between my legs, making my thighs stick to the leather seat. Sunlight floods through the windshield and lands on my wedding ring. The diamonds wink at me mockingly. They know my marriage is a sham. A cruel trick played on me, but that's what I get for thinking I could get a fresh start. Hysterical laughter bubbles up my throat and fills the empty car. It morphs into a choked sob.

What am I going to do?

I press the gas pedal to the floor and fly over the speed limit. I haven't been home since yesterday. All I've done since I spotted them kissing outside the restaurant is follow them around like a creepy stalker. I told myself to go home. To get in my car and go back to Belmont, but I couldn't. I had to know who she was. What she had that I didn't.

I was afraid they'd spot me in the restaurant, even though I sat in the far corner with my hair pulled back in a scarf and my sunglasses on, but Aiden didn't notice anything going on around him. Not the server.

Not the food. Definitely not me. He was oblivious and never took his eyes off her. He ran them up and down her body like she was his dessert as soon as they finished their lunch.

And she was.

I followed them to the elevator and watched as he nibbled on her ear and she nuzzled his neck. That's when I should've left. I'd seen more than enough. Instead I found a seat in the hotel bar and waited to see if they'd make another appearance. The hours passed in a blur. Around seven, Aiden snuck into the bar alone, and I almost rushed over to him. It had to be a mistake. Maybe I hadn't seen what I'd thought I'd seen between them. Maybe I'd exaggerated it. Aiden would never do something so horrible to me. He loved me. I was his angel. That's what he said when he asked me to marry him.

But then my phone rang with his call. I didn't want to answer, but I picked it up anyway. I watched from across the room as he lied to me, going on and on about how busy he was at the conference, that he had only been able to step out for a minute to call me. My heart shattered into pieces when he ended the call by saying he loved me and was counting the minutes until he could be home with me.

He lied too well for it to be his first time. A steady scream rolled through my head. Shame and embarrassment burned my cheeks. My brain sputtered, and every part of me went on pause. One minute I was sitting in the hotel bar, and the next minute I was lying in my queen-size bed on the floor below them all checked in for the night.

But I didn't sleep.

I didn't eat.

There was no light. No sound. No air.

Nothing felt real in the morning as I took the elevator down to the lobby. It was like I was sleepwalking underwater. I watched myself as I ordered coffee from the barista at the Starbucks counter and wondered how I was speaking to her so clearly. There was a roaring in my ears.

My soul was empty, like a pumpkin whose insides had been scraped out and discarded.

I rounded the corner and came face to face with her.

Her.

I stopped dead in my tracks.

She smiled like she'd been expecting me.

"Hi, Nichole," she said in a voice that I would recognize anywhere, even though it didn't match her face.

A chill ran through me. I took a step back. And another.

"I know, shocking, right?" She made a circular motion around her face. "Amazing what a nose job and a little bit of collagen can do for a girl, huh?"

My lungs stopped taking in air. I couldn't breathe.

Somebody help me.

"I was wondering how long it would take you to figure it out. I mean, I've only been sleeping with your husband for three years." Her familiar smirk lit with smug satisfaction.

I opened my mouth, but no words came out.

She came closer. I moved back until I was up against the wall. I ran my hands along the wall, searching for an invisible door as if she'd locked me in the barn again and I had to find my way out.

"Funny, my company managed the security systems for Aiden's company for years before I found out he was married to you. But I knew you were his wife the minute I saw your picture in one of the company newsletters." She tilted her head to the side and cocked one hand on her hip. "Remember when you cut the ribbon on the Edison building? Great dress you wore that day, by the way. The red went great with your hair. Anyway, that's when I knew I had to find a way to meet him. Make him mine." Her beady eyes were still the same up close, even though they'd changed color. She moved them up and down my body. "They must do some serious photoshopping because you're way more frumpy than in the pictures."

All these years I'd waited for Alice to return, but *she* was the one to come back. This couldn't be happening.

"Veronica?" My voice squeaked out in disbelief, barely audible. "You did this?"

She nodded. Pride written all over her now-beautiful face. "It's usually not so easy to meet the big boss, but everyone knows how much he likes a short skirt and high heels." She noticed the tears leaking out of the corners of my eyes and gave a little laugh. "Oh, but not you, huh? I'm sorry to burst the bubble in your perfect little world, but yes, your husband is a cheater. All it took was a few emails and a couple sexy pictures."

I recoiled in horror. "How could you?"

"How could *I*?" she said, pointing to her chest. "You left me on the side of the road like a dead deer you hit with your car. How could I?" She gave another laugh. "Do you know what I went through after the two of you left? Do you have any idea?" She took another step closer. She was so close it made my skin crawl. "After all that, how couldn't I? Do you want to know what he says about you?"

"Get away from me," I growled.

"He says having sex with you is like having sex with a dead fish. That you have no idea how to please him. He's only with you because he feels sorry for you."

I dropped my coffee and shoved her as hard as I could.

And then I ran. I didn't stop running until I reached my car. I don't remember leaving the hotel or the first ten miles of my drive.

But here I am.

The broken pieces of me are shards of glass stabbing my insides. I choke on my tears, coughing and spitting as I grip the wheel. It's a good thing I'm almost home because I can barely drive. Within seconds, I pull into the garage and park next to Aiden's Mercedes-Benz. I want to take a hammer to it. Knock out every window. Crush all the doors.

The vanity license plate reads MY LOVE. I had it made on our tenth anniversary when I bought him the car. It hurts too much to look at it.

I hurry out of the car and into the house. Grief pummels me when I open the door to the home we created—the one we were supposed to grow old in. Sobs rack my body, and I collapse on the mudroom floor, unable to go any farther. I don't want to go inside. I can't see the golden-framed pictures of our wedding day hanging over the fireplace in the living room and lining the hallway going up the stairs, the flowers sitting on the dining room table that he sent me yesterday before he went away. Just like he does every time he goes. Or the books lying on our matching nightstands in the bedroom that we read out loud to each other before we fall asleep. The bed that we sleep in together with me tucked underneath his arm like a baby bird.

None of this would be happening if it wasn't for Veronica. Every single bad thing that's happened to me can be traced back to her. She's a demon in disguise and destroys every person's life she touches. Anger boils inside me, working its way into a red-hot rage. I let it fuel me. Swallow me up and consume me. It feels so much better than desolation. The rage multiplies itself until it's all there is and I see nothing else. I rise from my heap on the floor.

Rage propels me into the kitchen, but instant calm settles over me as I grab the biggest knife from the chopping block on the counter.

I know what I have to do.